A MAN WITH
THOUGHTFUL EYES ...

Tansy, who loved beautiful things, stood gazing at the carvings.

She was startled when a pleasant voice behind her said, "those curious carvings represent the Holy Sepulcher."

She turned and saw a man with a handsome face and thoughtful eyes. He looked sensitive and approachable as he smiled at her.

"How do people know it really looked like that," she asked.

Suddenly a messenger ran into the room and dropped to one knee. Startled, Tansy became aware of a small group of men watching her with shocked expressions. Then she knew—she'd been talking to the King!

THE KING'S BED

Margaret Campbell Barnes

POPULAR LIBRARY • NEW YORK

For CATHY,
when she grows old enough

Chapter One

An angry sunset flamed over Leicester, as if reflecting the troubled heart of England. City walls and gates, gabled houses, and the massive Abbey of St. Mary might all have been but a flat template carved in black wood against the portentous sky. The heat of an August day still hung about oppressively, trapped in narrow streets by overhanging eaves.

It was the hour when the day's work was done and townsfolk usually strolled abroad to take the air; but a sense of tension and the threat of ominously piling thunder clouds kept the women grouped apprehensively about their doors, while their men sat elbow to elbow on tavern benches grumbling at the danger to trade and fidgeting for news of the invader.

At the sign of the White Boar seventeen-year-old Tansy Marsh, helping her father to serve their customers, heard all that they said. But she heard it with the half-interested ears of youth. National crises and party arguments about Yorkists and Lancastrians, over which her elders waxed so hot, concerned her less closely than the color of her new gown for Michaelmas, the lovableness of her new pony, Pippin, or the spells of breathlessness which had recently attacked her father.

"If this Lancastrian, Henry Tudor, has landed in Wales it could mean civil war again," declared William Jordan, the master of the grammar school, through the sweaty heat of the low beamed room.

"He be landed right enough," confirmed the Guild Hall watchman, who should know. "At Pembroke, so that Welsh merchant who rode in this morning told our Mayor. And marching nearer and nearer across Wales every hour, making towards Shrewsbury, he said. And because he marches under his father's banner of the Welsh dragon, men rush singing to join him, swelling his handful of invaders at every market cross."

"Ten groats to our Tansy's shoe buckle the King will bring an army down from Nottingham to stop him!" wagered Tom Hood, the dashing young fletcher, catching her about the waist.

7

"An' a pretty clash there'll be when they meet!" guffawed the blacksmith, tossing back his ale with relish.

To fletchers and farriers the prospect of approaching armies must suggest gain, supposed Robert Mash, the landlord. But having struggled for years against the ill effects of an arrow wound in the chest sustained on the Scottish border and being now settled in life with an extravagant second wife, he wanted no more Lancastrian troublemakers drawing men away to battle from his tavern benches. Business was chancy enough at it was, with that loud-voiced, enterprising rival Malpas over at the newly built Golden Crown, and he himself not able to work as he used. "Our Duke'll make mincemeat of the Tudor," he prophesied testily, beckoning to his man Jod to breach a fresh cask.

Richard the Third had been King of England for over two years, but to many a Midland man like Marsh who had fought under him he would always be *the Duke:* young Richard Plantagenet, Duke of Gloucester, who had spent most of his life soldiering to keep the peace for his elder brother, the fourth Edward, serving him loyally, from one campaign to another, with little time to join in Edward's court revels and philandering.

Because mine host was not one to speak lightly, his words lent graphic reality to the probable encounter. An uneasy silence hung in the room. "How far would King Richard's army have come by now, think you, sir?" quavered a first-year apprentice, voicing the fear in several minds.

"Not far as yet, my lad," replied Marsh kindly, as much to reassure his own young daughter as the questioner. "But he makes his men march swiftly, as I should well know."

"Do you suppose he will come through Leicester?" asked the fletcher, with more eagerness than fear.

"More likely westwards, towards Gloucester, so as to prevent this upstart Tudor from crossing the Severn. Though if he be too late for that maneuver, he might well make for the stronghold of Warwick so as to cut him off from London. It would be like his bold military skill to place himself in the very middle of his kingdom. But who can tell?"

What with the heat and the rumors and the distant thunder, it had been a trying day. Noting the landlord's weariness, and sharing it, the gray-haired schoolmaster rose and handed his empty tankard to Tansy with a half-sketched bow. There was a fair purity about her which made men of discernment treat her with respect, and even the roughest churl present knew that if he presumed to do otherwise in her father's presence he would soon find himself on the wrong side of the Boar's hospitable doors. "Our good friend Marsh is probably right," Master Jordan said. "And as even Warwick is over thirty miles away, there should be no bloodshed here. So I wish you all a peaceful good night."

The beloved old pedagogue's departure was the signal for a general scraping back of stools and benches. The Abbey bell began to ring the Augustine brothers to bed, the sun had sunk behind the castle walls, and—invasion or no invasion— many of Marsh's customers would have to be up at cockcrow. With a hubbub of "good nights" they left in twos and threes, going their ways along the darkening streets home to their nervous wives.

Jod bolted the door behind them and gathered up the last of the dirty mugs. Tansy, yawning, lighted a candle at the damped-down kitchen fire to light herself to bed. And Robert Marsh sat down abruptly on an upturned barrel, trying to hide his exhaustion.

Glancing across at him, Tansy forgot her own weariness in a rush of anxious affection. "Bring your master a cup of mulled malmsey, Jod," she called, carrying her candle to the table where her father sat. "Is it your heart again?" she asked anxiously.

"Or the heat." Robert Marsh shrugged, trying to make light of it.

"Small wonder, with such a fug of stale liquor and sweat!" said Tansy, pushing open a casement to freshen the air. "How horrible they all smell!"

"The result of honest toil," he reminded her. "But I wish that you did not have to wait on them."

"I like to, since it helps you. And it is only when Dilly goes home to her parents."

But they both knew that it was not so much the young serving maid's occasional absence which put more work on Tansy as her stepmother's proud idleness. While there were two unwed girls to serve drinks to half the louts of Leicester, let them do it until they dropped, thought Mistress Rose

Marsh, going her pleasure-loving ways about the town. It was a recognized factor in the household, but not one of which Robert or his daughter ever spoke. They merely held the time precious in her absence.

When Jod had brought the sweetened steaming wine and gone out into the yard to shoot the stable bolts. Tansy drew a stool close to her father. "You are not really worried about all this talk of more civil war?" she asked, seeing that the normal color had come back into his face.

"No need to be," he assured her, settling himself more easily with his elbows on the table. "This Tudor's claim to the throne is flimsy as thistledown. Descended from Edward the Third he certainly is, but only through the third son, John of Gaunt, and his children's governess, Katherine."

"Sister-in-law to the poet Chaucer, wasn't she? You remember how Mother used to recite to us lovely lines from his story of the Canterbury Pilgrims?"

"Aye. I remember." Robert Marsh sighed, and took up his tale. "And when John of Gaunt, Duke of Lancaster, had had a family by her, he married her. And their descendant, Margaret Beaufort, married one of these Welsh Tudors."

"And the Tudors themselves?"

"Owen Tudor was put in charge of the household of Henry the Fifth's widowed queen, Katherine of Valois, and had the effrontery to marry *her*."

"But everyone says they were so deeply in love that it wasn't just ambition," sighed Tansy romantically.

"That's as may be. But the fact remains that they married their elder son Edward to Margaret Beaufort and so became the grandparents of this present perfidious claimant, Henry Tudor."

"Who has French royal blood as well as Welsh."

"And has cunningly picked the propitious moment when our King Richard is widowed and his infant son but recently dead. There is no direct heir."

Tansy nibbled at a honey cake and spoke diffidently because she knew that her father would brook no criticism of the King. "They do say that the child's death was a judgment from Heaven because of those two poor Princes shut up in the Tower. Pratt, the packman, who is often in London, swears that they have been murdered. No one ever sees them now and——"

"A packman has to bring gossip so as to sell his wares. The apartments in the Tower are a royal residence like any other, and what profit would it be to the King to murder his own brother's boys after they had been declared bastards, because of their father's previous marriage, and the crown freely offered to him?"

"None, I suppose, though he might feel safer," agreed Tansy, her mothering heart still shocked by the packman's lurid tales. "And you think the people still like him well enough to stand by him, as you do?"

"They certainly should, seeing the good firm rule he has given them after all the wars of the red and white roses. Peace on the borders, a truce with Scotland at last, and protection for our trade abroad. Why, even our laws are written in English now, instead of highfalutin Latin, so that the meanest poacher can understand what he is convicted of. And this new idea he has organized for the safe posting of merchants' important letters from town to town—why, it may well be that even now our Mayor has news of Henry Tudor's movements by this very means."

"If only some of the aldermen had come in tonight, we might have heard," said Tansy, beginning to wipe the liquor-stained table.

"Most of 'em drink at the Golden Cross these days," Robert Marsh reminded her bitterly.

Tansy stopped polishing to watch a group of merrymakers, singing some catchy tune, lurch tipsily past the open window from the direction of the rival inn. She thought with a sigh of the comfortable rooms above, aired but sparsely occupied for weeks, which in her mother's time had been so constantly used by travelers. "Why, for pity's sake, does everybody go there now?" she asked.

"Something new," said Marsh, rising and standing before his own empty hearth and looking round at well-worn benches and old smoke-grimed beams. "A juggler and a singing wench hired to entertain them. And if she stops at singing . . . It's anything to get money, these days. A go-ahead man, is Hugh Malpas!"

"Yes," agreed Tansy, remembering how jocularly he had
pinched her leg as she had ridden into his spacious yard with
some message from her stepmother, who admired his successful ways. Careful not to add fuel to her father's envious
wrath, she forbore to mention the incident and, leaving her
task for Dilly to finish, went and slipped a hand through his
arm. "So that is why you have worked harder than you
should all spring, helping Jod to modernize the cellars and
enlarge the stables!"

It was the way his first wife used to stand beside him in
everything, loyally encouraging, helping him to overcome the
disability of his wound. "At least we can bait a score of
horses now." He grinned, looking almost young and eager
again.

Though for what use, when most of the stalls were so often
empty? wondered Tansy. But, hearing her stepmother's
warm, resonant voice in the yard calling good night to some
friends and almost immediately scolding Dilly for returning
late, she hastily took up her candle, stood a-tiptoe to kiss her
father's cheek, and went upstairs to bed. Up the wide oak
stairs, past the closed and silent rooms, and then up the narrow winding flight to her attic under the middle gable.

Tired though she was, her sleepiness had gone. The worst
of the distant thunder had passed over, and the few heavy
drops of rain which were falling had already cooled the air.
Gratefully she leaned from her window, with its small leaded
panes. Above her head finely carved timber came to a point
beneath a roof of blue local tiles, and within arm's reach
below her, from its spiked iron shaft, hung the inn sign. In
the still air the familiar White Boar, which usually swung and
creaked, looked dead as their diminished fortunes, and—even
Tansy had to admit it—sadly in need of a coat of paint. Beyond the city walls strips of unharvested corn in the peasants'
fields gleamed whitely against thick forests, and to the west
occasional flashes of lightning played over the flat land
around Bosworth beyond the river Soar. But light streamed
comfortingly from the tall windows of the Abbey and twin-
kled in dozens of windows along the darkening streets and
in the market place, where vendors were still setting up their
stalls and where on Monday she would go marketing. It was
the newly entrusted treat of her week, going to market on her

pony with a purseful of money for the inn's provisioning and
Jod lumbering on a packhorse behind. There would be
chaffering and chattering, and all manner of pretty things on
the chapmen's stalls, a performing bear perhaps, and plenty
of impudent apprentices bringing blushes to the cheeks of
every pretty girl. Apprentices and their like were beginning
to loom large in Tansy's secret, personal life. Their calls and
whistles had become a kind of judgment, like the apple
offered by the shepherd Paris to the most beautiful goddess.
And by the way they looked at her, Tansy was beginning to
realize that, in spite of her stepmother's unkind teasing
about a tiptilted nose and straw-colored hair, she could not
be so plain after all.

If I wash with the rose water which that extravagant Tom
Hood bought me last May Day, and put on my rose-sprigged
gown, I shall look very different from how I do now, she
thought, unfastening the crumpled bodice of her workaday
linen and fastidiously shaking her slender body free from a
clinging, sweat-damp shift.

She leaned farther out and looked half enviously towards
the Golden Crown on the other side of the street, where lanterns still flared and laughter still sounded. She watched the
better-dressed citizens leaving, some calling for their horses,
some in convivial groups afoot. Ostlers came and went, and
presently, as his popular inn emptied, Hugh Malpas himself
appeared, standing in his doorway, prosperous and capable.
A large man, dark and Levantine. He spread out a palm to
see if the rain had ceased and looked up at the sky. Looking
up his sharp eyes caught sight of his rival's daughter, hanging
slutlike and unbuttoned from an attic window. By the light of
the Crown lanterns Tansy saw his thick red lips widened in a
grin, the gleam of his splendid teeth, and the florid gesture as
his money-grubbing fingers touched them to blow her a kiss.
From any other neighbor it might have been a friendly greet-
ing to a young girl, but from him it was somehow mocking,
lascivious and nauseating. A fierce stab of anger tore through
her because his brash success had harmed her father. But,
being Tansy, with a maternal ancestry molded more in manors than in inns, she scorned to draw her disheveled head
back out of sight and turned it sharply in the opposite direction. And so she was the first to see the two horsemen,

cloaked against the spattering rain, come galloping down the street from North Gate. There was something so urgent about their behavior that she had no need to pretend that she had not noticed Master Malpas. She simply forgot him altogether.

They appeared to be strangers because, hard as they urged their tired mounts, they were looking to right and to left as if searching for something, hampered by the semidarkness. She quite expected them to canter past, but as they drew nearly level the leading horseman stopped, pulled his jaded beast almost to its haunches, and shouted back over his shoulder with glad surprise, "The White Boar!" He pointed up at the signboard as if it were some welcome miracle from Heaven, and his companion pulled up beside him.

Lights still streamed from the open door of the rival inn. The more ostentatious sign of the Golden Crown hung invitingly only a few yards farther on. But they ignored it and, dismounting, hammered urgently on Robert Marsh's door. Looking down from immediately above, Tansy remarked the fineness of their travel-stained clothing and realized that they were rich, belated travelers such as her parents had been used to cater for.

She heard Malpas's footsteps hurrying down the street to lure them away. "The Golden Crown has better accommodation, sirs," he was telling them persuasively. But they were not to be dissuaded.

"The White Boar is good enough for us," they said, almost in unison, laughing as at some private joke and brushing him aside.

Triumphantly, all maternal precepts forgotten, Tansy stuck out her tongue at him. Quick as one of those lightning flashes over Bosworth fields, careless of her appearance, she ran downstairs, fastening her bodice as she went.

Fortunately her stepmother must have been regaling Marsh with a vivacious account of her doings, as neither they nor Dilly had gone up to bed. The travelers had riden in under the archway of the yard, and the lardlord was receiving them with his usual courtesy. All was welcoming bustle. "There are excellent rooms upstairs," Rose Marsh was explaining, moved to eagerness by the evident quality of her unexpected guests and ushering them inside. "This is but the ale room, stale from the low kind who use it."

They seemed to appreciate only its cosy homeliness. Their minds were full of more important issues. "We shall want *all* your rooms," they said.

"Then you are traveling with a large party, sirs?" surmised Rose delightedly, signing to Tansy to take their cloaks while her husband called across the yard for Jod to come and take their horses.

"With an army," said the older of the two gentlemen. "They should be coming in through the North Gate now. Best ride back, Critchley, and direct his Grace here."

The younger man hurried out and galloped up the street again. Tansy, with the cloaks still across her arms, stood stock still and stared. Her father, closing the door after him, swung round with shining eyes. "The King's army!" he exclaimed proudly.

The same pride was reflected in Sir John Hungerford's face, drawn as it was with weariness. "Our men have marched down from Nottingham in the day with only one break."

"Like he made us march when he was Duke of Gloucester," said Robert Marsh, reaching for a flagon of his very choicest wine.

Sir John sat down gratefully in the high-backed chair which Tansy hastily pulled forward, relaxed for the first time and smiling over the sparkling Bordeaux which was handed to him. "Then you, too, mine host, have served under him? Which explains why you took his badge for your sign."

"And will serve him with my whole heart while his Grace is beneath my roof!" exulted Marsh, knowing that his inn would be famous for all time.

Chapter Two

"The *King*, coming *here!*" gasped whey-faced Dilly in the kitchen, so frightened that she almost vomited in the sink.

"I will have the best bed prepared," bustled Rose, poppy-red with importance in the parlor. "Get out the swansdown pillows, Tansy, and the new linen sheets——"

Tansy was halfway to the stairs before Sir John Hungerford stopped her. "No need, my girl," he said, kindly. "His Grace never travels without his own bed. You will remember, landlord?"

"Aye, 'tis true," recalled Marsh. "A wooden camp bed that took to pieces and always traveled on a special baggage wagon in charge of a handful of his trustiest men."

"Who will bring it in and erect it in a matter of minutes, mistress."

"And move the great four-poster that stands there now, I hope," said Rose. "Our great chamber is big enough to accommodate both, sir."

"Assuredly they will. The captain in charge of commissariat always sends them on ahead to arrange such things. I hear the creaking of wagon wheels now."

The whole street—the whole town—was suddenly alive with soldiery: with the clatter of hoofs, the tramp of men, and the shouting of orders. Heads were thrust out from every window. Families called to each other from the intimate proximity of overhanging eaves, and youths clustered on the steps of Leicester's High Cross. Every housewife, either for loyalty or gain, was making up beds of some sort. The inns, which had been about to close, were all astir again.

Tansy Marsh saw little of it. Hurrying from room to room with piles of bedding, trying to calm Dilly so that she would not spill the water pitchers, promising the flustered cook that she would go to market first thing Monday morning for more food, dodging soldiers who swore and sweated up the wide stairs with the King's bed and his followers' bundles, she shared in the excitement of her town only by coping with domestic chores behind the scenes, although she was there at

16

the heart of it. It was her stepmother, animated and capable when she chose, who dominated the activities downstairs and finally helped her overawed husband to receive their royal guest. It was russet-headed Rose who would be able to boast all her days that she had knelt to serve the King of England with wine. Admiringly, Tansy looked down from one of the courtyard galleries to watch her show dukes and lords up the outside staircases to their allotted rooms. But she herself caught only a brief glimpse of the King.

The innyard was a rare sight, packed with richly capar-isoned horses ridden in under the archway from the High Street and packhorses led in from the side gateway in White Boar Lane. Tansy was calling down to Diggory, the yard boy, to make room in her pony's spacious stall for the King's tall white charger when Dilly came tugging at her sleeve.

"Come and see!" she urged, in an excited whisper, drawing her away from the gallery and into the huge master room to watch the baggage men set up the royal bed. Miraculously the headpiece unfolded from the wooden boxlike base, and slender carved-oak pillars were raised to support the light-weight tester. The panels of the headpiece were painted in various colors and ornamented with golden fleurs-de-lys. The base formed a chest from which were taken bedding and the royal nightshirt. All was methodically done as if each man had performed his part of the act dozens of times.

"Does the King always take his own bed when he travels?" asked Dilly, gaping at the rich coloring.

"Always, except on actual battlefields, when he uses a tent like the rest of us," one of them told her. "His Grace sleeps but ill, and more so in strange beds."

"But it is so grand!"

"Yet very light to handle, and fits into a special wagon," he pointed out, amused by her rustic amazement. "You should see his great bed at Westminster! And the one he used to share with poor Queen Anne—God rest her soul—at Middle-ham, which they always counted their home."

There were voices at the foot of the stairs. He and his mates hurried away, beckoning warningly to the girl to follow them. Someone below was saying something about there being no room for Lord Stanley and his followers.

"Why can he not go to the Castle?" suggested someone else.

"It has fallen into a sad state of disrepair since there has been no resident Earl of Leicester."

"Then let him go to that large inn on the other side of the road. The Golden Crown, I think," said a quieter voice, with an intonation which suggested that the speaker could not care less where milord Stanley went. And then the same pleasant voice added, more quietly still, as if confiding in some intimate at his elbow, "If he comes at all, Francis. Since Thomas Stanley is married to the Tudor's mother, even though they live apart, I find it difficult to trust him."

Although half aware of this conversation going on and of the voices coming nearer, Tansy, who loved beautiful things, still stood bemused at the foot of the bed. She leaned forward between the two slender pillars gazing at the exquisite carving of two small gold panels above the pillows. As far as she could make out, each of them depicted a gilded doorway—a triumphal arch, perhaps, or some grand tomb. She wished that someone would explain them to her, and so intent was she that she remained unaware that two men had come in at the open door.

"Those curious carvings represent the Holy Sepulcher," explained that same quiet, pleasant voice from close behind her.

She started and turned. The speaker was of medium height and lean, with sharply cut features and remote, thoughtful eyes. Apart from a wide gold chain across his shoulders, he was plainly dressed in black velvet, and a flat-brimmed cap with a single jeweled ornament surmounted his straight brown hair. He looked sensitive and approachable. "How do people know that it really looked like that?" asked Tansy.

He smiled at her unexpected interest, and some of the strained tiredness went out of his face. "A crusading knight, back from Jerusalem, described it to my great-great grandfather, who always wanted to go there himself."

Before she could thank him, a mud-splashed messenger came running into the room and, dropping on one knee, handed him a letter. Startled, and with thoughts distracted from the intriguing carving, Tansy became aware of a small group of armed gentlemen standing respectfully by the door

—of the half-amused, half-scandalized expressions on their faces—and knew suddenly that she had been questioning the King.

With fluttering heart and a spread of inadequate skirt, she sank down in what she hoped might pass for a curtsy. But he had forgotten her existance. Quick as thought he whipped a dagger from his belt to slit the sealed ribbon and unroll a brief, urgent message. "Both our surmises are correct, Francis," he said. "The Tudor is marching towards London by way of Watling Street, the straight old Roman road. And Stanley's army, like his heart, is halted midway between us."

"What it is to have military experience and good spies!" gloated Francis Lovell, the good-looking young man nearest to him. "Norfolk here was so sure he would make more directly southward through Gloucester."

"Whichever way he is coming, the treacherous Tudor is making good time of it," growled the faithful Duke of Norfolk. "He could be here in Leicester in a couple of days' time."

"We want no butchering in Leicester. Tomorrow we will march out westwards to meet him," said Richard Plantagenet tersely. "If we must fight, give me flat open fields."

Greatly relieved, Tansy flattened herself through the crowded doorway and fled downstairs. Her stepmother was superintending the clearing away of their guests' hasty meal. In the small room which served as office she found her father trying to reckon up his unexpected expenses and to make a rough draft of an account against the royal exchequer. "I have seen him!" she cried, excitedly.

"Hay and straw for a score of horses, extra bread from Bakehouse Lane—say, one and a half gold angels. Two gold nobles for the meal," Marsh muttered diligently, over his spluttering quill. "That his Grace should have honored me by eating beneath my roof!"

"He spoke to me!" persisted Tansy. "He is not at all as I pictured him."

Not without relief, the honored landlord laid aside his efforts at such large-scale accountancy. "And how did you picture him, my girl?"

"Strong, big, fair and handsome, like people always describe his brother, the late King Edward."

"There is ten years' difference between them. They àre quite different types."

"Is he delicate?"

"I have heard say that he was as a child. But it has never prevented him from living hardily and being the finest soldier of our time."

Tansy's excitement had simmered down into sympathetic reflection. "His face is so full of suffering."

"He has recently lost a loved wife, and his eleven-year-old son," Marsh reminded her. "But I grant you he has aged too much since I last saw him. He certainly looks more than thirty-two. But then, consider all the heavy decisions he has had to make since King Edward died, leaving him Protector of England. Whether to declare the two young Princes bastards after Bishop Stillington of Bath told the Council that he had married Edward to one of his many loves before ever he met the Queen. Whether to have the Queen's brothers executed for plotting to deprive him of his Protectorship. Having to get rid of traitors."

"And the poor young Princes themselves, perhaps?" wondered Tansy.

But there was little time for talk or speculation. Long after she had persuaded her father to go to bed, she was helping to wash platters and strew fresh rushes on the floors.

"How long will these grand people stay?" moaned Dilly, who had had to give up her bed.

"When shall we get some sleep?" groaned the cook.

But to Tansy, who had really spoken with the King, events were beginning to assume the bright tapestried pattern of a piece of history. Life, before his coming, must have been uneventfully dull, she supposed, although none of them seemed to have noticed it. "They are marching out to disperse the Tudor's army tomorrow, and then we shall all have time to rest until they come back," she told them. "And think how exciting it will be if they bring the invader with them and parade him through the streets."

"They may have killed him," yawned Dilly gloomily.

"More likely they'll bring him in alive an' drag him at the cart's tail to Lunnon," predicted Cook, damping down the kitchen fire.

"So us'll miss all the drawing o' his entrails an' the quarterin'," added young Diggory, with gruesome regret.

Late that evening the Earl of Northumberland led in his belated men and put up at the Golden Crown. Until long after midnight people walked about the streets, careful not to waken the snoring troops, and staring up at the windows of the White Boar. And when at last Tansy dragged her tired limbs to bed, a light was still burning in the King's room. As she mounted the stairs she could see the glimmer of it beneath his door. "His Grace sleeps but ill," the man in charge of his bed had said. A pity, she thought, picturing him pacing the great chamber in his rich scarlet nightgown, worrying. Before fighting for his crown and country, surely even the most experienced general must need a good night's rest?

Tansy forgot the horrible stories about the two Princes in the Tower and remembered only how kindly he had explained to her about the curious bed carvings, and how the Plantagenet charm had lit up his face when he smiled.

Whether Richard slept well or ill, he was—like a good soldier—up and dressed right early, not in the sober travel-stained garments in which he had come from Nottingham but resplendent in a ceremonial tabard emblazoned with the royal arms so that not even the most illiterate baggage follower could mistake who and what he was. He had broken his fast in his own room, with only a few of his gentlemen in attendance. But afterwards Tansy saw him standing by the long oak table where he had supped, giving orders for the day, and accessible to all.

Dukes and lords stood about him, and he called the captains of his army by name. A rough map of the district was spread before him. He remembered the main roads between Nottingham and Oxford, but with a long ringed finger he pointed to the ruins of what had once been the Roman forum of the city when it was called Ratae. "The Romans must surely have made a road from here to join up with Watling Street by which our enemy is marching from Wales to London, and by which we could cut him off." He looked up with one of those alert gestures which so belied his quiet, thoughtful aspect, and stopped the passing landlord who was hurrying about his own concerns. "Tell me, Marsh, do you know of such a road?"

Robert Marsh thrust the pile of papers he was carrying into Tansy's arms and sprang to attention with military precision. "Yes, sir. A track which joins Watling Street at Mancetter."

"And if we go out by your West gate and take the bridge there over the river Soar, which is the first village we should come to?"

"Bosworth, sir. About fifteen miles to the southwest."

"Good, that is in the right direction. And there is flat open country between?"

"Yes, sir. Except for one small hill near the village. Our thick forests lie mostly on the other sides of the town. But to leave Leicester that way your Grace must cross two bridges.

"But you have only one river which is your city boundary on that side."

"Yes, sir. But just outside the city the Soar divides, forming a little island on which a small community of the Gray Friars have their canonry. On the far side of the Island is a narrow arched crossing called Bow Bridge."

"Aptly named, by the time all our bowmen will have passed over it!" laughed Lord Lovell. "Is the way easy to find after that, my good friend?"

But Robert Marsh's eager gaze was on the King. " 'Tis only a lane, overgrown in places. And boggy, down by a little tributary called the Tweed. If I might ride with your Grace as guide—" he suggested eagerly.

Richard's thin, clever lips curved into that too rare smile. "Nothing could be better," he agreed, with the willingness to listen which had always made him so popular with his tenantry and army. "And the Gray Friars will be conveniently at hand to give us their blessing as we go."

In spite of his practical ability, he was a man to whom all auguring meant much. Had he not said at supper that staying at the White Boar seemed a good omen for success on the battlefield? He rose and beckoned to a page to bring him the crown of England and Tansy, from the vantage point of the stairs and with her father's hastily fetched riding boots already dangling from her head, stopped awestruck to view the dramatic moment. She saw the King lift the golden circlet from its cushion and the morning sunlight from the latticed windows glitter on the jewels, and then the sudden commotion as John Howard, Duke of Norfolk, almost stumbled forward to prevent him. "Is it wise?" he entreated anxiously.

"Wise, milord Duke?" Richard's eyebrows shot up, the gleaming symbol still half raised.

"I mean, your Grace would be instantly conspicuous. With far less chance than any of us. It is not as if your Grace will ever keep out of the battle. Any Welsh archer might take aim——"

Richard Plantagenet's strong, slender fingers set the crown down firmly on his smooth brown hair. "Then if his aim be true, at least I shall die King of England," he said lightly, apparently taking no chances on the former Richard's fate. "And by the same reasoning," he added, in a different voice which none would dare to disobey, "go, one of you, and fetch milord Stanley's son, whom we brought down from Nottingham, so that he may ride with me." His face was inscrutable so that not even his friend Francis Lovell knew whether he had in mind to bribe the vacillating noble with an honor or to hold the popular young man as hostage for his loyalty. And almost immediately he led the way through the open doorway beneath the swinging inn sign to where his tall charger, White Surrey, was champing impatiently in the sunlit street.

Ever since dawn stragglers from the royal army had been coming into the town, and now gentlemen from manors in the district, each with his handful of followers, were arriving. "Give them some refreshment and direct them over the river towards this place called Bosworth," Sir John Hungerford told Mistress Marsh, who was standing in the entrance of the inn to wish her guests Godspeed.

"Is it to be at their own expense?" she asked cautiously.

"No, mistress. Charge it to the King's account, which we will settle on our return."

"And if they should arrive too late to fight?"

Sir John was already fidgeting to be away. "We shall probably encamp in a few hours, but I do not think the King intends to join battle today."

"Because it is Sunday?" asked Tansy, who was standing just outside in the street.

"Perhaps," said Sir John hurriedly, thinking that his royal master might consider the day inauspicious.

But there might well have been some other reason. The King had been standing by his horse, twisting one of the rings on his finger, as if lost in thought. Before taking the reins from his groom he turned and even came back a step or two. "If a gentleman named Gervase should come, tell him to ride straight to my tent, where the sentries will have orders to let him pass," he commanded. "A lean legal gentleman from London, who will have with him a youth of about this wench's age."

For the briefest moment his sword hand rested on Tansy's shoulder, and then he had drawn on his gloves and sprung up into his saddle and was clattering away at the head of twelve thousand men. Over West Bridge and Bow Bridge he led his army out from Leicester, his standard bearer, *Blanc Sanglier,* going before, the splendor of heraldry and banners all about him, and the Earl of Northumberland's less eager army bringing up the rear. So narrow and humped was the farther bridge, and so vast the army, that they seemed to be passing endlessly all that Sunday morning over the Soar. The Canon of the Gray Friars came to the riverbank to bless them, and an old blind beggar, pushed from his favorite pitch by the jostling press, called cursings after them.

And somewhere in that endless tide of armed men, closer to the King's stirrup than Stanley's reluctant son, rode Robert Marsh, innkeeper and sometime soldier, guiding them along the narrow lanes towards Bosworth.

Back in the disordered and deserted White Boar, a sense of anticlimax oppressed all whom he had left behind, but Tansy's thoughts followed only him in all that proud throng. "You think my father will be safe?" she asked of her stepmother, who had not witnessed his near collapse the evening before.

"Safe?" Rose Marsh tossed her brassy curls. "Why should he not be? He has not gone to fight, ninny, only to show them the way. And the closer he sticks to King Richard the more likely we are to get our money."

And that, thought Tansy, bitterly, is all she cares about.

Chapter Three

Ordinary life was at a standstill in Leicester when the army was gone. Most of the young people had followed after them as far as Bow Bridge. The older people, tired and bewildered by so much excitement, stood about in streets and talked. Battles and rumors of battles up and down the country had disturbed them during all the thirty years of the Wars of the Roses, while Yorkists and Lancastrains took it in turns to wear the crown. There had been bloody fightings at Towton and Tewkesbury. But nothing, since the terrible days of the Black Death, had come so ominously near to them as this.

Shopkeepers were sold out of food. Housewives left last night's makeshift beds unmade while for the first time they had time to talk. Hunters went after the wild hogs that roamed the surrounding forests. Although it was Sunday, farmers drove in what cattle they could spare from their grazing lands along the far side of the river, and butchers slaughtered them against the return of thousands of hungry men. And in the better inns work had to go on, preparing for the return of the more important guests.

In the White Boar, Dilly was still helping Tansy to make the beds. "And those grand people won't be back tonight, will they?" she asked.

"Nor for a couple of nights perhaps," said Tansy. "I heard one of them telling Mistress Marsh that the two enemies probably wouldn't meet until Monday."

"Please God they do meet!" whimpered the little maid shakily. "Suppose this Tudor dragon and his wild Welshmen slipped through in the night and got into the town and raped and murdered us!"

"Our King is too clever for that." Tansy laughed. "Pull your side of the coverlet straighter and plump up the pillows. We must go down and help serve the customers. All manner of important people are drinking here today out of sheer curiosity, and your mistress is singlehanded."

It was true enough that the inn was crowded, and that the men drinking on Sunday morning looked far more prosperous

25

than the regulars who had sat there Saturday evening. But
the landlord's wife was not singlehanded. Tom Hood, the
fletcher, was handing out pints with dextrous enthusiasm,
raking in the money and making himself generally useful.
With his adaptable energy and ready wit he might have been
selling ale instead of arrows all his life.

"Why, Tom, how kind of you!" exclaimed Tansy, nearly
bumping into him as he carried two foaming tankards to no
less a personage than the Mayor.

"Your father passed me on his way through Applegate,
and asked me to lend a hand," he whispered hurriedly.

Tansy lost no time in helping, too, until their chattering
customers began drifting away reluctantly for their dinners.
"Heaven send there be something left in our own kitchen!"
she said, sudenly realizing that she had scarcely eaten since
dawn.

"How you can think of food!" exclaimed Rose dramatically,
as Jod closed the doors. "I am so exhausted I could swoon!
The burden of everything was upon me last evening and now
come all those members of the City Guild, who haven't been
near us for months, asking impertinent questions about our
guests! Whether Lord Lovell is as handsome as they say, and
whether he seduced our daughter? What did the King eat?
Whether that old wives' tale was true about his having a
withered arm? And what is he going to do with Henry Tudor
when he catches him?"

Tansy crimsoned at her careless words, and Tom Hood
turned away tactfully to screw a cask sprigget tighter. "As if
he would tell us!" he muttered. "And if that gay devil
Lovell——"

But the mistress of the White Boar had said her say. "I am
going upstairs to get some sleep," she announced, careless of
the fact that her young stepdaughter would have to cope
with the depleted state of their larder.

"I will send you up some hot caudle or an egg posset,"
offered Tansy.

"Only a light meal. You youngsters can survive all this rush
of work, but my stomach revolts against food. Just some
breast of duck with peas, and a slice or two of spiced beef.
And some of that mulberry tart with cream, if the King's
table left any."

As she went towards the stairs Tom straightened himself from the dripping cask and winked at Tansy, turning the annoyance on her face to laughter. "I am ravenous," she admitted simply. "Let's sit down and eat."

There was nothing he had hoped for more than to be alone with her for a while, but being a generous young man he hesitated. "My mother will probably have something ready."

"I doubt if she has much in her larder either. And surely Cook can find us some remnants from last night's feast. The laborer is worthy of his hire, you know."

When she smiled up at him like that he was defenceless. "My stomach wouldn't revolt from umbles," he said, swinging a leg across the bench and sitting down opposite to her. "But take your mistress all that is left of the beef first, Dilly, and for God's sake see that it is tender!" Dilly grinned at him adoringly. As soon as she was gone he said, without beating about the bush, "How can you bear living with that woman, Tansy?"

"Since my father was fool enough to marry her, she has more right to live here than I, I suppose."

"He must have been lured by the flesh like many a decent, credulous man before him."

"You must admit that she is handsome."

"In the way which satisfies a man for an hour and leaves him heart-hungry and pitied by his friends for a lifetime."

"You should not say such things, Tom."

He shrugged and picked up his knife as Dilly laid a makeshift dish of eggs and beans before them. "I knew your mother," he reminded her. "When my father beat me for playing with his arrow butt feathers she used to comfort me with honey cakes."

Although she laughed, Tansy's eyes were momentarily moist as she looked across the table, seeing him again as the lively, curly-haired little rogue she used to play with. "She loved you, and when your father died and left you far too young to carry on the business she often worried about you."

"I was glad to be on my own, and I haven't done so badly," said Tom, with the frank self-confidence of his auburn-haired kind.

They were young and hungry and made short work of the few nourishing scraps which the cook had found them.

"And this coming of an army," said Tansy, after a while. "Were you able to make a profit out of that?"

"I hoped to. But King Richard does not leave things like weapons to chance. I might have had the sense to guess as much. Instead I wasted time going round to each of his captains and found they were all adequately supplied," the young fletcher told her ruefully. "But I managed to sell several hundred to some of Stanley's fellows out at Stoke Golding. An indifferent crowd and half of them Lancastrians at heart, I would say."

"And while you might have been busy scraping in a few more sales to stragglers you came and helped us here."

"I told you, your father asked me——"

Tansy laid a hand on his wrist beside his plate. "You mean, you suggested it, thinking that we women would be alone."

Tom's capable hand turned and closed over hers. "I often think of you, Tansy." Across the table they smiled into each other's eyes, but after a moment or two Tansy withdrew her hand. During these last few eventful hours she had had a feeling that life was opening up before her, and there were so many possibilities and so many likeable young men. For once Tom did not tussle with her reluctance in playful affection but rose, serious-faced, to fill their tankards. "When your father comes back and all this commotion is over there is another, more important, suggestion which I shall make to him. About us," he said. "That is," he had the grace to add, "if my sale of arrows mounts to anything like his sale of ale."

Being in a Yorkist inn, they raised their tankards to the King. Tom thanked her for the meal and thought he might be able to persuade the Castle steward to let the White Boar have some salted meat—at a price. But, like any up and coming young opportunist, he was in a hurry to be off and improve the profitable, warlike hour. "I am going along there now to talk the Castle captain into believing that his emergency supply of arrows is hopelessly inadequate," he said.

"You could talk anybody into anything, Tom Hood," said Tansy, suppressing a yawn.

"I never seem to succeed with you. But you must rest, my girl. Your cheeks are almost as pasty as Dilly's." Briefly he took her face between his hands and kissed her, before pushing her into her stepmother's cushioned chair. And so tired

was she that almost before Dilly had removed their plates
and he had closed the inn door, her eyes were closed.

Everyone in the White Boar was exhausted, and she must
have slept soundly for the best part of an hour when she was
wakened with a start by the clatter of horses coming into the
yard and someone calling impatiently to Jod, who was shamelessly snoring on a bale of straw.

Tansy's first thought was that they should not disturb her
stepmother. She suspected that the rest of the day would be
uncomfortable for the whole household if they did. So she
pulled herself hastily from the softness of the cushions,
smoothed down her crumpled gown, and went out to meet
them as they came indoors: a lean stern-looking gentleman
followed by a weary and rather bewildered-looking youth of
about her own age. "Can I do anything for you, sirs?" she
asked.

"We heard that his Grace the King stayed here last night,"
the middle-aged gentleman said stiffly. "Where has he gone?"

"Out westwards towards Bosworth. He directed that any
stragglers—any followers, I mean—were to be given refreshment and directed to ride after him," answered Tansy,
thinking how little use either of them would be to him.

"The refreshment to be added to the royal account," said
the mistress of the inn, flouncing down the stairs, ill-pleased
in spite of all Tansy's precautions.

The gentleman allowed himself a thin smile and bowed to
her. "I fear, Mistress, we shall need a few hours' rest as well
as refreshment. We are from London and have been on the
road for days, and this young man is much—er, discomfited.
My name is Gervase."

Rose's whole manner changed. "Then the King is expecting
you! Last thing before leaving he left a message for you to
follow him."

"To go straight to his tent, he said," added Tansy, recalling
the King's words and almost feeling again the light, insistent
pressure of his fingers on her shoulder. At the time she had
been too preoccupied with anxiety for her father to pay much
heed, but now she remembered perfectly. A tall legal gentleman from London, he had said, with a youth of about her
own age.

"Then it sounds as if we could rest ourselves and our

mounts awhile and still catch up with a foot-slogging army before they camp."

"Our rooms are all taken," said Rose, with the air of one accustomed to turning away mere knights. "But since his Grace specially mentioned you I will show you to a room which some of the Duke of Norfolk's officers used, where you could snatch a couple of hours' sleep."

"And I will waken you in time for dinner," promised Tansy, fervently hoping there would be some, and feeling that, since this appointment had been so much on the King's encumbered mind, the legal gentleman was behaving with insufficient urgency. Indeed, he seemed so much engrossed at the moment by his hostess's gracious smile that he forgot to invite his far more discomforted charge to accompany them upstairs.

"Do you suppose we shall be in time? Before the battle begins, I mean," asked the youth, as soon as their two elders were gone.

"They say the King is not likely to engage the enemy today and hopes to intercept him in twelve miles or so, this side of Bosworth." Tansy was calculating how long it would take Tom Hood to wheedle something reasonably edible from the Castle steward and added rather perfunctorily, "If you are so tired, why do you not sit down?"

There was a slight embarrassed silence. "Because I cannot."

"Cannot?" She looked him over from brown head to sensibly shod feet, but there was no sign of any particular disability about his slender, well-grown body.

For the first time he smiled. "My backside is too sore," he explained.

Tansy burst out laughing. "Oh, what a painful predicament! You have ridden too far and your saddle galled?"

"It must have been made for a fat knight in full armor, I should think! And you heard Master Gervase say we had been jogging along for *days*. But the fact is," he added, with a rather charming candor, "I have never ridden before."

"Not ridden before!" Leicestershire-bred Tansy looked amazed.

"Until a few days ago I was still at school," he confessed.

"I see. What is your name?"

"Dickon."

Invitingly, Tansy rearranged the cushions in Rose's chair to the best advantage of his bruised anatomy. "And in London, of course, one would scarcely need to ride. But surely on holidays, at home with your parents——"

"I have no home or parents." As he eased himself gratefully into the chair he saw, and loved, her quick gesture of compassion. "Oh, you need not pity me too much," he hastened to add, covering what she guessed to be a wound far more painful and private than any dealt by saddle leather. "I live in my schoolmaster's house, and he must have been very carefully—chosen. He is both wise and kind."

"Not that old——?" Tansy's head jerked backwards irreverently towards the closed door while she smothered the unflattering description which had sprung to her mind.

The lad laughed. "No, no, praise God! Master Gervase comes to see me occasionally and asks how I am getting on with lessons and arranges about payments, I imagine. But I do not know where he lives, and he is always very careful to impress upon me that he is no relation of mine—for which," added his graceless charge, with a wide grin, "I am truly thankful."

Tansy listened to him with that careful attention which made people tell her things. She felt all the more sympathetic because he showed no particular self-pity. "But, Dickon, it must be terrible to have no relatives at all. No one of your own to love."

"I loved the kind woman who brought me up in a cottage when I was small," he said, reminiscently. "It was there that I first saw Master Gervase. As soon as I was old enough he fetched me to Master Paston's school. I cried myself to sleep for weeks, but now it is home to me. My classmates are good fellows. But we shall soon have to part company. Most of them will be apprenticed by their fathers to some freeman or other of one of the City guilds."

"And you?" asked Tansy.

"Master Gervase always thought I should become an apprentice, too. But now he is not so sure." The bewildered look returned to blank out all his expressive eagerness. "Why should the King have sent for me?"

Tansy considered the problem, all housekeeping worries

momentarily pushed aside. "Perhaps, Dickon, your father was one of those many gentlemen who gave their lives for him in battle. My father says the King is always doing kindnesses to their families. Even sometimes to their bastards."

"That is what Piers suggested."

"Piers?"

"Piers Harrowe. My particular friend at school. And it would, of course, be very nice to think so. But why should King Richard be bothered with me at such an important time?"

"It might be some promise he made. A man going into battle must want to fulfill his promises."

They sat side by side companionably. "It could well be true," agreed Dickon, absently chalking a succession of attractive arabesques and corbels on the absent landlord's tally board. "Because some months ago Gervase took me to a very beautiful house. It had lovely colored windows and a hammerbeam roof. After we had waited a long time and all manner of grandly dressed people and servants had passed back and forth across the hall, we were called into a much smaller room where a gentleman spoke to me very kindly. He was dressed in black, I remember. He asked me about my studies and whether I went regularly to archery practice with the elder boys. He seemed particularly pleased because I had once hit the gold at two hundred and twenty yards and made me construe some Latin out of one of those new printed books. He seemed to be looking me over and testing me, if you know what I mean. Before we left he gave me a gold noble, so that I was able to return some of the kindnesses of my friends. Master Gervase told me never to speak of this visit, and I never have, except to you and Piers. And why I should be telling you, whom I have only just met and whose name I do not even know, completely mystifies me!"

"My name is Tansy Marsh."

Dickon repeated it carefully, as if committing something precious to memory. Then suddenly he laughed lightheartedly, all gloom and secrecy gone. "Do you know what Piers says? He says I must be one of Lord Lovell's numerous byblows! It is a wild sort of suggestion he sometimes comes out with."

But Tansy was too much intrigued to laugh. "How long ago were you taken to this grand house?"

"Oh, only a matter of months. It was a year ago this spring, just after young Prince Edward died. I remember because I had hoped to see some wrestling, but all London seemed to be in mourning."

"And what was this gentleman who spoke to you like?"

"Medium height and lean and brown-haired, like me."

"Then you can tell your imaginative friend it couldn't have been Lord Lovell. He was here last night, and he is stocky and fair."

For one who had no fond relatives and no rosy prospects, Dickon looked remarkably relieved, she thought.

"I believe you would rather stay in London with your friends and be apprenticed then be adopted in some wealthy manor."

"In a way I would. When one has no family, one cleaves to familiar friends. And although the life is often hard, 'prentices have plenty of fun."

"I imagine they do," agreed Tansy with a smile, remembering market days. "What craft or trade do you think Master Gervase will set you to?"

"Before there was all this mysterious going and coming, he said that I might choose. And of all things I want to become a master mason."

"A mason?" Tansy looked down at his long clever fingers, and at the odd drawings he had made, and decided that he would probably become a very good one. Because he had not yet been out into the world to earn his living, and she, as an innkeeper's daughter, was accustomed to meeting all kinds of people, she felt almost maternal towards him. But he certainly had individuality.

"Above everything else," he repeated, speaking to himself rather than to her. "I want to build gracious homes and exquisitely carved pillars upholding soaring arches that look as if they are reaching up to praise God."

Tansy stared at him, surprised and fascinated by an aspect of him so alien to her workaday world. But she was recalled to more mundane matters by approaching voices. "Well, when you have rested you will both need to eat," she said, rising hastily, "so I must not sit here wasting any more time."

In spite of his ridiculous disability, he rose with her. Evidently, although the school diet had failed to put much flesh on his bones, Master Paston had not omitted to teach him manners. "Do you really think it is wasting time listening—as if you really cared—while some lonely fool unburdens his inmost mind?" he asked. And although he grinned and raised a quizzical eyebrow, his voice was rather sad and, to Tansy, somehow reminiscently adult.

Chapter Four

That Sunday was a strange day in Leicester, a day of waiting and false quiet. Not having been able to attend Mass, Tansy slipped into the church of St. Nicholas to pray for the safety of her father. It was then afternoon, and by the time she returned Master Gervase and Dickon were gone. *And I did not even remember to ask his surname*, she thought, passing through the parlor where the lad had, as he had termed it, unburdened his inmost mind. But, because of some mutual liking there had been between them, she had remembered him briefly in her prayers.

People were all agog for news, and those who had ventured to ride out in the direction of Bosworth reported that the King's army was encamped and all was quiet, although some of them, who had scrambled up a small hill for a better view, insisted that they could see the tents of the opposing army in a meadow across the little river. Master Gervase would probably have had time to discharge his mysterious errand. As Tansy sat enjoying an unaccustomed hour of leisure, she wondered if King Richard would really see them, and whether she would see young Dickon again on his way back to London, and hear the outcome of it all. Far more urgently, she wondered when her father, who had evidently led the troops to the desired position, would return.

The opening of a door made her spring up hopefully, but to her surprise it was Master Malpas, their rival. He poked his head in, looked appraisingly to right and left and, seeing her alone, came forward. It was the first time for months that he had crossed their threshold and Tansy felt sure that, save for her father's absence, he would not have done so. "A comfortable, homely place you have here," he conceded ingratiatingly. "But I suppose, like the rest of us, you are eaten out of your last bite of bread?"

"With good friends in Bakehouse Lane we have little need to worry," lied Tansy valiantly.

"But think of the appetite those Yorkists will bring back in a day or two," he persisted. "I am sure Mistress Marsh will be glad enough then of a fat ox or two all ready for the spit. Urgent as my own need is, with all milord Northumberland's friends to feed, I can spare her a couple and welcome."

The landlord of the Golden Crown almost begging them to accept a favor! Perhaps he hoped that as their fortunes rose they would recommend to him guests they had no room for. It was certainly a straw in the wind, like the influx of all his most influential customers since the coming of the King; a sure sign that her father's fortunes would go up and up.

"A couple of whole oxen to spare—here, in Leicester—now?" gasped Tansy. "However did you come by them, Master Malpas?"

He laid a fat, conspiratorial finger against his nose. "Shall we say that Gladys, my pretty Welsh singing girl, has a father who is a prosperous farmer?"

"Or a lover, more likely," said Tansy, who knew very well that the painted hussy's father was the drunken old showman who ran the bullbaiting down in Swinemarket.

"How you innocent-looking poppets grow up!" laughed Malpas.

But she was certainly not innocent enough to risk his attempt at fondling. "I will call my stepmother and tell her of your kind offer about the meat," she said, making her escape.

Rose was putting on her best taffeta gown, with an admiring Dilly in attendance. Already she felt it incumbent upon her to play the part of successful hostess. "Everyone comes to the White Boar now," she boasted, well pleased with Tansy's news. "You must make yourself some new aprons, Dilly, and when that clever mercer next comes with all the latest fashions from London you must tell me, Tansy, so that I may get some clothes suitable for the kind of guests we shall be having. And as soon as the King's account is paid, we must get you some new shoes," she added, in a burst of exuberant generosity. She waved Dilly aside and gave her stepdaughter a perfunctory hug in passing. "Tansy, my girl, we are made! And shrewd Hugh Malpas would naturally be the first man to realize it. How sickening it must be for him to have to come offering gifts so as to keep in with us!"

Tansy was as glad as she and, encouraged by this rare burst of affability, hoped that prosperity would bring easier times in more ways than one. But she had lived with Robert

Marsh for longer and understood what kind of things enraged him. "Would my father like it?" she demurred.

"Like what?" asked Rose, with a final glance in her mirror.

"Accepting anything from him!"

"My good girl, the King will probably be back to supper tomorrow evening and we shall have to feed him somehow. We should be fools to refuse."

"There is the salted pork Tom got us from the Castle——"

Rose Marsh spurned it with a gesture. She could afford to, now. "Salt pork is all very well for common folk. But juicy cuts of prime beef for the gentry!" she chortled in that deep, throaty voice of hers. "Remember, we have a reputation to keep up now." Halfway down the wide staircase she turned and called back, "I tell you what, Tansy. After all this silly fighting is over I shall get your father to have a notice inscribed THE KING SLEPT HERE nailed to the wall beneath our signboard. That should put paid to the Golden Crown and the Three Cups and all the other inns in Leicester."

Flushed with success and full of rather overripe sexual allure, Rose went down to accept the offering of her defeated rival. He was her type of man. She had always admired his methods. When Tansy went out through the yard to feed her pony she could hear her talking and laughing more boisterously with their visitor than she ever did nowadays with her husband. Come to think of it, she should have married a man like Hugh Malpas, thought Tansy. If only she had met him in time, how happy we might all have been!

In the quiet warm stall which he had humbly shared with a King's horse, Pippin nuzzled against her with his soft pink nose, and while he champed contentedly at his oats she promised him that their ride to market was only deferred until life should become ordinary again. Then she wandered out into the sunny yard to find Jod busy with a hammer at the side gates. "I be fixin' a better bolt," he explained. "Come tomorrow night we'll have all them valuable horses in our stalls again."

"But they have their own men to look after them. You don't have to feel responsible, Jod."

" 'Tis true. But folks'll come pryin' in to look at the King's White Surrey, as like as not."

Tansy watched him approvingly and then, while the gate

was still open, they walked together a few yards along White
Boar Lane to the corner of the High Street. After their sudden breathless activities it was good to have time to loiter
again, and Jod had adored her since she was a child. "Do you
know what the Mistress says, Jod? That she will get a notice
made, saying that the King of England slept here, and have it
nailed beneath our signboard. I believe that young man from
London could have drawn one."

They stood at the corner looking up at the familiar front of
the hostelry which represented their life, the slender fair-
haired girl and the bent old man. "That there ole boar certainly did ought to be proud this day, Mistress Tansy," he
said, with a cheerful, toothless grin.

"We will give him a new coat of paint next week," she answered, with more truth than she knew. And then they both
gave a cry of relief as the Boar's owner came riding up from
Applegate and through the main arched doorway into the
yard.

They hurried to greet him as he slid wearily from his saddle. "We scarcely dared to hope you would come back so
soon!" cried Tansy.

"They were all well placed for the battle—just where the
King said, along that swampy little river Tweed by Bosworth.
There was nothing more I could do. So I thought I had best
get back and help you here. We are sure to have a busy evening, and then we must prepare for the King's return." Tansy
wondered if that had been the only reason. He leaned heavily
on her shoulder as they walked towards the inn, and turned to
her with a wry smile as they went indoors. "I wanted to
stay," he admitted, too quietly for his approaching wife to
hear. "But I doubt if I should be much good at fighting any
more."

Cold apprehension clutched at her heart. "Tom Hood came
and helped us this morning, and we took a mint of money,"
she said, to cheer him.

"A good lad, Tom," he said. Then, with a vestige of his old
teasing chuckle, "You might do worse than encourage him,
my poppet."

A busy evening they certainly had. The curious, the anxious, the secretly Lancastrian, the confidently Yorkist—everyone came to drink at the White Boar that night. And they

came for news as much as for drink. For had not the landlord of the White Boar—always a respected citizen—actually been with the King?

"Where were Lord Stanley's men placed?" asked the Mayor, anxiously.

"He and his brother, Sir William, came up later, as you know. They are midway between the two camps, you might say," said Marsh, handing him his glass.

"A clever move of his Grace's to keep young Strange, his son," remarked someone.

"Maybe. But a finer or more disciplined army than marched through our town never took the field," said Mayor Wigston proudly. "No pillaging, no interfering with our women——"

"I reckon they were too dog-tired for that sort of lark, the way he marches 'em," laughed Marsh, shortly.

Master Jordan, the schoolmaster, stirred in his accustomed seat in the chimney corner. "Seriously, Robert, what chances do you think Henry Tudor has?"

"Precious few, I should imagine, Will," said Marsh jauntily, but felt obliged to add on a more sober note, "While I was there our spies brought back a rather disturbing report that he had some of these modern cannon."

It was a topic bound to spark off general comment.

"Like we hear they have in France?"

"Barrels from which they expel stones by making an explosion with some kind of flintlock——"

"Great cumbersome things, beyond a man's strength to carry, surely?"

"They'll soon get bogged down in our watery meadows!"

"If they ever have a chance to use them, once our bowmen start," contributed Tom Hood.

"If I know the Plantagenet, he'll let fly at them as soon as it is light," chuckled Marsh.

The babble of discussion went on, but after they had all gone he sank down as he had before. This time the exertion and excitement of his ride, followed by such a press of questioning customers, had tried him beyond pretense. "I am a sick man," he admitted, and allowed his wife and daughter to help him to his bed.

Tansy took him a hot posset and sat by him while he drank it.

"I must be up and about tomorrow somehow," he said, gradually reviving as he spooned up the nourishing herbal mess. "The King promised to lodge here on his return. If the Tudor is taken alive everyone says he will be brought south to London for trial and execution. Speaking of London, Tansy, did that lawyer his Grace mentioned ever come?"

"Yes, and stayed to dinner. And the young man with him: Dickon somebody. I forgot to ask his family name."

"Odd visitors for the King to bother about at such a time."

"Yes. But he tried to explain it, as far as he understood it himself."

"Who? Gervase?"

"No, Dickon. In confidence." Because she trusted her father utterly, and partly in order to take his mind off the worry of his failing health, she related what the strange young man had said.

With bigger affairs on his mind, Marsh dismissed it with a laugh. "A likely story!" he scoffed. "Don't you know that Bedlam is full of lunatics who believe they are descended from John the Baptist or Julius Caesar or somebody?"

"But this young man was not at all mad," persisted Tansy, earnestly. "All he seemed to want was to live an ordinary life in London and be apprenticed to a mason."

"Then probably the Gervase man is using him as an impostor to claim some rich inheritance. All this tarradiddle about being taken to some grand house! In case I should be taken from you, you must learn to be less gullible, my girl. And if they should come back here for beds," he added wearily, "tell them we are full up, which we shall be. Turn them out and have nothing more to do with them."

The pain from his chest wound seemed to stab closer to his tired heart, and he spoke more sharply than he intended. Before leaving him, Tansy shaded the rushlight and pulled the covers more comfortably about him, hoping that her stepmother would soon come to bed.

But next morning Diggory was sent hurrying off for the doctor, who decreed that whatever excitement went on at the White Boar, the landlord himself must rest. It was a bitter blow to Robert Marsh, but at least he had the satisfaction of knowing, in the midst of his pain and weakness, that he had been right about the Plantagenet's beginning battle before cock-crow so as to take the enemy unprepared. The town was already astir with rumors. People swore they could hear the strange firing of cannon, and before *Nones* all the church bells had begun to ring.

"They be comin' back," Jod shouted up from the yard.

"Men marching along the road from Wales, a whole army of them," reported Rose, poking her head round the bedroom door to impart some of the news in the midst of her flustered preparations.

"How do you know?" asked Marsh, hating his enforced inactivity.

"Captain's lookout men can see them from the tower of the Castle church." In a flurry of excitement she slammed the door, in spite of the doctor's orders that her husband must be kept quiet.

"Then it is all over!" he murmured, sinking back against his pillows with a gratified sigh.

Yes, it was all over. Strangers exchanged scraps of news in passing, people who had been sworn enemies for years hugged each other in the streets, women rushed back to the meals they had been preparing. Then, quite suddenly, the bells stopped, leaving a strange, rather frightening stillness. It was as if some known way of life were suspended. Surprised, uncertain, more subdued, householders went to their open doors or hurried towards the West bridge. In the sudden stillness they could certainly hear the tramp of feet coming closer: the tramp of a whole army, as the Castle lookouts had said. Orderly and disciplined, if weary. But to their bewilderment it turned out to be a different army from the one they had cheered so lustily as it set out. Instead of the leopards and fleurs-de-lys of England and the familiar *Blanc Sanglier* of Richard, a great flaunting banner with the red dragon of Wales was being borne triumphantly across the Soar. And the man riding beneath it into their city was a stranger. Henry Tudor, the man with Lancastrian and Valois and Welsh blood, who had spent most of his thirty years in Pembroke Castle or exiled overseas, and whom few Englishmen had ever seen. Most of the people of Leicester stared at him with hatred, but some, whose fathers had fought at Agincourt, looked to him with hope. "Anyone, anyone," prayed the more thoughtful traders, "whose coming will put a stop to this bloodshed and ravaging of our country!"

"Victory went to Henry Tudor, Earl of Richmond!" yelled a gang of apprentices rushing past the White Boar to spread the news from the City Cross.

"It was his newfangled cannon and Stanley's defection that won him the day," corroborated Tom Hood, bursting into the inn parlor where Rose Marsh and her stepdaughter stood white-faced and arrested like statues in the midst of their eager preparations. "And now he rides in wearing the crown!"

Tansy stood uncomprehendingly halfway to the stairs with a pile of freshly laundered towels in her arms. "The lovely golden crown with the jewels that was here, in this very room, a few hours ago?"

"How did he get it?" asked Rose.

"Some archer found it in a thornbush."

"The Crown of England—worth hundreds of pounds—in a hedge!"

"That was after the Stanleys ratted. It seems Lord Stanley put it on Henry Tudor's head."

Tansy laid down the White Boar's best towels on the edge of the table. They would not be wanted now. "Then the King —" she faltered incredulously.

Tom crossed the room and took her cold hands in his. "King Richard was killed in the battle," he said, speaking slowly and distinctly, because it was so difficult for her—and for all England—to believe.

Chapter Five

The Marshes' bitter cup of disappointment was full when the new, self-appointed King stopped at the Golden Crown. The sign must have seemed as propitious to him as the White Boar had to Richard. There he collected scribes and messengers with as much ardor as Richard had collected skilled bowmen. While Malpas's cook kept hot the prime cuts of roast ox for dinner, he dictated news of his victory to all parts of the realm. "Henry, by the grace of God, King of England and of France, Prince of Wales and Lord of Ireland," he styled himself, staking his claim to everything. And he wisely began by charging his followers, upon pain of death, "to rob no man, nor despoil the people's common lands, nor to pick quarrels with any, but to keep the King's peace."

When at last he relaxed from his statesmanship, the alluring Gladys was sent to sing Welsh songs to him while he ate. But although he applauded the songs and complimented the cook, he scarcely seemed to notice the allure.

While Hugh Malpas expanded visibly with pride, across the street in the deserted White Boar only a few faithful old regulars came sheepishly to drink, and Rose Marsh was glad enough to take their humble groats. "What is this Tudor like?" she asked of those who had seen him.

"Very different from our fourth Edward," guffawed a sheep dealer who had been to London in his youth. "They say that Malpas' singing hussy all but undressed herself and he went on talking to Lord Stanley about the best way to raise taxes."

"At least he has not boasted about the battle," added a merchant's clerk with Lancastrian leanings. "In fact, he says very little at all. A secretive type."

"I mean, what does he look like?" persisted Rose, womanlike.

"Not particularly striking in any way," the sheep dealer told her. "Thin as King Richard, but fairer. Thoughtful-looking like he was—and thin-lipped, too. But without the Plantagenet's rare, warming smile."

"But in a way, not unlike him," added the clerk, obviousl rather taken aback by his own unexpected conclusion.

"Which is scarcely surprising," pointed out Master Jordan "seeing that they are cousins of a kind."

Tansy watched her opportunity. When the babble of con versation had died down a little, she went to take the school master's empty tankard. "Could you come up and talk a littl with my father, Master Jordan?" she begged. "He feels so ou of everything, laid low at such a time, and you could tell him so much that he wants to know. And naturally," she added lowering her voice, "we are all worried for the business."

He rose at once and followed her upstairs, and after she had set a chair for him she lingered awhile to savor her father's pleasure in his company and to hear their friendly talk "This is a sad day for you, Robert, even apart from your sickness," said Jordan, his finely drawn face full of sympathy.

"How that pushful brute Malpas must be crowing!" lamented Marsh weakly. "My wife and I were so sure that we were made. And God knows I needed the money, William!"

William Jordan knew it too, considering the debts Rose Marsh accumulated at the drapers'. "And now, will you ever see even what the royal party owes you?"

"I doubt it. Where are they all—Norfolk, Lovell, and the rest?"

"Scattered. Riding hell for leather to some place of hiding, I suppose, those of them who are still alive. No, I fear you will never be repaid."

"And the White Boar's takings will go down again. . . . For Rose, of course, it is the disappointment about success and the royal patronage. For party loyalties she does not care much either way. But for me it is the loss of a good master."

"Everybody says he died in personal combat, fighting furiously. That he killed the invader's standard-bearer and almost reached the Tudor himself."

"Would that he had! Where is his body? What did they do with it?"

The schoolmaster shook his head sadly. "I heard a rumor that the Gray Friars came out and begged to be allowed to give it sanctuary. Perhaps we shall know more definitely tomorrow."

Robert Marsh pulled himself up in the bed. "It is incredible! Not only that he lost the battle——"

"No one could have won it against such tremendous desertion."

"But that this usurper, this stranger, should be allowed to march unmurdered through England!"

"Perhaps it is because he is a stranger," suggested Jordan thoughtfully.

"What do you mean?"

"Oh, I know that we feel differently about this, Robert. You, like all men who actually served the Plantagenet, see only his ability, his decisiveness—the way he saw that his own people were properly armed and fed and personally looked into their grievances. Around Middleham, where he lived with his wife, and throughout all Yorkshire, he was God. But it seems it wasn't so in London, where people remember his easygoing brother. Where the Queen dowager and all her Woodville tribe tried to thwart and blacken him because they wanted the power themselves. And where the young Prince whom the Londoners looked upon as their future King has been set aside."

"He had to have traitors like Buckingham and the Woodville Earl Rivers executed. Woodville plotted for the Protectorship, which King Edward, in his last words, willed to his brother Richard."

"Admittedly. But personally I have always thought he would have been wiser to spare Lord Hastings who had been his brother's honored counselor for so long."

"You said because the Tudor is a complete stranger——"

"Yes. Just because to some people Richard Plantagenet is a god and to others a devil. Because this country has been ravaged and impoverished by civil war for years. Is it not possible that hundreds of farmers and traders and peace-loving folk see a complete stranger as a new hope? As the unknown quantity upon which some kind of agreement may be built? He has begun well by forbidding his followers to ferment disturbance. If he can get to London alive, I think he may pull off his impertinent venture. Start an altogether new dynasty with hope——"

Marsh drummed impatiently on the counterpane. "How can you be so impersonal?"

"Perhaps it is a kind of impersonal wisdom that Englan
needs just now. As a sick man, like you, needs soothin
drugs," said Jordan, reaching for a phial which the docto
had left.

Marsh waved it aside. "But what can a man called Tudo
care for England?"

"Perhaps the Plantagenets cared too passionately?"

Tansy left them arguing and slipped away. Most of th
customers had already gone, fearing violent disturbances. Fo
if Henry Tudor's immediate followers obeyed his humane or
ders, there were many who did not. Stragglers and citizens
local people who had always been supporters of the Lancas
trian cause, now began to make nuisances of themselves
Having drunk heavily to celebrate, some of the younger me
began brawling and beating up inoffensive citizens and wer
soon joined by the wilder elements of Henry's Welsh follow
ers.

"Best be going home, William. The streets may not b
safe," advised Robert Marsh, weary with talking. "Tell Tans
to make sure that Jod bolts all the doors," he called after him
chafing because he could not see to such things himself.

After thanking the old gentleman and watching him cros
the street to his schoolhouse, Tansy went out into the yar
and stood listening for a few minutes to the sudden bursts o
shouting. The last of the customers' horses had been taken
and Jod was just about to close the gates onto the lane. Fro
the direction of the river they could hear even more violen
shouting and the footsteps of many people running.

"Just as well I fixed them new bolts," said Jod, with hi
hands already on the gates to push them shut.

But just at that moment the yelling crowd swept round th
corner into the lower end of White Boar Lane, hot in the ex
citement of a man hunt. In the gathering darkness, Tans
could discern the unfortunate victim they were pursuing:
slight, darkly clad figure, doubling and stumbling with ex
haustion as he ran. "They will catch up with him in a matte
of minutes," muttered Jod, stepping out into the lane.

"And kill him," murmured Tansy pitifully.

"Aye, the poor wight is prid near finished."

The rabble were catching up on him quickly. "The telltal
Yorkist! Didn't even fight! But quick enough to spoil ou

sport!" were some of the things they were shouting. "Cut his wheedling tongue out! Throw him in the river!" And the river was very close.

He was stretching out a hand now to touch the innyard wall, either to steady himself as he ran or because it was the asylum he sought, and Tansy could hear the sobs of his panting breath. "Wait!" she whispered, as Jod would have slammed the gates.

"For Christ's sake, no! We shall have the whole cutthroat pack in here," he warned.

But, taking a risk on it, Tansy held one gate open a moment or two longer. She pulled the poor wretch in and slammed them with only a few yards to spare. In those moments she had caught a glimpse of his pursuers' cruel, drink-inflamed faces and knew that they would have killed anyone who stood in their way. As Jod shot the great iron bolt, howls of disappointment went up, as from wild beasts cheated of their prey, and blows from their fists rained on the other side. But the strong oak held.

Realizing her moment of danger, Tansy stood with wildly beating heart until at last the mob gave up and began to drift away in search of fresh entertainment. It was some moments before she turned to look at the man she had saved.

He had collapsed on the ground and lay there with arms outstretched, his body still heaving with the effort to draw breath. Jod fetched a lantern. He set it down on the ground and propped the panting young man against the wall. His clothes were torn, one hand clutched at his ankle, and blood gushed from a nasty gash on his forehead, almost obliterating his features.

"Get a pail of water and a clean horse cloth," Tansy told Jod. Then, kneeling, she began to wipe the wounded man's face.

Revived by the cold water, he opened his eyes and looked at her.

"Dickon!" she exclaimed.

"I didn't—think—I should make it!" he panted.

Unreasonably, she was immeasurably thankful that he had. "I shall have to tie this tightly to stop the bleeding," she said, pushing back his matted brown hair.

Her friendly presence helped him to pull himself together.

"It isn't much, really," he said. "They began throwing stones. It is my ankle that hurts. I tripped on the cobbles as I ran. When they all set on me, I ran for my life."

"Anyone would have," she assured him, remembering their murderous faces.

"Anyone, yes. But not my father. He wouldn't have been very proud of me, would he?"

"Your father?" repeated Tansy, mopping some blood from her skirt. "I thought you told me you'd never even seen him."

"I have now," he said, without embellishment. "He was the King!"

Tansy stared at him apprehensively, supposing him to be lightheaded. His eyelids had dropped shut again, but there was a small proud smile on his lips, a contentment where, when she had first met him, there had been only a kind of restless bewilderment. And because in his extremity his face looked older and bore the marks of suffering, the queer sense of some elusive likeness which had bothered Tansy resolved itself. With lantern light throwing into relief the fine molding of his cheekbones and the tightly compressed lower lip, she saw how closely he resembled the man who had explained to her about the bed carvings and who had touched her shoulder when he commanded so urgently that this young man should be brought to him. She suddenly knew, without logical explanation and beyond skepticism, that what Dickon had said was true.

All that was maternal in her, all that part of her which invariably rose up compassionately to defend even an animal in danger of being hurt, was terribly afraid for him.

She sat back on her heels in the starlit yard and wondered what to do. "A likely story!" her father had said, when she told him about mysterious payments and a fantastic visit to a grand house, and an ordinary schoolboy who thought he might be some nobleman's bastard. This story was more incredible still, yet she had seen the fleeting likeness and believed. "If they should come back, send them away and have nothing more to do with them," Robert Marsh had said. Never before had she deliberately disobeyed her father. But how could she turn out into the dangerous streets one so helpless, who had already been set upon, perhaps because he had been seen about King Richard's camp? How could she bring herself to do it even if he were of no particular interest to her? And honesty forced her to admit that he was.

Feeling far too young to have such an important decision thrust upon her, she shook the lad to full consciousness. "Where is Master Gervase?" she asked, in a last effort to shelve her feeling of personal responsibility.

"I don't know. He made off."

"After the battle?"

"As soon as he saw that the King was killed."

So there was to be no help from that quarter. Tansy thought furiously while she finished bandaging the damaged ankle with linen soaked in cold water. Jod, who had served her mother's family before ever he came to the inn, must be her only confidant. "Help the gentleman up the ladder into the hayloft and make him comfortable for the night. I will put something for him to eat on the rain butt outside the back door. And please, Jod, do not speak of this to anyone."

The old man's steady gray eyes met hers, and although she could not know how much she looked like her mother at that moment she knew that no verbal promise was needed, either for the hiding of a fugitive or for the strange thing which Jod might have overheard.

She stood up and said formally to Dickon, "I will not pretend that our rooms are full. They are empty—and probably often will be now. But it would be unwise to offer you one."

He caught at her hand, still wet from her ministrations, and pressed it to his lips. "Is it not enough that you saved my life just now?" he asked huskily.

She turned hurriedly towards the lighted kitchen windows, but by the time he had risen shakily with Jod's help, her curiosity had forced her to come back. "Why did they call you telltale Yorkist and yell that you had spoiled their sport? And then set on you?" she asked.

Because I ran to the Gray Frairs and entreated them to take the King's body from them, to give it decent Christian burial before they . . . It was at Bow Bridge. . . . The sadistic curs had . . ." Dickon shuddered and covered his bruised face with both hands. He was not much more than a schoolboy and he could bear no more.

"Tell me tomorrow, Dickon," said Tansy pitifully, and went back into the inn to find herself, as usual, the butt for her stepmother's strident wrath when things went wrong.

"Where have you been loitering at such a time?" she demanded. "With your father sick again and all those ruffians howling at our door and throwing stones. Huddling with some tipsy lout in the hayloft, I'll be bound. If the Mayor and Guild Masters do nothing to stop this broiling we shall all be murdered in our beds!" All the warmer expansion of Rose's good mood when prosperity seemed certain had turned to gall, which must be taken out on the absurdly loved daughter of the man, the ailing luckless man, whom she had been fool enough to marry. "At least in King Richard's time we could sleep in peace," she admitted, cooling down a little. "What have they done with him, d'you know?"

Tansy stood still and outwardly respectful before her. "He was killed," she said stupidly, battered by the torrent of the tirade.

Rose began to loosen her over-tight bodice preparatory to joining the sick husband who was of no use to her either by day or by night. "Of course he was killed, nitwit. We all know that. But what have they done with the corpse?"

Tansy did not like to think. "The Gray Friars took it, I was told."

"You were told! Who told you?"

His son—and he should know! thought Tansy, who had got into the habit of carrying on simultaneously a spoken and an unspoken conversation when her stepmother bellowed at her. Aloud she said, unromantically but truthfully, "Someone who came to the inn this evening."

"And ended up in the hayloft!" sneered Rose, who had been trying to drown her disappointment in malmsey.

When Tansy reached her attic she found that at least some of her stepmother's words were true. Exultant Lancastrian sympathizers paraded the streets so that decent citizens could get no sleep. They bawled ribald songs about dead Richard and Norfolk the lion and Lovell the dog, referring to their heraldic badges. And what better target could they ask for than the sign of the White Boar, gently swinging in the evening breeze? Stones were hurled at it until it rocked madly, and those which missed spattered on the timbered front of the inn. When one stone broke a pane of transparent horn in her casement and struck her bare shoulder sharply, Tansy, tired out, pulled the bedclothes over her head and whimpered. But her tears were more a general *miserere* for the misfortunes of her father's inn, and for slain King Richard and his lonely unacknowledged son, than for her own discomfort.

Chapter Six

"In his tent, the night before the battle, he told me that I was his son," said Dickon slowly, staring unseeingly at the hayloft wall.

Tansy had the good sense not to hurry him. It was as if he were trying to reassemble his memories: amazing memories only a day old which had been almost shaken from his mind by the violence which he had since suffered, memories which would alter the self-image of his whole life. He lay on his stomach supported by his elbows, with a half-munched apple in his hand, his face clearly visible in the early morning light from the wagon shed below.

A king's son eating bread and apples for breakfast in a hayloft! thought Tansy, squatting with her back to the wall and her feet curled up under her near the top of the ladder. "Were you alone with his Grace?"

"Except for Gervase. I think he was there all the time, somewhere at the back of the tent. It was late afternoon. There was an unlit lamp on the table beside the King's crown, an ordinary lamp like the one hanging up there above that bit of old harness."

He stared at the rusty, worthless thing as if trying to reconcile the familiar with the fantastic in all that he had seen and all that had happened to him in the last two days. With the same intent, perhaps, he bit again into his apple, chewed, and threw the core across the hay.

"He said that he fathered me when he was not much older than I am now. That from the time he could bear arms he lived a rough soldiering life with far too much responsibility, so that his elder brother could cease fighting and keep court at Westminister. He didn't even know who the girl was, but afterwards, when some of his friends told him she had died of the sweating sickness soon after childbirth, he arranged for me to be cared for by that good cottage woman I told you of. And they all laughed at him for a conscientious fool."

"Then you are his eldest son," said Tansy, wide-eyed.

"His bastard son," corrected Dickon. "And the only one, he

said, except young John of Gloucester whom everyone knows about and whom he made Governor of Calais because his mother was a lady. Only a courtesy title, of course, because he is not much more than a child. They say in London that the King never cared for any woman except Anne Neville, his wife. How cruel that their real son, Prince Edward, had to die!" Dickon rolled over on the straw and sat up. "Come to think about it, that was when he sent for me, just after his heir died!"

"But as you and John of Gloucester are both illegitimate, he could not possibly have thought of——"

"Oh, no, of course not. There is his sister's son, the Earl of Lincoln. And his elder brother Clarence's son, Warwick, has always lived in the royal household. His mother was Queen Anne's sister, as you know."

"Then why——"

"It was just perhaps because he did have a conscience, as they said—and some kindness. It must have been the King himself who chose Master Paston as my tutor, and I could not have had a better one. Do you remember, Tansy, saying that it must be hard to have no one of your own? It is almost harder to find a father one day and lose him the next. And to see his body so——"

"What did they call you at school—besides Dickon, I mean?" asked Tansy hastily, trying to divert his thoughts from whatever he had seen which had so grievously shaken him.

"Broome. Richard Broome."

Tansy wrinkled her small nose. "Not a very attractive name."

"No. But one with a useful implication. The bigger fellows at school often told me to sweep our classroom."

"Broom means a flower, too," she reminded him.

"Yes." Then suddenly he leaned forward and gripped her hand as she plucked idly at the hay. "Yes, of course. I see now. He even gave me his name! Chaucer's plain English for the Latin *planta genista*." His face was illuminated with the joyful pride of a child who finds his way home. "The lovely yellow bush which riots in Aquitaine, they say, and from which the Plantagenets took their name."

"And which riots on every English heath, too," said Tansy, glad that he had found some measure of happiness.

"Dick Broome. Richard Plantagenet," he said, experimentally, and added after a moment's thought, "A mercy he did not fully acknowledge me! It would indeed be dangerous to be called Plantagenet now."

A mercy all those hooligans last night did not know or they would have torn down our walls! thought Tansy. Aloud she said, to prompt his absorbing story, "So you and Master Gervase caught up easily enough with the army?"

"Well before sundown. Everything seemed quiet and orderly. The sentries let us through. His squire must have unbuckled the King's armor. It lay across an improvised table with some untouched food. But he still wore his sword belt. He spoke to me very kindly but could not spare much time, and I was too dazed by what he first told me to take in all he said."

"Why had he sent for you?"

"It seems that he was not displeased with me when I was brought to him in London. God knows why, for I have no courtly graces. But I remember—I shall always remember!— how he said, 'You have both modesty and intelligence. If the day goes well with me tomorrow, I will acknowledge you as being of my blood and will find you some position in my household. A few days ago I sent young John to Calais, that he might be well out of all this chancy bloodshed. I am a lonely man now, Dickon.'

"I mumbled my sympathy, about poor Queen Anne Neville and the Prince, and he turned away so that I could not see his face. But I think he was perhaps a little comforted because I was of his blood—and cared. For after pacing back and forth across the tent for a minute or two he came closer to me and stood twisting one of his rings—his wedding ring, perhaps—and spoke slowly in what must have been a rare, painful effort to explain himself.

"'Some say that it is a judgment. That I have been too harsh. I had two strong, handsome elder brothers and from childhood had to fight against delicacy to join in the sports of other boys. This is the sternest test of all. It probably hardened me, in more ways than one. Since I was your age, I have lived by my sword arm, and always successfully, until

my brother died and the accursed Woodvilles tied my arm by
treachery. I am still fighting treachery. But there is another
part of me that loves beautiful books and buildings, that
wants to watch Caxton's printing press and meet explorers
from far lands, a part which has had so little time. So little
time!' He sighed, and laid a hand briefly on my shoulder.
'Perhaps, Dickon, you will fulfill that part of me—the more
peaceful, creative part.'

"He became all terse commander again then spoke to Master Gervase.

" 'A tent is prepared for you. As soon as it is light, take the
lad up to the top of this hill. Ambien Hill, it is called. You
can see the whole of the flat ground from there and even the
Tudor tents. Watch how the battle goes. You will be able to
follow it by our various standards. If we win, join me in
Leicester afterwards. But if I should lose, go back at once to
London.'

" 'But, sir,' I cried, breaking in unpardonably, 'it is in just
such case that I should want to stand by you!'

"He smiled at me, patient with my meager understanding
of him. 'Do you imagine that I should let the Tudor take me
alive? If I should be killed'—he substituted the word, and I
think that he had some strong premonition then—'get away
from here as quickly as your horses can bear you, before the
soldiers disperse and all manner of revenges are taken. And
neither in boast nor jest tell anyone what I have told you.
There is always the dangerous chance that they might believe
you. You are too much like me, Dickon.'

" 'But, sir, there are so many who love you with loyalty,' I
croaked, hating the suggestion of losing him.

" 'And they would be the greatest menace of all. You have
no conceivable right to the throne, but it is of such stuff as
you—and even by means of chance likenesses—that pretenders are made. And there would be no mercy then. No more
than if one of my enemies happened to believe your tale.
No, do as I say. Go back to London. See Master Aeneas Paston, and he will arrange your apprenticeship to some prosperous merchant.' He took some gold from the wallet at his
belt—a handful of gold nobles, I think—and gave them to
Master Gervase, saying that in case the day should go against

him, there would be sufficient for our journey and for my indentures. And to me, he said, 'If I do not see you again, my
son, live the enviable life of an industrious craftsman, marry
some kind girl of ordinary station, mix with the uncaring
crowd, and forget all that I have told you.'"

Tansy sat very still, trying to enter into the extraordinary
experience with him. "If you live to be quite an old man, how
can you ever forget?"

"How indeed? It will make me always—different. But I
may often wish that I had never known."

"Yes." She had scarcely taken her eyes off him. The
strangeness of his story had drawn her out of her own life,
compellingly. The natural way in which he had shared it with
her now perplexed her. "Dickon, he told you to tell no one.
Yet you have told me."

"Somehow that does not seem a betrayal. Perhaps because
I have never before had anyone—'special,' I think you said?
No one who listens to other people's problems as if they
cared."

"People do tell me things," admitted Tansy, momentarily
wondering if it was always safe to speak of such peculiarly
important ones. For she had heard a furtive footstep in the
shed below. Glancing cautiously downwards she was just in
time to see Diggory, the yard boy, standing in the doorway
with a pitchfork in his hand. Probably he had been about to
mount the ladder to toss down some hay, but Jod came
hurrying across from the stables and called to him to take
Master Marsh's mare to the farrier's.

" 'Er be only just shod," argued the boy impudently.

"But 'tis a good opportunity while the master be laid up.
So get moving," called back Jod. "I'll get the hay myself
when I be finished with black Mopsy-and Pippin here."

Tansy blessed him silently, but she was worried because
Diggory, who usually stumped clumsily about the place, must
have come in between the two wagons very quietly, and she
could have sworn he had been listening. Whether he had
overheard anything or not, his curiosity must have been
aroused by hearing voices. She decided that she and Jod
would have to think up some way of keeping him out of the
loft if their secret visitor were to stay many hours longer.

Making sure that the boy had laid down his pitchfork and departed, she turned back to Dickon, warmed by his appreciation of her friendliness. "And then?" she prompted.

"Then we were hustled away. Important people were waiting for some eve of battle conference. I don't know who they were. But as soon as it was light we heard the trumpets shrill and saw the lion standard flying as the Duke of Norfolk and Surrey, his son, charged down Ambien Hill. They forced the attack before ever the invading enemy was astir. But soon arrows were flying and terrible cannonballs of stone. How I wished the King had been able to bring some of those great guns which now fortify the Tower of London! Or that the Stanleys and the Earl of Northumberland would move to support him!"

"You mean—they disobeyed orders?"

"I suppose so. Because after a while the King sent a few men to protect Norfolk's flank. Sir William Stanley was to the north and Lord Stanley to the south. And between them Norfolk's forces were spread out like a bow, having to face all fronts. At first they seemed to be gaining the day, reaping the benefit of a surprise attack. But because the King was obliged to spare some of them as protection against men who were supposed to be his own supporters, and because the heavy French cannon had wrought havoc among them, the royal bowmen became very sparsely spread."

"And Henry Tudor, Duke of Richmond?"

"He was on a small rise across the valley. As the sun rose higher we could see his great red dragon of Cadwallader flying there. The King must have seen it too, for he called his own special friends and followers, and just as Norfolk was being pushed back he charged right through the midst of them. Down the hill, across what they called Redmore Plain, and up the little rise, in a cloud of dust. He didn't use his sword. He made straight for the Tudor, hacking right and left with his battle-ax as he went. The sun glinted on its sharp blade and on his crown. There was a great shouting of men, and screams of wounded horses. Poor White Surrey was shot under him, but his squire caught at some dead man's horse and King Richard mounted. Lovell and Breckenbury and all his friends fought with him. But it was he who killed a great giant of a knight who, seeing the Tudor's danger, galloped up to bar his way; he who trampled both standard bearer and dragon banner in the dust. He was within a few yards of the pretender. Henry Tudor must have been a very frightened man. And then his squires yelled a warning 'and we saw the Stanley cavalry bearing down upon him from either side, scattering his personal followers. From right across the plain I could hear him yell 'Treason!' He tried to shake them off. He was still struggling to reach the Tudor, with only a few yards to go; one man fighting alone in a milling sea of enemies. But they closed in on him like hounds at a kill and beat him to the ground. We couldn't see him any more. They must have been stabbing at him as he lay dead on the ground. He had so nearly reached his objective that they butchered him with the terrible cruelty of fear. There were no priests in his camp, that maelstrom of death. He went unshriven to his Maker. But I tell you whatever sins the man ever committed must have been expiated by such a brilliancy of courage!"

There was a long silence in the hayloft. Then the Plantagenet's son said shakily, "It was as if I were lying there, living with him and then dying."

"Oh, Dickon!"

"I couldn't believe. My eyes were blinded with tears. It had seemed like an eternity, watching. But the whole battle was over in a couple of hours." It was as if some shutter had fallen between one scene and the next before he added, in quite a different kind of voice, "And when I turned round, that cur Gervase was gone."

"And the gold with him?" surmised Tansy, who had lived more than he among money and men.

Dickon nodded and reddened. Painfully, he pulled himself upright. "So that I am no more than a beggar," he admitted, glancing down at the empty platter she had brought.

Tansy picked it up. "We are not all cast in the Gervase or Stanley mold!" she said angrily, and then she saw that, with the same swift change of expression as had characterized his father, he was smiling down at her.

"No," he said. "Some ministering angel must have acted as model when Nature carved you. My first thought out at Bosworth was to get back to you."

"How did you get here?"

"I fled before the battle was well over. On that horrible

horse. Back to Leicester, which was the only place I knew my way to in these parts. To the White Boar, which had sheltered me. To you. And a sorry sight I must have looked! You know how ill I ride. I think I must have missed my way. The Tudor had long since ridden in. Some of his men caught up with me at Bow Bridge. They were bringing in their prisoners, those they had not butchered. I dismounted and ducked down into the monastery grounds for safety. And then I saw they were bringing—something else: the King's body, flung stark naked across a horse, torn all over with stab wounds so that the blood ran down and matted his hair. They'd put a halter round his neck, as if he were a felon, and forced one of his heralds to carry his torn White Boar banner before him. They were jeering at him—at him—who had shown more courage than both armies put together! And as he came over the narrow bridge——"

"Don't, Dickon!" she begged, seeing how it distressed him and remembering with what splendor the King had ridden out.

But he had to tell someone, this once, even if he never spoke of it again. "Down in the Friary garden beside the river my face was level with the humped roadway of the bridge. I was so close I could almost have touched him. They were all grabbing at the reins, pulling his bedraggled mount this way and that, so that his down-hanging head—his bleeding, battered head—banged against the posts of the parapets as he passed."

"His anointed head," murmured Tansy, bowing her face between her hands.

"I couldn't bear it. I ran to the Canon who was standing sorrowfully in his garden and fell on my knees, clutching at his habit and beseeching him to take King Richard's body for burial. Seeing me so distraught, he put a hand on my head and said, 'Do not worry, my son. I will send to ask permission of the victor, who calls himself King Henry.' It may well be that he would have done so anyhow."

"He did. This Henry Tudor had ridden in at noon, not at a cart tail as people had predicted but with the crown of England on his head. He gave his gracious permission," said Tansy scornfully. "Tom Hood, a friend of ours, says that he did so to ingratiate himself with the people of Leicester, but our schoolmaster thinks that he may not really have known until then with what indignity Richard's body had been treated. In any case, he has made it a condition that it must be on public view before burial."

"Wasn't it enough to kill him without gloating over him?" exclaimed Dickon, with clenched fists.

"Master Jordan, the schoolmaster, says that he was only being cautious. So that no one could start a rumor that he had escaped and set up some pretender."

"As the King himself warned me they might do."

Too late Tansy clapped a hand to her mouth, realizing the sense of danger which must always dog the son. But his mind was back in the horror of Bow Bridge.

"How could he show him, all bloody and mutilated? How would he dare?"

"Oh, the Gray Friars have washed his poor, brave body. He lies beneath a catafalque covered with a velvet pall. Only his face. . . ."

"How do you know? Have you seen him?"

"No! No! I couldn't. I remembered his kindness, when he spoke to me. But we have heard other people talking. That is where everybody has gone this morning. Where my stepmother has gone. Otherwise I couldn't have sat here talking to you." She got up to go, only then realizing how long they had been together, how absorbed she had been. "Your head is really better, Dickon?"

"It scarcely hurts. Good old Jod renewed the bandage. And, look, I can stand——"

"You could not walk far. And you have lost your horse."

"Yes. When those drunken brutes started chasing me. Though it was scarcely a grievous loss," he added, with an attempt at a grin.

"Except that you must somehow get to London," Tansy reminded him, beginning to descend the ladder rather hurriedly, as she remembered that her father might be needing attention and her stepmother returning at any moment.

Dickon looked down at her sweet, troubled face. Silently, helplessly, he acknowledged that she was far more practical than he, that she had hidden him and fed him, and that without the risk she had taken at the White Boar Lane gate, and her compassionate help, he would be dead. His self-esteem was at a very low ebb.

But when her chin was almost level with the hayloft floor, she smiled up at him enchantingly. "It took plenty of Plantagenet courage to go and ask the Canon, didn't it, in full view of all that excited, bloodthirsty mob? I am sure King Richard would have been well pleased with you!"

Chapter Seven

In the inn parlor Rose Marsh and her friends were all talking excitedly about the view they had had of the late King's body.

"Such a crowd there was that my new cloak got torn!" complained Rose.

"Where was he laid?" asked Tansy, coming into the room with some clean linen for her father.

"Outside the Guild Hall," Mistress Gamble, the shoemaker's wife, told her. "Erected almost beside the stocks, the bier was. And what with the people shoving and the Friars praying and the new King's men standing guard in case some of us takes a fancy to steal it, 'twas all we could do to see which was royal bier and which was felon's stocks."

Coming from the stark reality of grief, Tansy felt the woman's shrill, excited laughter cut through her like an uncaring wind. Although many mourned their King sincerely, to Rose and the friends who had gone along with her, his lying in state—if state there had been—seemed to have amounted to little more than a puppet show.

"They be showin' him down in Newarke by the Castle tomorrow, and close by here at St. Nicholas Church the next day, if so be as you wants to go, my dear," another woman told her kindly. "But I wouldn't leave it any later, or the poor corpse'll begin to stink an' the good Friars 'll be takin' him for burial."

Tansy hurried upstairs away from them all. On the first floor, which had so recently been all grandeur and bustle and which was now so sadly deserted, she put down her burden and opened the door of the great chamber. The chatter of voices no longer pursued her. Here all was quiet. She shut the door and stood leaning against it, thinking of the man who had slept here—the man who slept so ill—and who, incredibly, was Dickon Broome's father.

All her life she had been familiar with the room, but now it was as if she saw it for the first time, taking in every feature. As a child she had often played here while her mother and some maidservant made up the great double bed; her memory held a jumbled succession of wealthy travelers who had professed themselves comfortable here, but now it had housed the privacy of a king and must have formed the background to some of his last thoughts and hours. She looked appreciatively at the wide hearth with its two stone jambs, at the great beams open to the high ceiling ridge and ornamented with scrolls in red, black and yellow, and at the oak-mullioned window with its five glass lights projecting over the main entrance in the High Street. King Richard must have formed his first quick impression of all these things that evening when he came in with Lord Lovell and found her standing staring at his newly set-up bed. How right her stepmother had been when she had promised there would be room for it and for the existing four-poster, now pushed to one side, in this fine master room.

Tansy's gaze came back to the King's bed. She wished that she could show it to Dickon, who had so much more cause to be interested than she. She wished that he could see the whole room, just as King Richard had left it and so poignantly ready for his return! There was his splendid scarlet and gold nightgown lying across a carved chest, his soft, furlined shoes set by some squire before the empty grate—even the book he might have been reading, on the bedside table.

Tansy crossed the room to look at it. As she picked it up, the tooled leather was smooth as squirrel fur to her touch. She opened it and found it was in Latin. To her disappointment she could not read a word, except the name of William Caxton in a kind of printed picture. But on the front page of all the owner had written his name in ink: *Ricardus Rex.* That much Latin, at least, everyone could read. With a sudden sense of her own boldness, she stood staring down intently at the bold, flowing script, until the door was flung open and with a swish of skirts her stepmother came in.

"So you had the same thought as I did," she was saying, not unamiably. "It is not a bad bed. We don't need another bed, but we could sell it."

"Sell it?" echoed Tansy.

"But of course. Seeing it was a king's bed we could probably get a good deal for it. Sell it, I say, whatever your father thinks! It is the only way to deal with people who don't pay their debts."

Tansy held the open book protectively against her breast. "You can't pay them when you are dead," she said, with the moronic lack of expression which Rose's overbearing personality invariably produced in her. It seemed so unbelievable that anyone could come into this room and feel nothing of the recent presence or the subsequent tragedy of its last occupant.

But Rose was bustling round, pouncing upon a brush here and a pair of hose there, scrutinizing and valuing them, until finally she swooped on the gold and scarlet gown. "Real Damascene! Nothing like it has ever been seen in this town before, I'll warrant. I will have that man from London cut it into a gown for me. It will be the talk of the town if I wear it for the Christmas revels."

She threw the gorgeous thing about her shoulders and executed a dance step or two.

"Does it not become me?" she demanded.

"Well enough. But it is too bright a color for your hair."

"Meaning that it would better liven up your straw-color curls?" she teased, flicking an end of the priceless material across Tansy's face as she whirled past.

"Meaning that I would not dare to cut up a garment of the King's!" retorted Tansy, stung to anger.

"But it does not belong to him any more. No one came back to claim it. And, anyway, he is dead. And now, whether we like it or not, we have King Henry the Seventh." Rose, with the silk still draped about her ample breast and hips, stood with arms akimbo and launched into exasperated explanations. "Do you not understand, foolish ninny, that everything in this room—everything left in any of our rooms—is ours? I went to the Mayor and made sure about that. A mint of money it cost to entertain them that night, I told him. Twenty men and horses to feed, to say nothing of all the scriveners and servants. And having to bribe to get food at all, with the town so full. And the way I worked—the way we all worked!" she had the grace to add. "When I'd talked myself to a standstill and paid him a few compliments about the way he had managed things when a different king came back, he readily agreed that we'd a right to keep everything.

But I made him say it in front of some of the aldermen so that there should be no going back on it afterwards. Although really I suppose the only thing of any value is the bed."

"There is this book," said Tansy reluctantly.

"A book. And all in Latin, I'll be bound," said Rose, glancing at it without enthusiasm.

Tansy held it out for her inspection, but made no effort to show the royal inscription. If Rose Marsh imagined the silk gown of more value than a book, so much the worse for her. Neither Tansy herself nor her father could read it. But she had immediately thought of one person who would know both how to value and how to read the beautifully bound thing. "You can keep it if you've a mind, as far as I'm concerned," said Rose carelessly. "And these shoes look as if they might fit your father. Just the thing for an invalid, and he will probably cherish them as if they were the crown jewels."

She picked them up and departed. Tansy stood clasping her book. If she could not bring Dickon in to see this room and the fine carvings on the bed, she could at least give him one of his father's cherished possessions. Before leaving the bedside she turned for a closer look at the curious carvings which she had so much admired, and as she stepped back she noticed something shining among the rushes where her foot had disturbed the folds of the valance. Uncovering it with the toe of her shoe, she saw to her amazement that it was a gold coin. She bent to pick it up and saw another. Putting down the book, she went on her knees, to thrust her hand under the ede of the bed, and discovered some more. Five gold coins which, in their haste, the King or one of his gentlemen must have dropped. Tansy turned each one over carefully. There could be no mistake about it. Three rose nobles with King Edward's picture engraved on one side and his Yorkist roses on the other, and two half angels with Saint George and the dragon. She gazed at them as they lay in a row along her outstretched palm, considering the fine things they would buy. She, too, would like a new gown for Christmas, and a furlined hood like the Mayor's daughter wore, and a gay new harness for Pippin. And, as her stepmother had said, everything the royal party left behind belonged to the White Boar now. But, of course, she must hand the coins over to her father. They represented more than his normal takings for a month and would help to repay his expenditure for the royal party's visit. Never once did it occur to her to show them to her stepmother, and when she heard her calling angrily from the foot of the stairs she slipped the coins into her pocket, hid her book in a linen chest, and ran down.

There were some rough characters in the tavern, and more were shouting and quarreling outside. Most of them had already drunk too much, and one truculent young fellow was sporting a large red rose and shouting above the din, "We saw him come in here, the lousy Yorkist!"

"What is this about your letting a man in at the side gates yesterday?" asked Rose, turning sharply on Tansy the moment she appeared.

"We saw him slip in," corroborated another aggrieved youth.

"They are trying to make out we are hiding someone from the battlefield," explained Dilly.

"They were drunk and throwing stones at our house yesterday evening. Far too drunk to know what they saw. Jod and I bolted the gates to keep them out of our yard," parried Tansy, badly frightened and playing for time.

"And we'll get him out if we have to tear your White Boar down. And tan him for a spoilsport, sneaking on us to the priest!" they yelled.

"I know nothing about any priest, but you'll get out of here or I'll call my husband to put you out," bluffed Rose, who certainly did not lack courage.

Tom Hood, who could not abide her and who had kept out of the row until Tansy appeared, rose reluctantly from his stool. "Come along now," he urged, propelling the drunkest of them towards the door. "Any Yorkist who'd run in here for safety would be well on his way out of Leicester by now, if he's got any sense. Best get yourself another drink at the Crown, up the road—they've got singing girls up there!"

"Your stableboy says there's some stranger in your hayloft. Swears he heard whispering," persisted one of them, trying to turn back at the open door.

"And would it be the first time you've heard a man and girl whispering in a hayloft?" jeered handsome Rose Marsh, taking the center of the floor. "Maybe they think hay's only for horses in whatever parts you rowdy lot come from, but young folk have other notions here."

A general guffaw went round, and between Tom's persuasion and her ridicule their unwelcome visitors took themselves off. But Tansy was left standing in her own home with a nasty slur on her name. For Dickon's sake she had not dared to open her mouth in self-defence. All their regular customers knew that there was no love lost between her stepmother and herself, but they had always looked at her with respect. Now she noticed how they either looked with a warmer, more speculative kind of liking, or avoided looking at her at all. Unfortunately for her, Master Jordan, who would have known how to deal with the situation, was not there. Indignant anger for herself and fear for Dickon fought in her for mastery.

"Didn't I say you were always cuddling in the hayloft when you ought to have been helping, you slut? Taking advantage of your father's sickness! And tonight we shall probably have these hooligans stoning the paint off the place again because they think we're ardent Yorkists!"

Rose Marsh said it loudly in order to deny the imputation to any strangers who might be present and who were unaware of her husband's sympathies. It was safer for trade to appear neutral these days, and money mattered more to her than did the reputation of her husband's daughter.

With white face and chin held high, Tansy walked out into the yard and across to Pippin's stable. It was there that Tom Hood found her, as soon as he could slip out without seeming to follow her. As he came through the doorway his good-humored face was unusually angry. "What was this about the fellow in the hayloft?" he asked.

With all her heart Tansy wished that she could tell him, but the whole thing would sound so fantastic, "a likely story," as her father had said. And she had acted impulsively against his word. Caressing Pippin's soft neck, she wished that humans could be as comfortably dumb and uninquisitive as beasts.

"I will clip Diggory's ears for you. But was there really anybody there?" insisted Tom.

"Yes."

For a moment he was too hurt to speak, leaning against the manger. Then he laughed with curt bitterness. "Too slow, wasn't I? If I'd supposed that you wanted that sort of thing——"

"There wasn't any of that sort of thing!"

"I was fool enough to think you were the kind of girl a fellow waits for, in marriage. But it seems you're like all the others."

Tansy turned on him furiously. "I don't know what other sorts of girl you've known, Tom Hood! But this man in the loft is no lover of mine. And, if it interests you, he is still there."

"Is he old or impotent or something, then?" asked Tom after a moment's silence, half persuaded by her vehemence.

"No. Younger than either of us. Not younger than I in actual years perhaps, but less experienced. The way people are who don't have to do with earning money. And he was pretty badly hurt."

"One of these new light-flight arrows?" hazarded Tom, with professional interest, taking it for granted that the fugitive she had befriended was a wounded soldier.

"I had to bandage his head and his foot," Tansy told him noncommitally. "He wants to get back to London, but he has lost his horse."

"As far as I am concerned, he can't get back there soon enough! But I am sorry I spoke to you like that just now, Tansy. And furious that Mistress Marsh should have talked the way she did in front of all of us. If only you had told your father——"

"How could I worry him when he is already a sick man and the business so badly hit?" asked Tansy, who knew that she would have had his disapproval. "But I must get this poor lad away somehow."

"You certainly must now. Before your stepmother finds him, or these battle-happy gangs do any more damage. By what I know of Mistress Marsh, she'd probably be more concerned to learn you were harboring an unpopular Yorkist than a lover." He came and joined her in offering titbits to Pippin. "You've been a softhearted fool as usual, haven't you, my sweet? But if it's only a matter of a horse——"

Tansy turned and caught at his arm. "Oh, Tom, you mean you could get him one?"

"My dear girl, ever since Bosworth the roads around this city have been full of roaming, riderless horses. Only this morning one came ambling into the forge in Cank Street when I was there. A good enough beast, but plastered with mud. Old Matt the farrier tied him up, and I daresay he'd be only too pleased to sell him for a noble or two."

"And you will buy him for me?"

"Should I see my money back?"

"Yes, yes, he can pay," promised Tansy recklessly. "And I will send Jod to fetch it soon after dusk."

"So he is in this too? I might have known. The besotted old watchdog would pull down the church bells if you told him to. All right, Tansy, I will see what I can do—for a kiss." He pulled her to him and she lifted her face to his, rapturous with gratitude, but it was not gratitude he wanted. "Not such a halfhearted peck as that, or I shall still believe you have been squandering them in the hayloft."

He showed her the kind of kisses he meant and took his time over it, while Tansy stayed breathless and quiescent in his arms. It was good to be cared for, to let down her defences and be warmed by the exciting thrill of his love-making. And Tom was no novice. "You are my dearest friend," she murmured.

He had to laugh and let her go in exasperation. "Not quite the relationship I was aiming at!" he said, admitting defeat. Lifting her chin with a gentler finger, he looked quizzically into her trusting blue eyes. "I wonder will you ever learn to love me, Tansy?"

"I do love you, Tom," she assured him. But he knew that for all his efforts at instruction it was not the awakened love of a woman. And the gay, go-ahead fletcher of Leicester was not accustomed to failure.

"Yes, I know you do," he agreed, with a sigh. "Like you love Jod, or old Will Jordan or this precious pony of yours."

Chapter Eight

"You must take that signboard down," ordered Rose Marsh. "Even now, when the Tudor's army has gone, it is still the rallying point for every rough youth in the neighborhood, the target for local venom—encouraged, I wouldn't be surprised, by Hugh Malpas at the Crown."

What she said was true enough. There are always some who will hit at a lost cause. So Jod fetched a ladder from the yard and set it up against the front of the inn, and Tansy stood in the High Street steadying the foot of it. "The chains be set so fast to the iron shaft hooks 'twill need a chisel or summat to detach 'em," he reported from aloft.

While he had gone back for the necessary tools, Rose said to Tansy, "There's no need to tell your father we're taking it down. He's very low this afternoon. It would only upset him."

"When things get quiet maybe we can get it put back before he's about again," said Tansy.

"Much good a white boar will do trade now!" scoffed Rose. "And sometimes I doubt if he ever will get about again, or notice whether there's a boar or a bush hanging there. Sheer madness it was, dashing off like that to Bosworth, when everyone knew he was more sick than he said, and leaving us with all this work and worry."

"You managed splendidly—and seemed to enjoy managing —when the King was here," Tansy could not help recalling.

"There was some incentive then, when we thought the money was coming in. And that we would have the laugh over Malpas."

Tansy leaned her slight weight against the ladder while Jod ascended for the second time. "And you—really think— that my father is worse?" she asked, her voice jerky as much through anxiety as physical effort. "That he may not—get better?"

"Doctor Leigh thinks that it is doubtful. And what shall we do then, with half our customers slinking off to the Golden Crown?"

Tansy watched her go indoors, wondering how she could

care where the customers went when the beloved landlord's life was in the balance. Yet her own thoughts went to the gold coins in her pocket. They could help to tide over a bad time, but perhaps they would be spent on fripperies for her stepmother and not make much difference to her father. Like her, he would mind more about the well-known sign coming down than about the money.

"Poor beast be fair battered," Jod was saying, as he clambered down the last few rungs carrying the signboard.

Tansy held out her arms for it as she might have for a hurt child. Together they surveyed its chipped paint and pitted surface, deploring the venom with which it had been belabored, then stood looking up sadly at the wrought iron shaft which, now useless, gave the front of the building a lifeless look.

As Tansy stood clasping the ill-used white boar in her arms she suddenly decided how she would spend the money in her pocket.

"Go to the farrier's in Cank Street and fetch a horse which Master Hood has bought from him. Put it in the stall nearest the Lane gates and see it has a good feed. If anyone asks you about it say we are stabling it temporarily for Master Hood, but it is really for the wounded man in the loft, Jod. I will find an old cloak of my father's and fill a saddlebag with food. As soon as it is getting dusk, direct him through South Gate onto the road to London. And then bolt the yard gates after him."

"Just as well he be goin'," muttered Jod, "with that sharp-nosed Diggory pryin' around!"

There would be time enough to see her father and try to cheer him before he settled for the night. Tansy followed the ostler round to the yard and set the signboard down against the wall in the wagon shed. Calling softly, she climbed the ladder to the hayloft.

In her mood of depression it was good to be greeted by a cheerful voice. "See, I can walk!" proclaimed Dickon. "I've been practicing, back and forth. I shan't need to burden you any more. I must be on my way to London."

"You wouldn't get very far with that ankle," said Tansy, oddly hurt that he should sound so willing to go. "But Tom Hood has found you a horse."

"Found one?"

"Since Bosworth, all the roads around here have been full of roaming, riderless horses," Tansy told him, quoting what Tom had said.

"I suppose they may well be, judging by the slaughter I saw. But, even so, a horse is worth something. If he found it, he could sell it."

"It might even be the one you lost. And then you'd have every right to it!" Tansy laughed.

"Heaven forbid! And unless it were, how can I take it? As you know, I have no money."

"I assure you Tom will not be the loser."

"Is he so rich then?"

"N-no. But what people hereabouts call 'up and coming.' The sort of person who has his own business and plenty of initiative and doesn't let the grass grow under his feet."

"Not an ineffectual dreamer like me." Tansy was aware of the edge of envy in Dickon's voice and was glad when his attention was caught by the battered signboard standing below against the wagon-shed wall. "Looks as if they've been throwing stones at it again. I heard a lot of shouting."

"It was some of the same crowd who chased you. I recognized two of them drinking here midday. They swore they had seen you come into the yard, and that they would get you."

"They know I am still here?"

"That little beast of a yard boy heard us talking."

"Then Mistress Marsh knows?"

Tansy nodded. "That is why you must go—this evening, before your ankle is really well enough, I am afraid."

"I saw her when she was talking to Master Gervase. She looked brassy hard. If she thinks that harboring a Yorkist is dangerous, why doesn't she drive me out?"

"She doesn't believe them. She knows Diggory heard us that first evening. But she just thinks that you—that we——"

Dickon caught her arm and looked into her face, and she reddened with embarrassment. "And you let her think it, to protect me. Oh, Tansy!" He let her go, sullen with self-abasement, and began pulling his discarded shoe onto the foot with the injured ankle. "I will go now. I have brought you nothing but trouble. I can walk well enough."

"Of course you must go. The sooner you will get to London the better. For you, and for us. But it isn't because I want you to. I shall be sorry, truly sorry, not to see you again. But you must do as the King your father said."

"Oh, all that romantic stuff I told you! You don't have to pretend you believe it," he said roughly.

"But I do believe it. And to prove it here is some money which belongs to you." She drew the coins from her pocket and held them out before his astonished gaze. "The King must have dropped them. I found them on the floor beside his bed. I can only think that in the haste of leaving for the battle either he or some nervous squire who was dressing him let them drop from the purse at his belt. And now whose are they, if not yours? Take them. He would have wished you to have them, Dickon, all the more so since we know he meant you to use the money which that unspeakable Gervase made off with."

"Findings, keepings," quoted Dickon, waving it aside. "It is yours."

Tansy faced him gravely. "I am afraid we can neither of us make ourselves disbelieve now that you are the King's illegitimate son. I haven't had time to tell you this before. But he spoke to me. Standing at the foot of that curious camp bed of his, he explained to me about some small carvings which he said represented the Holy Sepulcher. He, the King of England, explained to me, Tansy, the innkeeper's daughter. And again just before he rode out to Bosworth he put his hand on my shoulder. So you must understand that I have seen him close to, close as I am to you now. And that evening when you stumbled into the yard——"

"When you saved my life. Yes?" He was now listening intently to every word.

"Well, when I wiped the blood from your face it was so drawn with exhaustion that you looked much older than you are. You looked just like him. However people might make fun of your story, I could never disbelieve it. So take your money, all except a noble which I will use to repay Tom."

He took her hands and kissed them and put the money slowly into the wallet at his belt. He made no further protest. "If ever I am able to repay it, I can find you here. But since I am so much your debtor—so unutterably your debtor for much more than this money—I should like you to be able to contact me. I will leave you Master Aeneas Paston's address in Wood Street. See, I will scratch it with my knife on the wall behind this old lantern. Whether I serve my apprenticeship in London or not, he will always know where I am. I suspect that he knows *who* I am. Is there anyone who would bring you a letter?"

Tansy thought about it while he scratched laboriously on the wall. "There is Gufford, the chapman, who brings silks and new fashions from London every two or three months."

"Where does he live?"

"In Cheapside. Near an inn called the Boar's Head. I remember his telling my stepmother about it. The coincidence, I mean. Is that near Wood Street?"

"Quite near."

In spite of her distress for her father and for the bad blow to business, a new happiness warmed Tansy's heart at the thought that this strangely made new friend might keep in touch with her. "But you must not write as a duty, because of anything which I have been able to do for you," she insisted, sensing his conscientiousness. "And listen, Dickon. I have something for you which I think you will value far more than money. It is one of the King's own books, which I found beside his bed."

Dickon thrust the knife into his belt and turned to her, his face alive with interest. "A book?" he repeated.

"In lovely leather binding, with a metal clasp."

"Printed or in manuscript?"

"Printed, I think. The name William Caxton was all I could read."

"With the sign of the Red Pale?"

"What is that?"

"A kind of crest, to show that it came from his press in the precincts of Westminster Abbey."

"I think so, Dickon. But I am sorry. It was all in Latin and I don't read even English very well."

"I must teach you."

"Nothing would please me better. But how, when we live so far apart?"

But he didn't seem to hear her. His usually sober face was wholly attractive in its eagerness. "I have never really possessed a book before, except one or two tattered school primers."

"You will possess this one," she assured him. "For there were two Latin words which any ninny could read: the King's own signature on the title page."

Dickon's joy was indescribable, until a thought began to nag at him. "Then it must be doubly valuable. And since it was left here, and he can never claim it, it must belong to your parents."

"My father was too sick to be consulted, and my step-mother gave it to me. She wasn't interested."

"Not interested!" he cried. "Why, it might well be the *Order of Chivalry*, which Caxton dedicated to King Richard himself. Or even Earl Rivers' *Sayings of the Philosophers. I* should never be lonely if I had that."

"How do you know so much about these books?" asked Tansy.

"Master Paston took us once to the Red Pale and we actually saw the printing press working. And then again I have a sort of personal interest. For although William Caxton is quite an old man now and spent most of his life in Bruges— although he has changed the world of literature and has royal patrons—he began as an apprentice in London like the rest of us. A mercer's apprentice, oddly enough. And when his first master died, the Mercers' Guild arranged for him to finish his term with a Master John Harrowe, who was my friend Piers' grandfather. So of course we all talked often about Caxton's work at school."

"I will trap the book carefully in a napkin and pack it in your saddlebag," promised Tansy, feeling sadly out of her depth.

With one of his swift changes of mood he came back into her world again, coming close to her and taking her hands in his. "If there is ever anything that I can do for you, Tansy, anything at all, you must send me word, and I will do it."

There was a depth of sincerity in his words but she supposed them to be his only means of expressing present grati-tude. "There is something which you can do for us here and now, if you have time," she said, speaking lightly in an effort to dispel embarrassment. "Indeed, I told Jod that I thought you were the very man to do it. That board down there."

"You want it repainted?"

"But not as it is. I suppose my stepmother is right. We must move with the changing mood of the times."

"I will make it over for you in no time at all. Before it is dark. I am so glad you asked me." He looked at it consideringly. "Now, why not a blue boar, which—since the great Duke of York's death—has no particular significance to stir up party feeling? And which would probably hurt your father's feelings less than having his sign changed altogether?"

"Oh, Dickon, can you do that?"

"Easily. Tell your man to bring the board up here and to fetch me some blue paint and a brush. Why do you laugh?"

"Because it is the first time I have heard you give an order, and you sound so much like—your father."

"Do I?" This was a new possibility which seemed to intrigue him. But he did not dwell on it. With something constructive to do—something which he could do—he seemed a different being. He stripped off his doublet and began rolling up the sleeves of his shirt and clearing the only part of the loft where there was light. When she told him that she would send Jod with the paint but would not, herself, be coming back, she thought that he bade her a rather preoccupied farewell. But when she would have run down the ladder he caught her by the arms and stopped her. "Tansy, who is this Tom Hood?" he asked, frowning prodigiously.

She had to laugh. "Heaven help me! Do I have to spend my life explaining each of you to the other?"

"Did he ask about me?"

"But naturally. Wasn't he getting the horse?"

"Of course. And I will not forget it. But you said he was 'up and coming.' Do your parents want you to marry him?"

It was the first time the question had come to her so definitely, and she jibbed from it. "I think so," she admitted, trying to turn from him.

"And do you love him?"

She pulled herself angrily away. "How should that concern you, who have only known me a bare three days?"

"Because I may be leaving you for as many years. All the time that I serve my apprenticeship. I must know."

Slowly, beneath the warm gaze of his brown eyes, she was coerced to speak the truth as far as she could tell it. "I have always been fond of him since I was a child. But I do not think that I love him—as you mean love." She felt the pressure of his hands relax as the breath came out of him in a vast sigh. "But why must you know? How can it matter to you so much?"

"Because I shall always carry your image in my heart."

"So much can happen in three years. You would be a fool to do that," she told him, hoping desperately that he would.

Chapter Nine

In the morning, when Tansy went to the wagon shed, Dickon was gone. All that remained of his strange visit was a newly painted signboard, expertly repaired, picturing a sagacious-looking blue boar. With no money, but using his innate skill, he had left an offering to protect her and her family from annoyance. And as the weeks passed she almost needed this tangible proof that she had really received an incredible confidence and a brief friendship which had made so much difference in her life. Other citizens of Leicester might comment or jest about the inn's changed sign, but every time she looked up at it she felt oddly warmed by the possession of a precious secret.

At first on a more material level, the board was an embarrassment as well as a safeguard, since she had to make some sort of explanation as to how she had managed to get the thing repainted. Fortunately, Rose Marsh was so relieved to have it, and in such a hurry for Jod to rehang it, that she accepted without much question Tansy's vague references to one of their customers who had been both kind and artistic and clearly associated the gift with the amorous episode which Diggory thought he had overheard in the hayloft.

To her father Tansy tried to tell the truth, but he was past taking much interest in the return of a guest at whose fantastic story he had already scoffed. "He was welcome to a night's lodging if that foolish charlatan who hoped to profit by him left him penniless and stranded," he said weakly. "But it was a good idea to make him pay for it by repainting our sign. I have been meaning to have it done for months. But there are so many things I have been meaning to do. . . ." He lay musing sadly, and Tansy was glad that he seemed scarcely to have taken in the fact that the sign had been altered as well as repainted. "But there is one thing I have done, Tansy, my child," he went on, rousing himself. "Some months ago while I still had the strength I got Lawyer Langstaff to draw up my will. You ought to know about it. The business and house and everything in it goes to Rose, of course, during her lifetime—

unless she marries again, in which case a half of the profits go
to you. I know you do not get on with her. But that is why I
want you to stay as long as you can and do your best for the
Boar. At her death it becomes yours anyway."

"But I should not know how to run it. She may be lazy,
but I am not really as capable as she is when she chooses,"
said Tansy, painfully conscious of her youth and inexperi-
ence.

"That is the sadness of having no son," sighed Robert
Marsh. "But you, who have helped me in so many ways,
should know better than most. And you will marry."

"My husband may not want to be an innkeeper."

"Then you could sell it. Through Langstaff. He would see
to your interests, for my sake. And whatever your husband's
trade, the money will not come amiss."

Tansy sank to her knees beside the bed and sobbed in the
weakening shelter of his arm. "What do I care about marriage or money? I don't know how I can live without you,"
she cried brokenly.

"I think your stepmother will, all too easily. . . ." He lay
silent awhile and then added with labored breathing, "Always go to Will Jordan, in any difficulty, as you would to me.
And there is Tom. . . . You two have always been good
friends. I ought to have arranged a marriage for you, while I
had the strength. . . ."

But somehow, in spite of the insecurity of her position,
Tansy was thankful that he had left her free.

Although Robert Marsh lingered for several weeks, that
was almost the last time he was able to speak to her coher-
ently, alone. He never knew that with the fall of the last
Plantagenet his inn had become the Blue Boar, or that his beloved daughter had formed more than a passing attachment
for King Richard's illegitimate son.

His death was a much-regretted event in Leicester. And
when the contents of his will became known, relations between his widow and his daughter grew increasingly difficult.
Resenting Tansy's promised interest in the business, Rose
made use of her in every possible way yet tried to keep her
subservient. Although she was well provided for during her
lifetime, it infuriated her to realize that her value as a comely
and well-to-do widow would always be diminished in the

eyes of any matrimonially minded man by her stepdaughter's ultimate inheritance. Her good-humored moments of expansion became rarer, her tongue sharper. When Hugh Malpas, calling ostensibly with neighborly condolences, not only omitted his usual lavish compliments, as was proper enough in the circumstances, but made a point of treating Tansy with a new, ingratiating respect as a grown person, she found it hard to take. Enraged, she retaliated on Tansy afterwards when her friend, Druscilla Gamble, came to proffer sympathy and gather gossip. They were sitting near the parlor door, and Tansy, who was chopping herbs for Friday's fish by the open kitchen window, could not but overhear them.

"At least I didn't give him the satisfaction of asking how custom was going at the Crown," Rose was saying.

"No need to ask. Anyone can hear it every night," said Mistress Gamble, the shoemaker's wife, who had the misfortune to live hard by in Cordwainers' Lane. "What did Malpas say about your changed sign?"

"Thought it was the best thing we could do in the circumstances—and mind you, he's a shrewd businessman—and wanted to know whose idea it was to keep the Boar but turn it blue. I gave credit where credit was due. Said it was Tansy's, or some artist lover of hers. And that although his night's lodging wasn't marked up on the slate, we couldn't grumble at the way he had paid for it."

Tansy dropped her knife with a clatter, and even spiteful Druscilla Gamble protested, "Oh, no, Rose!"

"I thought it would cure him of casting such calculating looks in her direction. When Hugh Malpas has that calculating look he is usually thinking up some dangerous mischief. He was treating her altogether too much as though she were already mistress of the Boar."

"And no longer treating you as if he wanted you to be mistress of the Crown, eh?" giggled Druscilla Gamble, who could also play the cat. "But seriously, Rose, do you suppose our prudish Tansy really let some man tumble her in the hay that night when the town was full of soldiers?"

"Diggory says he heard them, and a man doesn't spend two or three hours restoring an awful old signboard for nothing," said Rose, with more determination than conviction. "But you'd better ask Tansy herself if you're so much interested."

"Chit as she is, I wouldn't dare," admitted Mistress Gamble, in spite of her proclivity for minding other people's business. And, as if struck by the oddness of the admission, even she kept silence for a few moments, wondering what there was about the girl. "Tansy," she repeated ruminatively. "How did she come by such an odd name?"

"Her mother must have been full of pretty whimseys. There is some cock-and-bull story about Robert having met her in a manor when he came back from the wars."

"She must have found the talk on the tavern benches a bit differentl" sniggered Druscilla Gamble.

"Perhaps they toned it down a bit, same as they do for her daughter."

"I never could abide those fancy flower names myself," said Mistress Gamble, forgetting that she was addressing a fullblow rose.

"'Tisn't a flower. It's a weed. A tall, quick-growing, coarse, yellow-topped weed." Tansy could hear the spite in her stepmother's voice and found it frightening. "Come to think of it, the name just suits her."

"She certainly is growing up, the way the lads begin to look at her," agreed Mistress Gamble, with less animosity.

"Even Malpas." Evidently that was a sore point too.

"He'd look at anything that had two breasts."

"And, of course, there's Tom Hood always hanging around."

The shoemaker's wife laughed indulgently. Most women had a soft spot for the young fletcher. "He'd make a kind enough husband if she didn't mind his shooting off at a tangent sometimes. Not unnatural, I suppose, for one in his line of business. Or that he should like his quiver full of girls as well as arrows."

"At least he's the sort to get on. I thought her father would have fixed it up. If I were her I'd snap him up. But the girl's got no gumption. All whimsey, high-flown fancies like her mother before her, no doubt. She'll probably marry some conscience-ridden, steady-going stick-in-the-mud like I did for the sake of his looks and end up worse off than she began."

Tansy banged down her knife, scattering herbs, bowl, and

chopping board in all directions, and flung open the parlor door. Like a slender fury she faced the two astonished women. "Throw whatever slime you like from your horrible mind over me, now there is no one to stop you," she told her stepmother. "But you can't talk that way about my mother in this house where everybody loved her before you came, nor about my father whom everyone in Leicester respected—and grew sorry for, after he married you!"

"You common little eavesdropper!" accused Rose, too taken aback to think of anything else to say.

"I should think every passer-by in the street must have heard without trying to!" said Tansy contemptuously, too proud to explain what she had been doing.

"My, what a temper we have! I didn't know you had it in you, child," said Mistress Gamble, half soothingly, half admiringly.

"Imagine her talking to me like that, the ingrate—living in my house, eating my bread!"

"And earning it!" snapped Tansy.

Before such unexpected anger, even the indomitable hostess of the Boar began to weaken. Tears of self-pity welled in her periwinkle blue eyes. "And me still wearing black for him," she faltered, appealing to Tansy's well-known pity.

But for those who maligned her loved ones Tansy had no pity at all. "Because black suits your red hair," she said coldly, "far better than a dead king's scarlet silk."

For the first time Rose saw her as a person to be reckoned with. She got up from her chair and planted herself before the girl as she would have stalked out of the room again. "Listen, Tansy," she said, almost civilly. "This is not an easy time for either of us. Wisely or unwisely, your father has left us both an interest in the Boar, and however much a stepmother is inevitably disliked, we must pull together if we are to make any money out of it."

"I am always willing to do my share of the pulling."

"I know. And I do not think too badly of you for taking your fun sometimes. Some parents would have beaten you."

"There was no cause. But after what you said in the tavern the other day all our customers must suppose there was."

"And think none the worse of you, seemingly."

This was probably true, since Rose's cruel words had but

increased her own unpopularity. And during that sad autumn, Tansy was to find what good friends she had.

Partly because the name of the inn was changed, travelers no longer feared to put up there, and out of sympathy for a respected citizen's affairs most of Robert Marsh's local customers continued to come. Master Jordan crossed the street every evening to pass an hour, seeming to bring something of his friend the innkeeper's genial spirit with him. And Tom Hood looked in whenever he could and tried to cheer them, but business was bad with him too. He rode as far afield as Warwick trying to sell his arrows but, excellently made as they were, no one in castle or manor seemed to be wanting any.

"Only a few score sold here and there to civic authorities who are bound to provide them for weekly archery practice, and they want only the cheapest," he reported, stretching his long legs wearily before the cheerful fire in the Boar. "Now that the new King is accepted and crowned in London everyone seems to think that the barons will stop skirmishing about England in support of Yorkist or Lancastrian, and settle down under a Tudor dynasty."

"And crafts and trade and shipping will have a chance, and the ordinary people will come into their own," added Master Jordan, regarding him with an affectionate smile.

"It may be very good for England, sir," admitted Tom ruefully, "but devilish bad for fletchers!"

"Poor Tom! Your wallet is empty and your hose wringing wet," commiserated Tansy, ruffling his rain-soaked hair as she handed him a warming drink.

He caught at her hand and kissed it. "The long-term trouble is that if we do have battles again everybody will be wanting to buy cannon," he said, pulling her down beside him on the settle.

"You really mean that?" asked Jordan.

"I am afraid so. They are difficult to make and cumbersome to move, but they turned the tide at Bosworth. I shall have to start an iron foundry. I understand there is iron ore to be found down in Sussex. It is always as well to have a second trade at one's fingertips," he added more lightly. "By the way, was that fellow who repainted the sign a master craftsman as well as a soldier?"

"He couldn't have been. He wasn't old enough," said Tansy, cautiously.

"Well, he made a masterly job of it," allowed Tom generously.

"If you want a second trade you could always make your arrow feather into pillows for the ladies," teased Tansy.

"And show them how to lay their pretty heads on 'em. It's an idea." He sat down his empty tankard and, as if reminded by some association of ideas, announced abruptly, "I spent an hour in the Golden Crown last evening."

"Surely you're not going to desert us!" exclaimed Rose Marsh, coming to join them as the last of her other customers departed.

"As I said, if your own business isn't paying, it's best to take a look at the methods of the man whose is."

"What did you find to do there?" asked Rose.

"Oh, plenty. Note how they run with the times by disguising their flea-bitten performing bear as a fierce Welsh dragon. Watch how they pour the drinks short when their customers are too sozzled to notice. Manage to take a rise out of old Malpas sometimes. Squeeze the alluring Gladys."

"Tom!" squeaked Tansy, pulling away from his casually proprietary arm.

"Your fault for being so unkind. A man must find some consolation. She blackens her eyelashes with some eastern paint. Did you know? And she has a new song, Mistress Marsh. I'll see if I can remember it. It ought to be sung in a fierce, rollicking double bass, of course, not in her enticing love notes. But it doesn't matter because she makes all the men sing with her." He sprang up from the settle and stood with his back to the leaping fire, embellishing an indifferent singing voice with fine dramatic gestures:

> " ' My Gold Crown *shall crush the* Boar,
>   *And make the* Angel *fly.*
> He'll *drown the* Bow Inn *in the* Soar,
>   *And drink the* Three Cups *dry.*'

There are several more verses, of course. But there's competitive advertising for you!"

"Oh the venomous bitch!" cried Rose, sinking down into the nearest chair.

"She probably has to sing what she is told. Malpas works her hard, poor mopsy. No doubt he composed the lines himself."

"And now we shall hear every tipsy lout who passes chanting them."

"Which won't do us any good," sighed Tansy, wishing she could think of some riposte.

"There's one way in which you can score," said Tom, as if reading her thoughts. And when they all looked at him expectantly, he began to explain. "Hugh Malpas may have a luscious singing wench, and a performing bear patched up as a dragon, and a ready turn for verse, but what he doesn't have is a King's bed."

"We shan't get much for that——" began Rose, doubtfully.

"Don't sell it. Not on your life!" advised Tom. "Keep it just where it is and make it the showpiece of Leicester. And so enhance your trade. The country is at peace again, the Tudor is making more stringent laws against road and river thieves, and people are beginning to travel about their affairs again. As the roads improve with the spring, they will be coming back. Put up a notice over your door. State boldly that the last Plantagenet King stayed here, which in no way indicates which way your sympathies lie. Offer to show them the King's bed at so many groats a time."

"But who would want to see it?" asked Rose.

"Quite a number of people, believe me, either from loyalty or curiosity. Keep the door of your great chamber locked, Mistress Marsh, and make a great to-do of taking down the key from the wall and leading them upstairs as a special privilege. Leave everything in the room just as it was. Let Tansy show it to them." Warming to his idea, he began to see it not only as a financial enterprise, but as something which might help to take the sweet girl's mind off her unhappy loss. "Like this, Tansy." With his gay gift for mimicry, he became Tansy, showing it. Turning a key, throwing wide a heavy door, then standing aside to give her audience a full, impressive view of the interior. "Our best bedroom, just as King

Richard the Third slept in it. The folding bed which went with him everywhere, no matter where he was fighting. Note the fleur-de-lys and the carving and the box beneath the mattress for his possessions. And see, here are his nightgown and his shoes—everything, just as he left them, the night before Bosworth, when he had only one more short night to live. Here, you will tell them, his squires dressed him in tabard and armor. Here he put on the crown of England. . . . Yes, yes, I know it was downstairs, but what matter? . . . And from here he went forth in splendor. And for an extra groat or two you could tell them how he came back."

"Oh, no, no!" protested Tansy.

"But it is what they really want. The Bow Bridge part. And showing of his corpse afterwards. Most people are morbid."

"We could try it," agreed Rose, feeling that she herself would rather enjoy describing the lying-in-state. "Have another drink, Tom, on the house."

Tansy sat in silence. She had promised to do anything to help, and here was something which she should be able to do all too well. For whereas to the others the King's room was already becoming an interesting background to a fragment of history, for her it held heart-shattering reality, kept alive through the existence and the shared emotions of his son. And only sensitive old Will Jordan, without knowing the cause, suspected how much she shrank from the part so blithely assigned to her.

Chapter Ten

If the King's bed did not make a fortune, for months after the
battle of Bosworth it helped to keep the Blue Boar going.
Tansy tried to be always at hand to take visitors upstairs and
to say her piece, more or less as Tom had instructed her. The
people who came were very varied—some were staying in
the inn, some just happened to be in Leicester, and some
were brought by relatives who lived there. Some were curious, some skeptical, and a few much moved.

At first Tansy hated telling strangers about something
which had touched her so profoundly. She often found herself wishing that she could show it to Dickon, who would
have felt about it as she did, and to whom in a sense the bed
belonged, since no man could have died more bereft of close
relatives than had King Richard. But gradually, as she said
the same words over and over, they became automatic and
lost their poignancy. And gradually, also, she became aware
that the Yorkists still had a strong following. They came
mostly from the north and midlands. Many men who had
served under him came, as on a devoted pilgrimage, from Yorkshire. Tansy always sensed this because of the way they
listened when she told them anything about the Plantagenet's
last hours. They knew as well as she did what he had looked
like and would stand in silence drinking in every detail of the
room and, as like as not, cross themselves in prayer for his
soul. But outside their own county such ardent adherents
would not dare to show their feelings because of the smooth
success which the first Tudor King was enjoying in London.
The Duke of Norfolk, Brackenbury, and the majority of Richard's closest followers had been killed, and Sir Francis Lovell
was thought to have escaped to the court of the Duchess of
Burgundy, Richard's sister, so they lacked a leader. And as
Henry the Seventh had put out a false report that Richard's
nephew, the Earl of Lincoln, was dead, they lacked the inspi-
ration of a Yorkist heir for whom to fight.

Weapon makers, like Tom Hood, whose fathers had
thriven during the years of civil war, were hard put to it to

make a living. "I should come to you only as a beggar," he said to Tansy, too proud to urge her to marry him even when her father had been dead a year. And Tansy, liking him the better in his misfortune, had begun to wonder why she had held out so long against him. Certainly it was not on account of the advances which Hugh Malpas had been making to her, which were not only unwelcome in themselves but invariably became a cause of still more dislike from her stepmother.

But riding to Lutterworth market one spring morning she was to learn the reason for the dullness of her present life and for the reluctance of her heart. Gufford, the London chapman, was there with all manner of attractive women's finery laid out on his stall, which looked all the more enticing after a year of economy and mourning, and when she had dismounted to finger and to admire he produced a small packet for her. "I should have brought it to you in Leicester next Saturday when I have my pitch there, if I hadn't recognized you in the crowd," he said. "A likely looking young man brought it to me in Cheapside and more or less threatened to kill me if I didn't deliver it at the Boar. But, more important than his urgency, was the fact that he paid me well for my pains. You've changed the name of the inn, he tells me. Which I shouldn't have known, not having been up this way for months, with trade in London so good."

So that was why she hadn't heard! Tansy looked at the neat script bearing her name and knew that after all Dickon hadn't forgotten her. The spring sunshine was suddenly brighter, her heart lighter. She thanked the chapman effusively, promised him all manner of extravagant purchases from her stepmother, and cantered home with half the week's provisions forgotten. Not until she had shut herself into the privacy of her own bedroom could she bring herself, breathlessly, to open her package.

To her mingled dismay and happiness four gold coins rolled out. She was dismayed that he should have repaid the amount which she had so willingly given him, yet happy that he was the sort of person who would do so. Never once had she expected it, never once wanted it; but a warm security wrapped her about like an ermine cloak because she found him to be utterly dependable, and because she could now base her feelings for him on the fact that all he had said had been sincere and durable and not just an emotional expression of gratitude. It made sense of her strange reluctance to accept a marriage proposal from anyone whom she liked even as much as she liked Tom Hood.

With eager, trembling fingers she unrolled the letter—the first she had ever received.

My sweet Tansy, wrote Dickon. *Weeks ago I sought out your chapman, but he has been too busy selling silks for the Coronation to the ladies of the new court to find time for his provincial round through the Midlands. Which is no doubt as well because only now am I able to repay the money which your lovely generosity persuaded me to accept. Without it I could never have been so well set on the path to a usefully creative life. The road to London was not too badly beset by thieving stragglers from the battle, and I received from Master Paston a most kind welcome, he being overcome by the King's tragic fate and eager to hear all the last news of him, and indignant at Master Gervase's dishonest desertion.*

Good Master Paston disclosed to me that he still had in hand some money on my behalf, and with this and part of that which you lent me he has managed without too much difficulty to arrange for my indentures to a master mason named Hurland Dale, living in Old Jewry. For a year now I have been one of his apprentices, living in a part of his house reserved for us. The work is such as I have always craved to learn, the rules of our Guild insure our fair treatment, and although we work hard my fellow apprentices make much sport on their holidays. For myself, much as I enjoy this, I would fill a part of my life with more serious occupations and so have been reading both the invaluable book which you gave me and some which my master has lent me.

Having done fairly the tasks set me, I have been chosen to assist Master Dale's head mason in the building of a town house for Sir Walter Moyle, a Kentish gentleman and judge of the King's Bench. This Sir Walter, seeing some quaint toy beasts which I have carved and colored in my spare time, was pleased to buy them for his small nephews, which is how I have been fortunate enough to earn money. And by the same token, and remembering a kindness concerning a horse which I later sold in order to buy suitable clothing, I would

*have you mention to Master Tom Hood that, should the
arrow-making craft become less necessary in the Midlands,
this same Sir Walter Moyle is in need of a good fletcher, he
being charged with raising Kentish men for the defence of
Calais, and his own fletcher having but recently died.*

*This letter is all about me, dear Tansy, but my thoughts
are all of you. I would that I were a chapman bound for
Leicester or, better still, that I might have you here to show
you the sights of London. I envy even that foolish painted
creature the Blue Boar who is ever near you.*

> *Your friend, who would be more,*
> RICHARD BROOME.

Tansy read her first letter through again, and then sat still
on her bed with a happy smile on her face. Her mind reached
far beyond the sloping walls of her clean, sunlit attic. In
imagination she was walking with Dickon in London, being
shown all the sights: the houses perched on the bridge, the
crowded masts of foreign shipping in the river, the grim
Tower, the open space at Smithfield where the 'prentices held
their sports, the gracious palace and grand Abbey away down
the Strand at Westminster—all the places she had heard travelers talking about. The fact that he wanted her to be there
made it all real. And was his message to Tom pure altruism,
or a lover's precaution, preferring to have him out of Leicester during his own absence? Tansy laughed aloud at the
thought and carefully locked the King's money in the small
box in which, since childhood, she had kept her treasures. At
the back of her mind was the notion that one day those gold
coins might help her to get to London, which was now, since
her father's death, beginning to be the city of her dreams.
Even killed, how much King Richard was still helping them!
she thought, for the first time coupling herself and Dickon as
a united pair. In fact, it was the King's tragic fate which had
given her Dickon. And then a frightened diffidence gripped
her, for how could she, Tansy Marsh, consider even in the
privacy of a young girl's dreams the possibility of marrying a
king's son?

She did not have long to worry about it. Stridently, intru-
sively, a voice cut across her interesting dilemma. "Tansy!

Tan-see! Aren't you coming down to help?" called her step-mother, from the bottom of the attic stairs.

The sloping whitewashed walls became part of an inn again. The pretty comb with which she tidied her fair curls was, rather accusingly, a fairing which Tom had given her. Downstairs, the lamplit tavern room with its broad local speech and laughter and its human warmth was part of her real, familiar life, a friendly place, lacking only the loving welcome of her father. But Master Jordan and Tom were there, and there were things she wanted to say to them both.

"Where have you been?" asked Tom, drawing in his long, sprawling legs to let her pass.

"In London," she whispered mysteriously. "I have a message for you presently."

"Someone left you a fortune?" inquired Rose, noticing with grudging admiration a new radiance on the girl's quiet face as she deftly picked up a tray of tankards.

"A fortune and a handsome husband," said Tansy, and everyone laughed goodnaturedly.

After serving for a while and spreading something of her new happiness among the Blue Boar benches, she went back to speak to Tom.

"You remember the man you got the horse for? I had a letter from him."

"So that is why you still have star dust in your eyes," he deduced glumly.

"He reached London safely and is apprenticed to a mason in Old Jewry. He was so grateful for your help about the horse that he sends you a message."

"A message to me? But he didn't even know my name."

"Oh, yes, he did. I often spoke of you."

Tom perked up considerably. "You did, Tansy?"

"And he was just as absurdly jealous of you as you are of him," she teased, with new flirtatious confidence born of the assurance of a lasting love. "He called you, quite enviously, 'that up-and-coming young man.' You see, he has less experience—less confidence. But, on the other hand, he is very deliberately thoughtful. And it occurred to him that since all the fighting seems to have ceased and prospects in the building trade are very good, perhaps your arrow business may be very bad."

"Very kind of him, I'm sure!" raged Tom, hit on the raw again.

He sprang to his feet and reached for his cloak, but Tansy calmly produced the letter from the bodice of her gown. "He himself, being apprenticed quite unadventurously to a mason, and helping to build a house for a justice of the King's Bench called Sir Walter Moyle——"

"I have heard of him," muttered Tom, half in and half out of his cloak.

"'This same Sir Walter Moyle . . . being charged with raising Kentish men for the defence of Calais,'" went on Tansy imperturbably, reading from her letter. She was aware that the cloak had fallen at her feet and that Tom's attention was well and truly caught; he had turned and was staring down at her. "'And I would have you mention to Master Tom Hood—he who was so kind about the horse, which I later sold for suitable clothing——'"

"Yes, yes. Go on. Never mind about the horse. Give me the letter!" He reached for it, but Tansy deftly held it out of his reach.

"'—this same Sir Walter Moyle is in need of a good fletcher,'" she concluded calmly.

But Tom was anything but calm. "But surely a man in Sir Walter's position, who is always raising bowmen—whose name is a byword in the trade—has a fletcher?"

"The poor man has just died," related Tansy, in tones of suitable regret. "He was probably quite old and experienced. That is why, as you seem to have gathered, the Moyle family would need a good fletcher."

"Died, has he, poor devil!" Tom said perfunctorily. But she looked up then and, seeing the twinkle that belied the solemnity of her voice, he hugged her excitedly. "Tansy, do you suppose that if I packed up now and rode hell for leather to London——"

"I don't suppose. I know," said Tansy, and hugged him back. "Haven't I always said that you could talk anybody into anything? You'll be making arrows for this personal body-guard the new King is forming before you know where you are."

"It's a chance. Where is this fellow's address? I ought to thank him," said Tom, all animosity forgotten. Indeed, every-

thing forgotten in the chance to get on, thought Tansy, a
trifle hurt.

"He works for a Master Hurland Dale of Old Jewry." She
turned and raised her voice. "Master Jordan! Stepmother! It
is Tom who is going to make a fortune. He is going to
London!" she announced.

"We can only hope, about the fortune," said Tom, with a
rare access of modesty.

They all wished him good luck, and since he had always
been the first to help others their wishes were sincere.

"But what about your business here?" William Jordan reminded him. To him they both seemed very young and optimistic, but then, with a new dynasty upon the throne, perhaps it was a brave young world.

"I will go and see my head man, Brewster. He is quite
capable of dealing with the regular orders that come in. And
after all, I may be back in a few days."

"I half hope you are," admitted Tansy, clinging to him.

He kissed her before them all, though it might well have
been a kiss of gratitude. "If you could spare Tansy to help me
pack, Mistress Marsh?" he asked audaciously. "I want to get
away within the hour."

But the landlady of the Blue Boar knew her world. "While
wishing you a prosperous and speedy journey, Tom," she
said, with an acumen which drew laughter, "I rather think
you will get away considerably quicker if you pack by
yourself."

And some hours later, Tansy, lying wakeful and excited in
bed, heard the hoofbeats of the fletcher's horse as he cantered
along High Street towards the Cross and South Gate. He whistled a stave of a song as he went past, and she ran to
the window and waved. Long after the town was quiet, her
thoughts and prayers followed him through the hazards of
night on the road towards London. But her heart was there
already, in a dormitory full of tousle-headed sleeping 'prentices, one of whom was a king's son.

Chapter Eleven

Life seemed lonely indeed to Tansy without her father, Dickon or Tom. She would have liked to send Dickon some answer to his letter, but Tom had seized his opportunity so quickly that there had been no time. Dickon would have news of her, of course, if the two of them met; he would know that Gufford had given her the letter and would hear the sad news of her father's death. But that was not the same thing as a personal written response which she was sure the chapman would take back for her. Dickon would look for one. He would be disappointed if his words of steady affection drew no response from her. But Tansy had to admit, to her shame, that it would indeed be a labor of love. Her days had been filled with domestic affairs, and since her mother's death she had forgotten any book learning which she had ever had. Save in her missal she seldom read anything, and she knew that her spelling was atrocious. Good enough, perhaps, to leave an urgent note for the apothecary or the wine merchant, but shame-making when writing to a man who knew all about Master Caxton's books.

Tansy pondered the problem, while going about her morning occupations, and decided to enlist the schoolmaster's help. As soon as she had heard the children come running and shouting from his door after lessons, she said firmly that she was going out for a while and asked Rose if she would show the King's bed to anyone who might come to see it.

Grudgingly Rose agreed, remarking that she had been going to take a rest and that, in any case, she knew none of the romantic nonsense which Tansy told her gullible clients. But for once Tansy paid no attention and slipped across the street to the schoolhouse.

Beyond the bare and empty schoolroom, with its desk and forms and hornbooks and the birch rod which she imagined kind Will Jordon was more inclined to spare than to use, she found him in his own little book-strewn room. "I am glad that you have come to see me here, Tansy," he said, drawing up a stool for her. "It is perhaps easier for us to talk freely than at the inn. Is there something you want to tell me?"

"It is only that I want you to help me with a letter: to write the address clearly and show me how to seal it. It is to go to London."

"So soon?" he said smiling.

She realized that he took it for granted that her letter was for Tom, and that somehow she would have to explain. Embarrassed and blushing, she drew Dickon's letter from her gown and laid it on his table, pointing to the address.

"Well, that should be easy," he said, looking down at the excellent penmanship. "But what is the name?"

"Master Richard Broome, apprentice. I have not seen him since the week of Bosworth. It is he who sent a message to Tom about Sir Walter Moyle needing a fletcher."

"I see. And you want to thank him," said Jordan, relief chasing anxiety from his sensitive face.

But his kindness and her own innate honesty forbade the easy subterfuge. She knew that Will Jordan was utterly trustworthy, and remembered how her father had told her to go to him in any difficulty. And so she told him the whole story, swearing him to secrecy on Dickon's behalf. To her pleased surprise he listened to it all with grave attention, asking a pertinent question now and again, and not scoffing at it as her father had done. "I can well imagine his calling it a likely story. It certainly sounds like one. But it is by no means impossible," he said, turning over the letter in his hand to admire the fineness of the script. "All the more so because no one seems to be trying to make anything out of it."

"He even returned the money," Tansy reminded him.

"And now, very sensibly, is trying to live down all pretensions, false or genuine, by following a useful craft among the busy population of London."

"That is what the King himself advised for his safety," said Tansy, "You see, Dickon is dangerously like him."

Jordan looked at her sharply, appraisingly. He knew her to be full of common sense, without high-flown fancies. Her last remark convinced him more than anything else. And although he was concerned for her, and not unmindful of poor Tom, he recognized how apt it was that she should seem to care for a lad whose father had meant so much to her own.

He set paper and ink before her and left her to compose her first letter as privately as possible, only helping her when she asked and finally addressing it for her. "I suggest that we do not seal it now, in case you should want to add anything before the chapman goes," he said, looking down at her diligently bent golden head with tender amusement. What he really meant was that he would leave her opportunity to add some spontaneous, ill-spelt love message which he was sure any lively 'prentice, whether king's son or not, would appreciate far more than all his own correctly phrased thanks or items of news.

Warm with gratitude, Tansy reached up to kiss his cheek and left the schoolhouse far more happily than she had come. She knew now that a friend was close at hand to take her father's place, and possibly one who was wiser than her father. But time had passed so quickly while she was with him that she had stayed longer than she intended, and she re-entered the inn with misgiving. Rose would have missed her afternoon nap, people might have come to be shown the King's bedroom, and she would probably be in a vile temper. But to Tansy's surprise she found her stepmother still up in the best bedroom, examining with apparent interest a belt which the King had left behind and singing, of all things, Hugh Malpas's ballad about the rival inns. Just as if its ribald triumphing had no power at all to hurt her.

"Did anyone come?" asked Tansy apprehensively, peering in at the door.

"Yes. Two parties of people. Quite pleasant folk, they were."

Tansy went right into the room, staring at her unpredictable stepmother in surprise. The setting sun shone through the wide mullioned window, making a russet aureole of her hair. All signs of disagreeableness and fatigue were gone and, apart from the fact that she was rather too plump, Rose Marsh looked a comely and pleasant enough woman to attract any man's attention. "Were they interested?" asked Tansy, at a loss to account for such a welcome transformation.

"Not particularly. Which was just as well, as they paid as much but didn't stay long."

Then why in the world are you staying up here instead of

resting or gossiping with Druscilla Gamble in the parlor?
wondered Tansy. But it was too good an opportunity to be
missed. Now, in such a moment of good temper, was the opportunity to confess about her lighthearted promises to the
chapman.

"I should have told you yesterday, but so much was happening, with Tom going off like that. I saw Gufford the chapman in Lutterworth. He'll be here in the market place on Saturday. He had some lovely things. Rose-patterned damask for
gowns and some cosy hoods lined with miniver. Silver chate-
laines with filigree work and some amusing shoes fashioned
like animals. I told him I was sure you would want to see everything."

Rose laid down the leather belt, all interest diverted
to feminine fashions. "Had he anything suitable for a
medium-weight cloak for Easter?" she asked eagerly.

"Yes. Something I thought was lovely: a roll of Venetian
velvet in the new shade of Tudor green. All the ladies were
wearing it in London at Coronation time, he said, and this
was the one length he had over. It was terribly expensive. Almost half an angel a yard." Tansy almost stammered with
nervousness, remembering how shamelessly she had tried to
curry favor with the useful letter-carrying chapman from
London. "But I said I thought you would like him to save it
for you."

"Indeed, indeed, I should!" cried Rose, to Tansy's vast relief. "I only hope you were quite definite, so that he isn't persuaded to sell it to some other eager customer first. I should
go green myself with envy if I saw the Mayor's wife flouncing
about in it!"

"It is certainly just the right color for your hair," said
Tansy, laughing and half envious too. "I will get up early on
Saturday morning as soon as the stalls are set up and make
sure of it for you," she added, wondering where the money
was to come from.

But that did not seem to be bothering Rose at all. "That is
good of you, Tansy," she said, "and I will come later and
make my purchases, and then be here all tomorrow afternoon
again in case anyone should come to see the King's bed. It is
rather magnificent with all those fleur-de-lys, isn't it?" She
went singing and humming to the window to look down into

the street. "You know, since you and Dilly and Jod managed to push it more into the middle I like this room much better. It gets all the sun. I think I shall move in here myself to sleep. My room looking over the yard is very dull."

"Then I expect you would like Dilly and me to bring your things and make up the other bed," offered Tansy, seeing that it was a sensible idea but not at all pleased at the prospect. Somehow the constant presence of her stepmother, who had never shown the least sympathy for the late King, seemed an intrusion.

Before the sun was well up next day, she had handed Gufford her letter to Dickon and secured the cloak length. But the Tudor green velvet was not the only thing which Rose was tempted to buy from Gufford. Later in the morning she came back from the market place followed by a packhorse laden with all manner of extravagant adornments and fripperies. She felt that she had every excuse. She was still a good-looking woman, the widow's mourning was past, and it would soon be springtime. She gave away some of the cheaper ribbons and gewgaws with a lavish hand and completely refurbished her own wardrobe.

Tansy tried to admire the purchases with good grace, but could not prevent herself from seeing in them the whole winter's profits for which she had worked so hard. When Jod had bolted the doors behind the last customers and her stepmother was upstairs peacocking before a mirror, she slipped away to the little office where her father had kept his accounts and for the first time gave her serious attention to the figuring. Since his death her stepmother had kept them in a flourishing and erratic hand but, as with most things in which she had an interest—and money always interested her—she contrived to do so with a certain amount of efficiency. To Tansy's untrained mind the figuring was difficult to understand, but it seemed clear enough that there had been no unusual spate of success on the credit side, nothing to warrant the spending of so much on luxuries. While big money flowed into the Golden Crown, it was evident that the Blue Boar, even with the popular attraction of the King's bed, contrived to make a steady, respectable living and no more.

She put away the books and was going to bed, wondering whether she dared remonstrate with her stepmother or not, when she noticed there was a light in the kitchen and heard someone impatiently opening and shutting cupboard doors. She went in, to find Rose, half undressed, impatiently searching for something. "What are you looking for?" she asked.

Rose started and turned, ill-pleased and flurried. "I thought you had gone to bed ages ago," she complained. "But, since you are here, where in God's name is the chisel?"

"The chisel?" repeated Tansy, wondering what anyone should want with such an implement at that time of night.

"Yes, the chisel!" snapped Rose, without vouchsafing any further enlightenment. "It ought to be in this drawer with the meat chopper and basting spoons, but some interfering hussy must have moved it."

At least Tansy could help her there. "Don't you remember Jod fetched it when he took down the signboard?" she said. "Probably it is in the wagon shed. I will go and see."

She went out under the stars across the still and empty yard, found it on the bench where Jod mended harness, and took it back to Rose. Her mind was so full of memories of other visits to the wagon shed and hayloft that she scarcely resented the scant thanks she received or the harsh railing against 'that forgetful fool' Jod. But she did notice the almost greedily eager way in which Rose snatched at the tool and hurried upstairs with it to her new bedroom, and how annoyed she seemed because she had not been able to find the thing for herself. But as more and more of the running of the inn fell upon Tansy's shoulders, she soon forgot about the incident.

Rose seemed to be always upstairs, or buying and trying on new clothes, or out pleasuring about the town. "She probably means to get married again," said Druscilla Gamble, watching her bustle out of the inn one morning in her becoming green cloak in company with one of the aldermen's wives.

Tansy turned to stare at the shoemaker's wife, letting the new and rather frightening idea sink in.

"And I shouldn't be surprised if she lands Hugh Malpas this time," added Druscilla, spitefully jealous of both cloak and exalted company.

"Oh, Mistress Gamble!" exclaimed Tansy, "You don't really think that?"

"Why not? Did you want him for yourself?"

"God forbid! But with the two of them, what should I do?"

"What indeed, your poor child!" agreed Druscilla Gamble, who was not completely heartless.

And only the next day when the inn door had slammed angrily behind its owner and Tansy was hurriedly making some honey cakes for a family of children who were staying, Dilly came to her in the kitchen in floods of tears.

"Why, Dilly, what's the matter?"

"She's been beating you again?" asked Cook, looking up from her pastry.

Tansy took the trembling girl into her arms, and Cook yanked the torn, shabby dress from her thin shoulders and smeared some soothing lard on the angry red weals.

"But what did you do, Dilly?" asked Tansy, knowing full well how irritatingly stupid the maid could be, and how much patient encouragement she needed.

" 'Tis the clothes. I be no good with 'em. Allus now she wants me to stand by and help her dress. Brush her hair, and pull in her corsets. Says she's training me to be a proper maid, like Mistress Wigston has. But I'm no good. I spill the rose water and spoil her freshly ironed laces with my hot hands, and then she gets mad at me and says I'm an imbecile fit only for Bedlam, and beats me. What is Bedlam, Mistress Tansy?"

"Oh, a kind of hospital. But you are quite useful really, Dilly."

"I'd do anything for you and Cook. But I don't know anything except about washing platters an' feedin' hens an' handing ale. An' there's some customers beginnin' to come in now, and me with my eyes all red an' my dress all down."

"You sit there by the fire and I will go and serve them," said Tansy, hastily pushing her cakes into the oven and asking Cook to see to them. But before she had reached the door Dilly said something which pulled her up sharply.

"She be gone out to buy a cupboard."

"Who is buying a cupboard?" asked Tansy.

"Why, the mistress, o' course."

"What sort of a cupboard?"

"One o' they wardrobe things. To put all the dresses in. An ar-moy or somethin', she kept callin' it. It's to stand against the wall in the King's bedroom, where she sleeps now."

Tansy came slowly back towards the fire. "Are you quite sure about this, Dilly? How do you know?"

"I heard her talkin' to the carpenter. Had him up there to measure. Real fussy she was about it. Had to have a drawer here an' hooks there." And, the pain having worn off, the girl began to giggle.

When Rose Marsh returned she was escorted by Hugh Malpas, which gave color to Mistress Gamble's surmise. He stayed for a drink, asked questions about Rose's latest purchase, and it seemed to Tansy that he looked round the place with a new proprietary interest. Partly because she could not abide his presence, and partly because she was so worried, Tansy slipped across the street to the schoolhouse and unburdened herself to Will Jordan.

"She always was extravagant, as you know. But my father wouldn't let her exceed the profits."

"The whole town is certainly talking about her and wondering where she gets so much money from," he admitted, seeing no kindness in pretence.

"They must know it isn't from the Boar," said Tansy. "And at the end of the month the vintner's bill will be coming in, and if she is really having this armoire made we shan't be able to pay it."

"But has it occurred to you that Malpas could? If she expects to marry him it would perhaps account for her extravagance. That may be the solution."

"Yes, it may be the solution. But either way," said Tansy slowly, "it would mean my home gone. If we get into debt I shall have no home, and if he marries her I could not live with them. I would rather hire myself out to work."

"No, you could not live with them," agreed Jordan. "But you will marry, Tansy."

"Men cannot take wives while they are still apprentices," she said, the color burning up into her cheeks.

"No. But up-and-coming fletchers can," Will Jordan reminded her, knowing what her father would have wanted.

Chapter Twelve

When Tom's man, Brewster, came with the news that his young master had been engaged by Sir Walter Moyle and had been given temporary accommodation in the London house which Master Hurland Dale was building, and that the supply of arrows for Calais looked like being one of the best paid assignments in the trade, Tansy saw the wisdom of Will Jordan's remark. With life at the Blue Boar becoming more and more difficult, and the future more uncertain, she was at times sorely tempted to let Tom know that she had changed her mind. Married to him, her future would be secure and, even if he were occasionally lured into gay affairs with other girls, he would always be kind to her. She had known him long enough to be sure that all his attractive good points far outweighed his shortcomings. She would go to London, perhaps later on she would even cross the sea with him to Calais, and life with Tom, wherever he was, would certainly never be dull. If it seemed like taking him in panic as a refuge from her troubles, she reminded herself that she would probably have married him anyhow, if Dickon had not come along. And what were two or three days of intense shared interest, a few hours of intimate talk, to pit against an easy companionship which went back to childhood?

But something had happened during those few hours with Dickon which gave a new set of values to her world. So she sent no message back by Brewster save sincere congratulations. And Brewster, almost as an afterthought, set her mind at rest as to how Tom and Dickon had liked each other when they had met. "My master sent word to you that he can never be sufficiently grateful to Master Broome who told him of this chance. He went straight to this young man's lodgings and now sees him every day at Sir Walter Moyle's house. I do not know who this Master Broome may be, Mistress Tansy, but it seems they have visited several archery contests together and had good sport."

I expect Tom was delighted to pay all the expenses of their outing, thought Tansy, knowing how little pocket money most apprentices had. But she was glad that she had said no more to encourage him, nor let herself panic into buying security. For somehow the vintner's bill was miraculously paid, and as the weeks went by her stepmother showed less and less inclination to marry Malpas. Or, indeed, to marry anybody at all. She seemed very well content as she was, spending money as and when she fancied and leading feminine fashion in Leicester. The only fly in the ointment was that this orgy of self-indulgence she ate prodigiously of everything she fancied and grew too fat to become her expensive clothes.

With the coming of spring, Tansy tried to put all worries behind her. She rode on Pippin through the fresh green lanes and, whenever possible, exchanged letters with Dickon. But a completely unexpected difficulty lay ahead. Coming back from Bosworth one day she was surprised to find Gladys, the singing girl, sitting sewing in the parlor.

"Whatever are you doing with Mistress Marsh's best head-dresses?" she demanded.

"Altering them," said Gladys coolly. "She asked me to."

Tansy suddenly experienced again that frightening feeling of insecurity. "I should not have thought that plying a needle was exactly your trade," she said.

The girl glanced at her calculatingly from beneath her long dark lashes. If she had intended an impudent riposte, she bit it back. Tansy of the Boar had grown to womanhood, and there was a steadfastness about her which commanded respect. It would be as well, thought Gladys of the Crown, not to run foul of her from the start. "I am no needlewoman, but I have some flair for clothes, even if it is rather—dramatic. And I am hoping that Mistress Marsh will engage me as her maid," she said, making a show of laying all her cards on the table. "You see, Master Malpas has dismissed me from the Golden Crown."

"Dismissed you!" echoed Tansy almost incredulously. "But you attracted so much custom!"

"I might sing here, Mistress Marsh thought, as well as doing"—the showman's daughter waved a contemptuous hand across her present occupation—"this sort of thing."

"I see."

"Not quite the same type of songs, of course," Gladys hastened to add, seeing the distaste on Tansy's face. Her own had been carefully cleansed of paint, and her mien was almost meek, but Tansy still distrusted her. She laid down her riding cloak and gloves and went towards the stairs to find her stepmother, an intention which the girl was quick to suspect. Gladys swept aside all the finery and thread and sprang up, following her urgently. "You will not try to dissuade her from engaging me?" she implored. "My father has said that he will not keep me."

"I daresay there are plenty of other men who will," flung back Tansy, without stopping. "You need scarcely fear to starve." But, true as that might be, the Welsh girl's urgent desire to stay seemed real enough.

Tansy, her temper up, was no longer the biddable young daughter of the house. She flung wide the door of the best bedroom without ceremony. "Is this true, that you are having Malpas's girl here?" she asked.

Rose swung round on her, a pot of Gladys's mascara with which she was experimenting still in her hands. "Yes. And why not?"

"Because the sly slut is not fit to live in my father's house."

"Don't be sanctimonious, Tansy. In any case, your father is dead and we must do the best we can for ourselves. Dilly is a hopeless fool, and Gladys is clever about clothes."

"And about plenty of other things besides."

"Oh, come, Tansy! Give the girl a chance. At the Crown she always had to do what Hugh Malpas ordered. Now, it seems, he has turned her out."

"I always supposed she was worth her weight in gold to him."

"Perhaps she wanted to find a little gold for herself."

"You mean, you bribed her from him?"

"Certainly not. But I shall make it worth her while. She came to me last night when you were over at the schoolhouse, discussing me with old Jordan, no doubt. She was in tears. Said she only knew inn business, and Malpas had thrown her out. She had heard Cook or someone say I wanted a maid, and would I take her?"

"As a maid or as a singer?"

"Both, I hope," said Rose, preening herself on her acumen. Although it would probably change their type of trade,

Tansy could not deny that it might well be a smart move for
the Blue Boar. "But where will you find the money to make it
worth her while?" she asked.

"Nobody is asking you to pay," snapped Rose.

"You mean it won't have to come out of our takings?" persisted Tansy, once more up against this mystery of where her
stepmother got her money from.

Rose turned on her in sudden fury. "Your tongue needs
slitting. You ask far too many questions!" she cried violently.

Tansy, half cowed, turned away. "At least tell me this," she
asked from the doorway. "Where is she to sleep?"

Rose shrugged as if the matter were of little consequence,
showing herself, perhaps, less clever than she had supposed.
"I don't use my room overlooking the yard any more. The one
at the head of the outside stairs."

"My father's room," remonstrated Tansy. But Robert
Marsh's widow did not seem to hear her. She was busy
painting her sandy lashes black.

All that summer Glady's Grumbold was with them and
carefully minded her manners. She was accustomed to work,
kept out of Tansy's way as much as possible, and served Rose
assiduously. In fact, her clever fingers were into everything.
In her quiet way she tried to learn all about the running of
the Blue Boar, wanted to know where everything was kept,
and asked all manner of unexpected questions, eliciting admiring cooperation from Dilly and Diggory and completely
unhelpful monosyllables from Jod. Tansy even caught her
prying into the account books. But the girl had soon made
herself indispensable to Rose. She followed her mistress into
shops, admired and advised, and carried all the wildly extravagant parcels home. On summer evenings she sang for the
customers out in the inn courtyard, choosing romantic ballads
or gentle love songs, keeping her bold eyes lowered and setting her cap at no man.

"But her bawdy songs brought in twice the money at the
Crown, and her being here does not seem to have lured any
of their custom to us," grumbled Rose, sitting by the little
mulberry tree eating sweetmeats while Tansy served the
usual number of drinks.

"It is strange that Malpas has never tried to get her back," commented Tansy, pausing, tray on hip, beside Tom Hood, who was home on a brief visit to set his local business in order.

"He probably caught her in some one else's bed," suggested Tom, eyeing the sultry little beauty with mild interest.

"You think she was his mistress?"

Tom shrugged a careless affirmation. "What else? A lecher like Hugh Malpas and an exciting wanton like her. Not that he was the only one"—he laughed—"judging from some of the men's boasting."

Tansy looked across at Gladys, plucking with boredom at the strings of a lute as the sun went down, and was nagged again by something which she could not understand. "Then how can she endure living decently here?"

For the first time it occurred to Tom to wonder the same thing. "She must have some very good reason, I suppose," he agreed slowly.

Tansy turned her back on singer and audience, put down her tray on a horse trough, and faced him. "I hate living here since my father died," she said, with queer intensity.

Considering the bright prospects which he now had, he might well have seized on her heartfelt confession and urged her again to marry him, but his mind was seething with inventions and ambitions which he wanted to satisfy first. He was at that high moment of a young man's life when a successful career was opening out before him. He took her free hand in his and looked up at her with his devastating smile, but he did not mention marriage. "My poor sweet! It must be unbearably grim. And worse, I wager, since that sly wench came into the household. You must see more of dear old Master Jordan, and get out more on Pippin."

It was wonderful to have him there to talk to again, someone to whom she could say any foolish thing which entered her head, even the half-formed fancies which she herself could not understand. "Lately I have had a feeling of——"

"Of what, dear Tansy?"

"A kind of foreboding. A sense of something sinister going to happen."

"Like your stepmother splitting her best gown in church through stuffing herself on sweetmeats."

"Oh, Tom, I wish you were not going back to London! Just

your foolishness and laughter make everything wholesome and normal again."

Reluctant as he was to leave her, at the mention of London Tom's mind was instantly filled with enthusiasm for his new work. "I must go. Sir Walter said it was difficult to spare me even for these few days to set my business here in order. I may be sailing to Calais with him soon, to meet the captain of our garrison there. He is interested in a new kind of arrow shaft, more on the cannon principle, which I am working on."

"And then?"

"Then, who knows? I may come back to England a reasonably rich man. And I shall owe it all to Dick Broome, who is still only an apprentice," he had the generosity to add, half reluctantly.

"But he is doing well?" asked Tansy, trying to hide the eagerness in her voice.

"He should go far. His term is nearly finished. He will soon become a freeman of his Guild, and his master, Hurland Dale, thinks highly of him. I overheard him and Sir Walter discussing some arches which Dick had built, and Sir Walter referred to him as 'that clever young 'prentice of yours.'"

"Then you see how right he was in wanting to be a mason!" And because she wanted them to be friends she looked searchingly at her companion. "You really like him, don't you, Tom? Apart from being grateful?"

"It would be difficult not to. There is something about him different from the rest of us."

Knowing what she knew, Tansy felt this to be scarcely surprising. "How do you mean, different?" she asked, pursuing a subject of which she could not tire.

"Oh, as if he thought and felt more deeply. I know his fellow apprentices respect him. They may laugh at him sometimes for studying or putting his whole self into his work when he might be out with them, painting the town red. But I've noticed they always go to him if they have some personal trouble, or there is some communal decision to be made. As if he had authority—which is odd, since there never was a more retiring sort of fellow."

Tansy glowed with pride. "You don't think he is working too hard?" she asked, managing to achieve an admirable casualness.

"Dickon? Oh, no. He is strong as a horse, really. When he gives time and mind to it he can beat most of us at the butts, or wrestling, and is the very devil at that football game they are forever playing through the streets, to the fury of the staider citizens."

"You spend a good deal of your free time with them, don't you?"

"I did at first. Dickon was extraordinarily kind to me when I arrived, a stranger in London. But I shan't be there much longer."

Because the obliging chapman would not be coming to Leicester for some weeks, Tansy seized her chance. "Would you take a letter to him?"

"Not if it is a love letter," stipulated Tom promptly.

"An ordinary friendly letter," Tansy assured him. "After all, I have written to him before, and Master Jordan helped me, thanking him for his quick thinking on your behalf when Sir Walter Moyle's fletcher died."

"Using that as an excuse, you mean, you artful jade! And you don't have to hold my obligation to that young man over me forever."

"I am sure Dickon himself would be the last even to think of it. He was so very grateful about the horse. It meant a lot to him, getting out of Leicester just then."

"I was well paid for getting him that horse at the time. In kisses, remember?" said Tom, pulling her farther into the shade of the mulberry tree.

"But you don't need such payment now, I'm sure. And only for a letter," teased Tansy. "Aren't the girls in London prettier?"

"No prettier, but much bolder."

"And so you make love to them all?"

"At least they're not so tantalizing as some I know in this deadly town," he complained, as she managed to slip from his arms.

For either kisses held more meaning for Tansy now, or Tom let her go more easily. Even with the girl he loved best against his heart, a sickle moon sailing up through the mulberry branches, and the plaintive notes of a love song in the air, the up-and-coming fletcher's mind was already halfway to Calais.

Chapter Thirteen

Tansy took Tom's advice, went out more often for rides, and spent more time with friends. There seemed no need to make extra money by exploiting the King's bed, and since the room was usually full of feminine gear it was difficult to do so. It ceased to be pushed as an attraction, and only when visitors were very insistent was it shown.

One afternoon when she had planned to watch a company of mummers performing in the open space of the Newarke opposite the Castle, Tansy found it particularly difficult to be patient with a party of merchants' wives from York. They wanted to pore over everything that had belonged to the late King as if they were viewing sacred relics, and she herself was worrying over a grazed knee which Pippin had sustained and which Jod had been poulticing. To her annoyance, just as she was at last getting rid of them, she was aware of another potential viewer waiting on the landing. He must have come up the stairs very quietly for so big a man and, instead of looking round quickly while they were still there, he seemed to be standing about waiting for their departure.

She took their money, bade them farewell, and turned to him with ill-concealed annoyance. To her surprise it was Hugh Malpas.

"I came around because your maltster's new driver has delivered me your load by mistake," he said. "They told me you were up here, and, ridiculously enough for one who lives so near, I have never yet seen this money-making royal bed of yours."

And I've no mind to show it to you now, thought Tansy, although he held out his money and assured her that he had no desire to trade on his propinquity. Aloud she said, none too civilly, "This is Mistress Marsh's own bedroom now."

"Oh, so this is where the fair Rose sleeps," he said facetiously, looking round with interest.

"It is larger and sunnier and looks onto the street," explained Tansy, at her most matter-of-fact.

"It certainly is large. Finer than any room I have at the

Crown," he admitted handsomely. "And does she sleep in the royal bed?"

"She does now."

"They say it takes to pieces very ingeniously for traveling. Did you see it being set up?"

"Yes. It took the men only a few minutes."

"And that fine cupboard. Does that take to pieces too?"

"Not so far as I know. Why should it? It is nothing to do with King Richard. My stepmother bought it afterwards for her gowns."

"Those expensive gowns with which she so much enlivens Leicester. She is fortunate to be able to afford such a well-finished bit of furniture as well."

His flippant condescension annoyed her, and all the time he was poking fun at Marsh possessions he was running those repulsive-looking fingers experimentally along the cupboard door, the chimney breast, the wooden sides of the bed, and even the wooden bolt on the inside of the door.

"You don't give away much information, do you?" he complained, as she stood silent.

"You are not in the least interested in King Richard, so you had better take your money back," flared Tansy, holding it out to him.

"Oh, come, Tansy," he protested. "I was listening outside and thought your patter excellent. Why else should I have come in?"

"Because you are the kind of man who would take a leering interest in any bed slept in by an attractive woman."

He stared at her in surprise, having always thought of her as the simple, gullible daughter of the house, and never as an observant, spirited woman in her own right. He had no means of knowing that something bigger than her upbringing, and outside of her quiet provincial life, had changed and strengthened her. Even Tansy herself was sometimes surprised how quickly she saw through people's motives and pretences and how fearlessly she could speak up about them.

"You did not like my verses about the local inns?" he suggested, half apologetically.

"Nor the jade who sang them," she answered, throwing his money on the window seat since he would not take it.

"Though I cannot imagine why you, with such a keen eye to business, turned her out."

"Well, your stepmother seems to like her, so you are stuck with her now," he said with a grin. "I believe she even sings up in this room—having heard her when I have been passing, of course."

"Yes, she sometimes sings to her mistress. My stepmother often cannot sleep of late."

"Must be the bed. They say King Richard couldn't."

"That, or eating too richly at supper," said Tansy, suppressing a shudder, yet trying to speak lightly.

"Or counting her gold."

They both laughed and went out of the room together on rather better terms, and Tansy was contemptuously amused to see that he picked up his money after all. But when he had gone and the matter of the malt had been put right, she asked Dilly, who was polishing floor boards near the foot of the stairs, why she had sent Master Malpas up.

"I never sent him nowhere," remonstrated the girl in surprise. "Never see'd him till you come down with him just now."

"And you've been here all the time?"

"Since them other folk come in asking to see the bed."

"Perhaps your mistress sent him?"

"She been out since dinner."

"Then I suppose he must have come up the guests' outside staircase from the yard," said Tansy.

"Like his impudence!" snickered Dilly.

When Rose came back from the Newarke she was full of the excellent show she and her friends had seen and mimicked the mummers for the delight and envy of her household, so that Tansy thought only of how much she would have liked to be there and little more of Malpas's visit. But late that same evening the whole question of his mode of entry took on a new significance.

She had heard Pippin whinnying several times, and, guessing that Jod would be fast asleep, went quietly downstairs and opened the back door preparatory to going to the stable. To her horrified amazement, as she stood there in the shadow, she saw Gladys flit across the deserted yard, unbolt the lane gate to admit her former master, go up the outside staircase with him, and disappear into her bedroom. The room, because of its convenient position above the kitchen and at the top of the stone stairs, had always been Tansy's parents' room. Neither Malpas nor the girl said a word, but it was clear from their movements that this was a frequent proceeding. Tansy stood still, taking in the full, unpleasant significance of it. No wonder she can manage to live here so respectably! she thought, remembering her own conversation with Tom. But it was not so much the Welsh girl's known immorality which shocked her, as her deliberate deceitfulness. And the horror of Malpas. And the growing mystery. For if Gladys was still his mistress why in the world had he pretended to turn her away? And why had she sought employment at the Blue Boar?

Tansy's fingers dropped from the lantern she had been about to light. It was a starlit night and she found her way quietly across to Pippin's stable, making no sound. All the time she was changing the bran poultice and the affectionate beast was nuzzling her gratefully like a comforted child, her mind was on this chance revelation. She felt her home abused, soiled, spied upon. And all for what purpose? As Tom had said, "If she comes to live here she must have some good reason." Or rather, thought Tansy, some bad reason. She stood for a long time with her cheek against the soft warmth of Pippin's neck, wondering what she ought to do about it.

Gladys would have to go. Surely, Rose herself would be the first to agree? Or would she, favoring the girl as she did, only laugh and tell Tansy, in her jibing way, that it was just a case of the pot calling the kettle black, except that some people preferred a bed to a hayloft? She was quite capable of it, thought Tansy, but not when the lover happened to be Hugh Malpas: Malpas, her rival, on her own business premises; Malpas, admitted nightly by stealth. All the sharp money-loving part of her would be up in arms. Suddenly, Tansy wanted to tell Rose—Rose who was more worldly wise, less vulnerable, who would know what to do and do it quickly and stridently.

I will tell her now, she decided. She always says she can-

not sleep until late. At least I can see if there is candlelight
showing beneath her door. If there isn't I will leave it till the
morning. But how much better to tell her now, when I know
they are there, in my father's room! When there is proof of
what I say. When she can catch them there, and sharpen her
tongue on the odious wretch, and throw the bitch out onto
the street with every justification!

Tansy went back into the house and slowly, reluctantly,
mounted the wide stairs. As she neared the top she saw a
glimmer of light beneath the bottom of the best room door as
she had seen it late that Saturday night when the King slept
there. She would go in and tell her stepmother now, and the
responsibility of this unpleasant affair would no longer be
hers. She would have to knock on the door for Rose to unbolt
it. Rose would undoubtedly be cross. Yet by the time she
reached the quiet landing Tansy felt she could not tell her
soon enough. She wanted to be with Rose, to have told her.
As if impelled by desire for company, she almost ran across
the landing.

She raised her hand to knock, but to her surprise noticed
that the door stood the merest fraction ajar. Then she saw
that the wooden bolt had been sawn through. Fearing she
knew not what, she pushed the door open noiselessly and
went in. Candlelight flickered in a pool beyond the shadows
thrown by the tester of the bed. But the mistress of the Blue
Boar was asleep. Tansy could see the outline of her obese
body outlined comfortably beneath the coverlet, and the
rhythmic rise and fall of her breathing. At first she believed
her to be alone. Then, as she tiptoed farther into the room,
she saw two figures kneeling on the floor on the far side of
the bed—the very two about whom she had come to warn
her stepmother—Malpas and the girl, Gladys. Between them
was the gold! A carpet of gold pieces spread out across a
shallow, secret drawer almost on the level of the floor; a
drawer only about an inch deep, which was so cunningly
made that it had always looked like the solid bottom of the
bed itself, beneath the box so obviously meant for keeping
clothes and bedding; the drawer in which the late King must
have kept his money, the secret of which Rose Marsh must
have discovered.

In a flash, as she stood there, enlightenment came to

Tansy. She remembered the gold pieces which she herself had found on the floor. Probably, after the bed had been moved again, Rose had found some more, which was when she had bought the cupboard and the expensive cloak. But either she had been more practically minded or it had been too long after Bosworth for her to imagine that they had been dropped from any king's or courtier's purse. She must have suspected their source. She had moved into the room herself, to have time and opportunity to search. And then there had been the evening when she was looking so surreptitiously for a chisel. Everything fitted into the explanation. But, having made her welcome discovery, Rose Marsh was not the woman to curb her extravagance for the sake of caution, and the whole town had begun to wonder where she got her money from. Malpas, the enterprising, had managed to find out. His reason for parting with Gladys became abundantly clear. With a clever, favor-currying spy on the premises the solution could not have been difficult.

He and Gladys were bent so low over the money, scraping it so greedily into a couple of sacks, that for a few moments they did not know themselves to be observed. It was easy game for them, in an inn run by women. And they had chosen a night when there happened to be no travelers sleeping on the first floor. With mounting terror, Tansy realized that there was no man within call. A few more minutes and their task would have been done, and they would have been safely away and unsuspected in their own beds—had it not been for a pony whinnying in pain.

She backed silently towards the door, meaning to run and rouse the neighbors. But just at that moment Malpas's pudgy hand dropped one coin upon another with a sharp click, close beside the bed, and its owner waked. She saw them in the candlelight and sat up with a startled cry. But the moment she set eyes on her precious gold gleaming in the candlelight, fear turned to fury. While they knelt back in momentary surprise she yelled at them for dirty thieving dogs. One plump knee was already out from beneath the coverlet and she had caught Gladys a smart blow on the cheek before they had recovered their wits. Her courage shamed Tansy. But Malpas sprang at Marsh's widow, pushing her back against the pillows. She struggled violently but Gladys came to his aid and, feeling their united strength, panic seized her. Looking past them she saw her stepdaughter standing just inside the doorway and called to her desperately for help. Tansy might still have slipped away and fetched the neighbors. But, seeing Malpas's fingers closing about her stepmother's throat, instinctively she ran forward to try to save her. She saw the fear of murder mount in Rose's eyes, and then their piteous appeal, and—small love as she had for the woman—she would always be glad that she had answered it. If time should be given her to be glad!

It was then that Gladys's quicker wits took charge. "No, take that girl, before she rouses the household," she ordered, in an urgent, callous whisper. "I will see to this one and leave no mark." Quick as thought she picked up one of Rose's extravagant silk shifts and thrust it down her throat, stifling her last scream. Held roughly in Malpas's arms Tansy saw her die; saw the large body struggle convulsively in the King's disheveled bed, and then gradually lie still; saw the terror in the wide staring eyes, and then their gradual glazing. Never, as long as she lived, would she forget those awful moments.

"God's blood, you have killed her!" she heard Malpas say, when the landlady of the Boar breathed no more.

"What else could we do, once she knew?" scoffed Gladys, with a cool villainy greater than his own.

And, since she too knew, Tansy supposed that her own hour had come. But Gladys's cunning saved her, and Dilly, running screaming down the stairs, giving the alarm.

"No, leave her with the corpse," hissed Gladys. "It is our only chance now people are coming. Everybody knows they hated each other. Hit the interfering fool—but not too hard."

Malpas's fist seemed to crash down on Tansy's temple. She staggered across the foot of the bed. Half dazed, she saw them push back the drawer and pick up the two small sacks. Then they were gone.

And when people began to run excitedly into the room, and the night watchman from the Guild Hall pushed his way forward with an air of authority, they found Tansy sitting there, weak and frightened, alone with her stepmother's still warm body.

Chapter Fourteen

The murder of the landlady of the Blue Boar was the biggest local excitement since Bosworth. Coupled with the discovery of the source of her recently acquired wealth, it left all Leicester both horrified and amazed. Crowds hung about in the streets outside, staring up at the best bedroom window with macabre curiosity. Sheriff and doctors passed importantly through the front door to examine the corpse. It was difficult to believe that anyone as vital and exuberant as Rose Marsh was dead. Alive, she had provided a wealth of gossip. Now, at her death, the talk of the whole town centered on who had done this dastardly thing.

Thanks to the quick wits of the Welsh girl, there was nothing save Tansy's word to pin the crime onto the guilty pair. Soon after she had poured out her improbable story they were found, apparently sleeping peacefully, in their respective beds, one at the Blue Boar and one at the Golden Crown. Save for a few scattered coins the secret drawer was empty, but although Gladys's room and even the cellars of the Golden Crown were searched by the Mayor's orders no sack of gold was found, and their air of amazed innocence seemed strong defence against an accuser who could produce no proof.

Although the Mayor looked into her honest eyes with pity, it began to seem certain that Tansy herself would be brought to trial.

The crime was discussed at every street corner and over every meal.

"The Grumbold girl was cunning enough for anything," the men said. "But she had broken with Malpas. He had turned her out. Is it likely that they would have plotted this theft together?"

"More likely the Marsh girl picked on two people she had good cause to be jealous of," suggested some of the women.

Everyone who knew Tansy personally liked and respected her, and her father had been a popular citizen. But justice must be done, insisted the Mayor, who, out of common humanity, had taken her from the scene of the crime into his own house.

After it had been established by the doctors that Rose Marsh had been suffocated with her own shift, and she had been given decent burial in the same grave as her late husband and his first, less spectacular, wife, a Court of Inquiry was held.

The questioning went on for days.

All Dilly could tell the sheriff and the jury was that she had been wakened by her mistress crying out "like as if she was bein' murdered." She had tried to wake Cook, who slept like a log. She herself had run down the attic stairs. The door of the best bedroom was a crack open and there was a light in the room, but she had been too scared to look in. So she had run on down the lower flight of the stairs, unbolted the front door, and gone out into the street, yelling all the way for help.

Jod tried to make an alibi for Tansy by saying that she must have been in the stable at that time because afterwards, when the noise had roused him, he had found her pony's bandages had been changed. But this seemed only to rouse more suspicion because people wanted to know why the murdered woman's stepdaughter had been wandering about at that time of night when she ought to have been in her bed.

And when Cook was questioned she made matters worse by saying how difficult the dead woman had been to work for.

More and more witnesses were called.

It was established that there was no love lost between Tansy and her stepmother, that things had become even more difficult between them since Robert Marsh's death. Even Tansy's friends could not deny it.

Men in the ale room remembered how Rose had called her a slut and made insinuations about her being with one of the soldiers in the hayloft after the battle of Bosworth. Druscilla Gamble recalled how Rose had spoken of her as a coarse yellow weed, and two people who had happened to be passing the open window at the time remembered hearing the spirited way in which Tansy had repudiated things said about her parents.

And then the gossips really came into their own. "Often we heard 'em quarreling, and most times lately the girl seemed to have learned to give as good as she got. Not as anyone could blame her," they said. "For 'twas past bearin' the way that extravagant, sharp-tongued redhead tried to keep her down. An' true it be, though I do be speakin' of the dead."

Master Jordan had not waited to be asked anything. The first moment he saw the crowd pushing and shoving and ex- claiming outside the Boar, and leaned from his window to hear what it was all about, he had hurried round to Brewster, in the fletcher's workshop. "Leave your arrows and ride hard to London. Tell your master what has happened and entreat him to come as quickly as possible," he said. And Brewster, who had been a pupil of his, had set off immediately.

"For whatever comes of it, Tansy will need all her friends at such a time," Will Jordan said to the priest of St. Nicholas Church. "Tom is an able young man, and has always been like a brother to her. If he has any sense he will marry her and take her right away out of this horror."

Although she was kept under surveillance, he managed to let Tansy know that his messenger had gone, and during the terrible days that followed she was sustained by the thought that Tom would surely come. Many people went out of their way to be kind to her, and most of the respectable citizens believed in her innocence, until Hugh Malpas said to the sheriff, with reason, "You have searched my inn and the Welsh wench's room and her father's house in Swinemarket. Why don't you search the Blue Boar?" When this had been done, although no hoard of gold had been discovered, a locked trinket box in Tansy's bedroom was found to contain three rose nobles and two half-angels. Not an impossible amount for an innkeeper's daughter to possess, but enough to arouse suspicion, particularly as business was known to have been bad.

And so the guilty pair, who might in those first days have attempted a getaway, deemed it wiser to stay where they were and put up a show of unconcerned innocence. Malpas ran an inn even more packed than usual, and Gladys went to live with her father, where her presence drew unheard-of crowds to watch his indifferent bullbaiting shows in the Swinemarket. Both she and Malpas were confident that a ver- dict of guilty would be brought against Tansy, whose sudden appearance in Rose Marsh's bedroom had been the sole cause of their being suspected at all and, it seemed, might well turn out to prove their salvation.

In the courthouse the questioning went on.

"Is it true that you did not get on well with the deceased?"

"Yes. But I tried to obey her."

"By the terms of your father's will the Blue Boar was to become yours if your stepmother married again, or when she died. Is that not so?"

"Yes."

"So I put it to you that you, and you alone, stood to benefit financially by her death?"

"Yes, I suppose so. But I didn't think much about it."

"And you were alone with her when she died?"

"No! No! As I keep telling you, they were both there— Master Malpas and Gladys Grumbold. The door was ajar and I went in."

"Why?"

"I wanted to tell my stepmother something."

"After everyone had gone to bed?"

"It was urgent. I wanted to warn her."

"Warn her about what?"

"About *them*."

"Then you were not surprised?"

"About their being in her room, stealing the money, yes. But I had just found out that they were both in the house, that Malpas was in the girl's bedroom."

"And you wanted to get her into trouble," suggested the sharp-faced attorney, whose pockets were being well lined by the landlord of the Golden Crown. "As your own ostler has already testified, you were prying about the house and yard late that night. And after your young maid ran screaming down the stairs and roused the neighbors, you were found alone with the murdered woman, whereas the two people you accused were found asleep in their beds."

Tansy's defense foundered badly. Who would believe her if she repeated that her pony had whinnied and she had got up and gone to him? How could she explain that she had wanted to convince her stepmother of Hugh Malpas's presence while he was actually there, or how badly she needed the assurance of a stronger personality to deal with the situation? How explain her own mounting sense of foreboding?

Her late father's lawyer, Master Langstaff, came to her assistance. "Perhaps you can explain to us how you came by the gold coins in your trinket box?" he prompted gently.

Tansy turned to him with swift relief. "Oh, easily. I found them on the floor beside the King's bed after he and the gentry who stayed with us had left for Bosworth."

"And kept them unspent for two years or more?" scoffed the other attorney.

"A likely story!" sniffed his clerk, shuffling some papers.

Tansy remembered that actually they were not the same coins and hoped they would not question her about that. The courtroom was hot and stuffy and packed with unfriendly faces staring up at her. She began to feel faint and wished that she could sit in some quiet garden and stop answering questions. Her eyes sought Will Jordan, but his kindly presence was blocked from view by the figure of a burly civic guard, just as his efforts to help her had been blotted out by the judge's certainty that he must be prejudiced. She longed for the comfort of her father. But if he had lived this dreadful nightmare situation would never have arisen. Hadn't she told Tom weeks ago that she felt a presentiment that something horrible was going to happen in her home? From the raised platform where she stood, she looked down on the Levantine face of the landlord of the Crown watching her with a kind of smug indifference, and on Gladys, sitting righteously on a bench with her long lute-playing fingers folded calmly in her lap, those slim, deft fingers which she had last seen stuffing swift, silken death down her stepmother's throat. Tansy's thoughts began to wander. She was glad that Rose, with eyes desperately imploring help, had known in her last moments that she, Tansy—the tall coarse weed—had risked her life in an endeavor to give it. She realized that had she slipped quietly away she would not be standing here in danger of being condemned. For the first time in all that nightmare of tortured days she realized fully that the judge sitting up there might declare her guilty, and that if he should do so she would be put to death publicly as a murderess. That would be a far more terrible death than she would have sustained from the fist of Hugh Malpas. Her hand went to her mouth, stifling a scream. Hysteria rose in her. She wished desperately that Tom would come. Common sense told her that he would

scarcely have had time. But why didn't he come? Though he
could not yet know the full danger in which she stood, why
didn't he come to help her? He had wanted to marry her. He
had always professed to love her. . . .

"You resented having Gladys Grumbold in the house, did
you not?" someone was asking.

"Yes." If the question sounded as if it came from a long
way off, the dangerous admission was almost inaudible.

"Did she ever behave badly while in the deceased's service
at the Blue Boar?"

"No," admitted Tansy, wearily.

The courtroom seemed more packed than ever. A surplus
of curious people had long since been turned away and were
no doubt waiting out in the street. But now someone was bat-
tering open the door again. The burly guard went to prevent
him but somehow he forced his way in and was pushing his
way through the angry crowd already jammed there; another
sweating body to make the air yet more stifling, another face
to gaze at her with calculating curiosity, wondering whether
she were capable of committing murder or not. Tansy could
not see him for the press of people, but at least the half-open
door had momentarily let in a breath of God's clean air and
she had caught a glimpse of sunlit street and heard the familiar whinny of a weary horse: something of the ordinary outside world where carefree, kindly life went on.

People were turning away from her to look at the intruder,
some of them giving vent to angry exclamations as they were
inadvertently buffeted by each other's elbows. The judge was
rapping on his desk for silence. But the man who had caused
the momentary confusion was extraordinarily persistent. Suddenly Tansy felt certain that it must be Tom. The haze of
faintness began to clear. Her heart was uplifted by hope. She
was aware of a resolute young man standing his ground
firmly at the back of the courtroom in the face of all opposi-
tion. That must have been his horse which she had heard outside the door. He had ridden as fast as he could from London
to Leicester. Dusty and urgent, he had come to help her. The
guard shrugged and lowered a detaining arm. The crowd
grudgingly made way. For a popular fellow citizen like Tom
they would, of course, thought Tansy.

But it wasn't Tom, the fletcher. It was Dickon.

In that glad moment she rejoiced not only in his presence, but at the change in him. He was no longer a bewildered, gangling youth, for whom she needed to feel motherly concern, but a purposeful young man, less tall than Tom, darker and more serious. He was a man who had acquired poise by the mastery of a craft, and sensitivity by some extra cause for thoughtfulness; a man whose concern was for her, who had come at the most awful crisis in her life to take care of her.

Dickon's eyes searched for Tansy. He seemed to be momentarily unaware of anyone else. Finding her standing suspected and alone, he looked straight at her and smiled, and she knew that in her ordeal she would be alone no more.

"If you did not steal the money now, but found it two years ago, why were you hoarding it?" persisted the sharp-faced lawyer.

"For a journey."

"Where did you want to go?"

"To London." The faint, wavering voice of the accused had miraculously become clear and steady.

"And why should you want to go to London? Have you relatives there?"

"No, sir."

"Is there perhaps some man there to whom you are betrothed?" asked Master Langstaff, who knew that his late client had hoped it would be Tom Hood.

But Tansy could not say she was betrothed, nor could she explain, except to her inmost heart, why she had hoped to go to London. A silence of uncertainty hung in the court, undoing the good impression her new air of confidence had created. And out of that damaging silence the intruding young man spoke. "*I* am going to marry her," he said.

Everyone turned to look at him. His words seemed to put a new complexion on the whole affair. The elderly judge leaned over his desk, cupping an ear with his hand. "And where do you come from, young man?" he asked.

"From London. And I intend to take her back there as soon as these people have finished tormenting her."

"These gentlemen are but acting in the necessary course of justice," reprimanded the judge sternly. "What is your name and occupation?"

"Richard Broome, apprenticed to the mason Hurland Dale

of Old Jewry, and now working on the town house of Sir
Walter Moyle," said Dickon, as if his credentials scarcely
mattered. "Do you not see, milord, that she is at the end of
her tether? I pray you, let her sit down!"

He spoke with such quiet authority that, after a moment's
hesitation, the judge beckoned to an usher to bring a stool.
Gratefully, Tansy sank down on it. The tension was still further eased for her because people were no longer staring at
her. This strange young man who wore the travel-stained
garb of an apprentice and yet recommended humanity to a
King's Justice of the Peace, and who had calmly announced
that he intended to marry the accused, was now the center of
attention. The questioning was transferred to him.

"If you have come straight from London, how did you
know that this trial was going on?"

"I didn't. But Tom Hood, your fletcher, waked me in the
early hours of the morning three days ago and told me about
the murder. He, too, works for Sir Walter Moyle." Dickon
turned from his questioners to Tansy and spoke gently as if
trying to soften some blow. "He was deeply concerned but
was on the point of leaving for Calais."

Everyone knew about the young fletcher's fortunate appointment, so the stranger's explanation rang true and held
the interest of all.

"And you say that you are going to marry Tansy Marsh,"
said Langstaff, with understandable surprise. "How long have
you known her?"

"About two years."

"Did you know that she had this money in her possession?"

"Yes."

"Do you know how she came by it?"

"She told me that she found it on the floor beside the late
King's bed soon after he left the Boar for Bosworth."

Although he had not been present, his words exactly
confirmed Tansy's own explanation. A gasp of relief went up
from Tansy's friends. Master Langstaff spread the gold coins
triumphantly across the table. "Then these have nothing to
do with this recent robbery. For whatever purpose she may
have hoarded them, Robert Marsh's daughter has been in
possession of them since August, 1485."

"Not all of them, all the time, sir," corrected Dickon. "Dur-

ing the first year she could not in any case have spent most of
them because she had lent them to me."

"Why?" demanded the defendant's lawyer, swinging round
on him.

A new fear assailed Tansy, but Dickon faced him imperturbably. The truth, and only the truth, would clear Tansy of
all the slurs which both murderer and murdered had somehow
managed to cast upon her. For himself, he had no guile. "To
get away from Leicester after Bosworth," he said.

In that Lancastrian court a shocked hush followed his
clearly spoken words.

"Then you were on King Richard's side?"

"Most ardently," admitted Richard's son.

"And you repaid the money?" There was a new gentleness
in the judge's voice which possibly revealed where his sympathies lay.

"Certainly, milord. As soon as I was able to earn it."

"Is there any witness to this transaction?" blustered Malpas's lawyer, for want of something better to say.

"A chapman from Cheapside named Gufford. He comes
often to Leicestershire and may be known to some of you."

By the way people turned to each other and mouthed the
familiar name, he certainly was. The whole story was becoming entirely credible. Even those who had discussed all the
suspicious evidence with relish began telling themselves that
of course they had never for a moment doubted Robert
Marsh's daghter.

Relief swept over Tansy. The nightmare experience was
nearly over. No one was going to condemn her. They were
looking instead at the guilty pair she had accused. They believed her. She dared to raise expectant eyes to the judge's
face. But what she saw there froze her with a new fear. Not
for herself, but for Dickon. What was it his royal father had
said? "If I should be killed, leave Leicester and never come
back. You are too much like me." But he had come back, for
her sake.

The little old judge was peering shortsightedly at Dickon,
peering with a curiosity which exceeded any interest he had
taken in the routine court proceedings. Slightly deaf and
shortsighted he might be, but his intellect was still acute. He
had been on that circuit ever since Tansy could remember

and must have served under the last two Plantagenet kings, and now his eyes were like probes on Dickon's defenceless young face. "*What* did you say your name was?" he asked.

Something in his trained, retentive mind had been set in pursuit of some elusive memory, some likeness. A mere hint —the name of Richard or the suggestion of Broome—might give him the clue. Dickon and Tansy looked at each other in sharp mutual anxiety. Dickon took time to answer. And in those few moments of time the judge's mind was diverted and the situation saved.

For at that instant, with no scapegoat to suffer for her own sin, Gladys Grumbold's nerve broke and she made a dash for the door. Her hands were no longer folded in her lap but clawing wildly for freedom. There was the crash of an over-turned bench as Hugh Malpas fought his way after her, to be trapped neatly at the door by Jod.

The whole attitude of the court was changed. There was no need of further evidence.

Chapter Fifteen

Immediately after the trial, Will Jordan took Tansy, who was almost in a state of collapse, to his home. But later in the day she crossed the street and went back alone to the Blue Boar, which now belonged to her. She wanted to say good-bye to the only home she had ever known. There were plenty of congratulatory friends who would willingly have accompanied her, but she took only Dilly and, except to Jordan, said nothing of her intentions. Weary with emotional strain, she was thankful to be alone, and, averting her eyes from the closed door of her stepmother's bedroom, she went up to her own familiar attic.

The little room was flooded with late afternoon sunlight, just as it had been that August day before Bosworth. She closed the door behind her and opened the two narrow casements. Leaning out, she remembered how King Richard's two gentlemen had come riding down the street looking for accommodation for their royal master, how gladly they had exclaimed at sight of the White Boar sign, and how Hugh Malpas had tried to inveigle them into the Golden Crown. She had stuck out her tongue at him, she remembered. And she remembered too, almost dispassionately, that this sunny evening, two years later, he was to hang. Once his guilt had been established, the administrators of justice, more outraged at the way he had shielded himself behind an innocent girl than by his original crime, had lost no time in carrying out the death sentence. People were even now gathering in the square by Gallowgate to enjoy the gruesome spectacle.

Wrapped in an apathy which was a reaction from all she had been through, Tansy felt strangely apart. Leaning from her window, she looked out over the familiar city and back over her life. It had been like a placid stream until King Richard came. And ever since then it seemed to have been gathering momentum until this terrible week. Before Bosworth she had been a girl, full of common sense but singularly trusting and unsophisticated. Now she was a woman who had learned to see through the smooth deceptions of

126

human selfishness, a woman who would in future have to make her own judgments and shape her own destiny. In this difficult hour of decision she prayed for strength to shape it wisely!

Slowly, almost abstractedly, she opened the fine oak chest which her father had given her on her seventeenth birthday and began laying out her clothes upon the bed: the low, narrow bed upon which she had cried herself to sleep when each of her parents had died, on which she had whimpered fearfully when the White Boar sign was being stoned, and on which she had afterwards lain awake thinking about the strange story of Dickon Broome; the bed on which she wanted never to sleep again.

Hurrying footsteps began clattering along the cobbles below. Scraps of conversation drifted up to her, spoken in voices high-pitched with nervous excitement and accompanied by the false laughter of those who try to hide their horror while morbidly wanting to watch a hanging.

Tansy would not listen. She began sorting and folding some of her best garments. She had finished with Leicester. What would women be wearing in London? she wondered. She had packed most of her possessions into the capacious pannier basket which was usually attached to Pippin's saddle for marketing, when there was a tap on the door and Dilly stood there, scared and panting. "Everybody's hurryin' past. Goin' to Gallowgate."

"I know," said Tansy, wrapping her best new shoes in a kerchief.

"They're goin' to see that wicked Master Malpas hanged. An' worse." The girl's eyes became wider still in the wheylike pastiness of her face. "Diggory's just rushed into the yard on his way to see it. I heard him shout to Jod to come too because they've built a pile of brushwood alongside the gallows. For that Grumbold cat! They're goin' to burn her alive!"

For a moment Tansy's strange calm deserted her. She sank down on the bed. "God be thanked I shall be getting out of this town!" she murmured, covering her face with both hands. No one could possibly have been more wicked to her than Gladys Grumbold. No one could possibly have been more wicked to poor Rose. But that this terrible thing should happen to someone who had lived in this house . . .

Dilly was down on her knees, clutching at her in tears, providing a merciful distraction. "Oh, Mistress Tansy, you b'aint goin' away? Not yet? Not leavin' us! I can't bear it!"

Tansy's comforting arms went round her. "But you will have your parents, Dilly, which is more than I have. And Cook, who is always kind to you. And I'm sure whoever buys the inn will employ you both. I have left a special message with Master Langstaff to recommend you."

"But it won't be the s-same!" sobbed Dilly.

Remembering past scenes, the new owner of the Boar had to smile. "It should be much better. Surely, you remember how Mistress Rose used to scold and beat you?"

"I was scared out of my wits of her. Still am," admitted Dilly, rising from her knees and preparing to depart with singular reluctance. "Truth is, I'm mortal feared to pass that best bedroom door. Fair bolted up these attic stairs, I did, in case of what ghosts might appear. Hers, or maybe poor King Richard's."

"Then why did you come up here?" asked Tansy, returning to her packing.

"Because Master Broome, who put everything to rights this mornin', be come. Went first to see about his poor, overtired horse that Jod's been cossetin' for him. An' now he be waitin' for you in the parlor."

Tansy suddenly came alive from her trancelike tiredness. Reminiscences of the past gave place to plans for the future. "Oh, Dilly, Dilly, you little fool! Why didn't you tell me?" she chided. "Here, find room for these shifts in the basket, be sure it's fastened securely, and carry it down to Pippin's stable. And then make us some kind of meal. If there's nothing in the larder, you're sure to find some eggs in the hen run." And pushing the pile of underwear into the astonished girl's arms, she ran down the stairs even quicker than Dilly had come up, without a single thought for ghosts.

She found Dickon waiting by the parlor hearth, looking serious and carefully refurbished from his hurried journey. It was the first time they had been alone since the old days in the hayloft. "I had no opportunity to ask you first," he began, with something of his old diffidence.

"To ask me about what?" said Tansy, halting in the middle of the room.

"What I said in front of all those people. That I was going to marry you."

She went to him and laid both hands upon his breast, setting his mind at rest with a beautiful gesture of surrender. "There was no need," she said, looking into eyes as honest as her own.

Then she was in his arms, the strong arms of a remarkably resolute young man, and he was kissing her with all the hunger of long abstinence.

After the ecstasy of a long embrace which helped to assuage his passionate yearning and assured Tansy of the reality of her own, a few coherent thoughts began to come back to them. "Your coming saved me," she whispered, when at last he allowed her breath.

"If I had known that suspicion had fallen on you——"

"You would have winded that poor horse past hope!" She laughed happily, between his renewed kisses.

"I would have stolen a whole string of horses to get here. . . . But all that horror is over for you now, my love."

"And you are taking me away."

He released her abruptly. The glow of love's inconsequent laughter faded from his face, as he pulled her down beside him on the settle. "I ought to let you wait here, with friends," he said soberly.

"Wait!" Tansy sat bolt upright, proud and hurt.

He took both her hands in his but made no more attempt to embrace her. "What I said was to protect you. For effect before the court and all those devils who were tormenting you."

"You mean, you were just sorry for me? You don't want to marry me?"

"Before God, I want it more than anything on this earth. Did I not tell you, when I was little more than a bewildered boy, that I should always carry your image in my heart?"

"And I have always remembered, and cherished, your words, because you have a habit of always doing just what you say, Dickon."

"But you must know, Tansy, that I cannot marry you while I am still an apprentice. It is forbidden by my indentures. And the humiliating truth is that until I am a fully trained mason I do not earn enough money to keep you. Only pocket money. It is Master Hurland who is paid to teach me."

"The sheriff returned our gold coins, and I shall have money from the sale of the inn."

"If you ever get any."

"But, Dickon, surely you know that at my stepmother's death the Boar became mine?"

"I know now. I didn't know when I left London," he said, inexplicably beginning to laugh.

"Well, what amuses you about it?"

"Only the way I first heard about it. As I came down the steps from the courthouse some hulking great friend of Malpas's came up to me. It was a small wonder, he said loudly, that I had ridden in such a hurry so as to get in first and marry a girl who was going to inherit one of the best inns in Leicester."

"Oh, Dickon, what did you say? And in front of all those people, too! Though when you arrived I certainly couldn't have looked much as if I were going to live long enough to inherit anything."

"I didn't say anything. I just hit him on the jaw and left him."

"And where is he now?"

"Still lying in the gutter, for all I know. Truth to tell, I've been so crazed with joy at seeing you again that I've only just remembered him."

"My dear idiot! And you so patiently reasonable!"

"After all you'd been through, I felt the need of hitting something," he explained calmly. "And though the inn is yours, Tansy, you must realize that these legal negotiations sometimes take months to go through. Even if anyone wants to buy it, after all that has happened here. Which most people seem to doubt."

"That's just what Master Langstaff has been warning me about," agreed Tansy sadly. "He says there will be a kind of curse on the place. That even though men may come in to drink, travelers won't want to stay here. And I can see now that because we did everything possible to make the King's bed famous, everybody within miles is sure to hear about the landlady of the Blue Boar who was murdered in it."

They sat hand in hand, considering their difficulties.

"It will be only a few months before I become a member of my Guild, and then we can marry," said Dickon. "In the meantime, I may be able to persuade the wife of one of our masons to take you into her house."

"I could work for hire," said Tansy eagerly. "There must be plenty of work for a girl to do in London."

"And I should have persuaded you to leave a good home, and friends like Master Jordan, to work, perhaps, like Dilly," he objected, as the girl came in bearing two steaming platters.

"It seems as if it is I who am doing most of the persuading." Tansy smiled, drawing him to the table. "Come and make a good meal before we start."

After a mouthful or two he was still objecting, but she was scarcely listening. An idea had come to her. "Tell me, is there not an inn called the Boar in Cheapside?"

"Yes. How did you know?"

"Gufford, the chapman, used to speak of it to my stepmother. And I told you he lived near there, do you not remember, so that you could send me letters. Somehow the name of that inn in London always seemed to make you feel nearer. Is it anything like this one?"

"Yes, now you speak of it. But I suppose all good inns look much alike."

Tansy set down her glass and turned to him eagerly. "Then probably it is run much like ours. I could help there. It is the only kind of work I am familiar with."

"It is possible they might have a vacancy," he admitted. "London becomes increasingly full of foreign merchants looking for lodgings. The Tudor encourages them, and I suppose one must admit he has done much for trade. In any case, it is a respectable place where you could get a bed for a night or two until we have time to look round."

"I should like to have sold some of my stepmother's expensive gowns. But Master Langstaff is sending someone here tomorrow to make an inventory of everything, and he says I mustn't take away anything except my personal possessions. I have packed my clothes in a basket which hangs on Pippin's saddle."

Clearly she was not going to profit by her lover's unselfish solicitude. But yet another difficulty confronted him. "Jod thinks my hired horse won't really be fit to ride for days."

"There is my father's fine black mare. Dear Dickon, surely I can give you that if you leave yours in place of her."

He lifted her hand from the table and kissed it. "Then I shall certainly be the proudest 'prentice in London. I saw her in her stable. A horse fit for a king!"

Their glances met, full of secret laughter at his unintentionally apt remark, and as soon as Dilly had withdrawn to eat her own supper they rose and stood closely embraced again.

"Then you really trust me?" sighed Dickon, persuaded at last.

"After this morning, how could I not trust you? You paid back that ridiculous money, although in a sense it was more yours than mine. You came when I so desperately needed you."

Conscientiously, he warned her that, once in London, he might have little time to look after her. "When Master Dale gave me leave to come I promised I would make up the time on the work I am doing for Sir Walter Moyle's house," he explained. "My master has contracted to finish it before Sir Walter comes back from Calais."

The place name turned the thoughts of both of them to Tom. Dickon released her and said with scrupulous loyalty, "I want you to know that there was nothing Tom could do, short of losing this fine new appointment. Otherwise he would have come himself, instead of rushing round in the early hours of the morning to tell me. You do believe that, don't you? He was even then due to start for Dover. He will have had to ride hard to catch up with Sir Walter's party."

"I know that Tom had a fine appointment and is a fine horseman," said Tansy. If she spoke coldly it was because her heart was aching with tenderness for the man who was only a penniless apprentice and an inexperienced horseman on a hired nag, and who had yet come to her.

Dickon laid a hand on each of her shoulders and looked searchingly into her face. "This hasn't made any difference—about your feelings for Tom?"

"No. If he were here in this room, with his gaiety and

laughter, we should both be adoring him. But he isn't. It is you and I, Dickon."

He kissed her hands with gratitude. "I have always thought—been mortally afraid—that it was he whom you cared for."

"I did. In a different way. I have always turned to him, shared every foolish joke with him. Sometimes he could charm the heart out of me. . . ."

"And will again?"

"No." Tansy kept silence for a few moments as if trying to be quite sure of this herself. "No," she repeated, looking up at him with smiling reassurance. "If I trust you enough to come to London unwed, you will have to trust me in this and never let a single twinge of jealousy mar the friendship of you two. I know now that our love, yours and mine, is something of body and soul which transcends anything that happened before."

"So that you are now prepared to leave all your familiar friends and go out into a new unpredictable world with me," marveled Dickon, out of the lovable depths of his essential modesty.

They stood before the open window as if making some silent, informal marriage vow. Everything was very still, in the house, and still out in the streets. The hurrying footsteps and the excited voices had all passed by—to Gallowgate. In the midst of their own urgent affairs they suddenly became aware of this, and then of the stench of burning flesh drifting faintly on the evening air. Suddenly Tansy's resolute calm broke. She turned and clung to him, hiding her face against his breast. "If you hadn't come, it might have been me!" she cried, in a choking voice.

He held her tightly in his arms, while gazing out over her head into the gathering twilight with a kind of awe. "You and I have been called upon to suffer more than most young couples," he said. "Yet now we have much to thank God for."

But, after resting acquiescently for a while, Tansy tore herself from his arms in a fresh frenzy of horror. "Let us go now!" she cried, in an unnaturally high-pitched voice. "I can't stay here another moment! Always when I try to sleep I see Gladys's clever, strangling hands, Rose's eyes, beseeching me. . . . Leicester is too full of memories!"

Leicester was full of memories, too, for Dickon, but he had the sense to recognize that it is better to come to terms with even the most terrible memories than to try to evade them. "You always said you wished you could show me the King's bedroom," he reminded her gently.

She almost shrank from him, and from what she thought was his lack of understanding. "But not any more, now."

He drew her towards the door and up the stairs. "You will be doing me a great kindness," he persisted.

Outside the best bedroom she stopped and shook her head piteously. "I can't go in there—again."

"You can, with me. Together we can do anything." He pulled her inside. "Pretend you are showing it to some traveler. You need not think what you are saying."

Obediently, Tansy began the familiar patter, pointing out all the tokens of his father's last night beneath a roof. Gradually, though she kept her eyes averted from the bed, she began trying to endow each souvenir with reality for him. And gradually, as if her last experience in the room were being exorcised, she herself began to see it as it had been, hospitable and ordinary, on the night of the late King's arrival, before Bosworth. "He explained to me about those carvings of the Holy Sepulcher," she said, surprised to find herself looking at them with interest again, without seeing her stepmother's red head against the pillows. "So kind he was, and with a pleasant voice. I liked him instantly." She turned and looked at her future husband, standing at the foot of the bed. "Standing just where you are, he was," she added, marveling afresh how much they were alike. "And in this fading light, you might be he," she added, with no supernatural fear, but with only anxiety for the man she loved.

The fine fingers of the younger Richard caressed the coverlet. There was a smile on his lips, as if he saw someone he loved lying in the bed. It was doubtful if he even heard her. "I shall sometimes remember him now in a homely room, not always as he looked being brought back across Bow Bridge," he murmured gratefully.

They closed the door on that part of their life and went side by side in silence down the stairs. Out in the yard their mounts were waiting to take them into their unknown future, mettlesome black Mopsy and the lovable pony, Pippin. And there with them was the bent old man Jod, serving her as he had been all her life, but now with the tears of parting running unashamedly down his wrinkled cheeks.

It was nearly Tansy's undoing. She clung to him, weeping, and saying through her sobs, "I can't! I can't!"

But there was the comforting thought that she would have news of him in letters from Will Jordan and be able to send him messages.

"Be good to her," muttered the old man, knowing well enough that he was tersely ordering a king's son.

Dickon lifted her into the pony's saddle and pressed the ostler's gnarled hand. The last half angel of a 'prentice's pocket money would have passed between them, but Jod would have none of it. "Keep it for her comfort on the journey," he said. Years spent in an innyard had taught him which types he could trust.

Chapter Sixteen

The journey to London was so great an adventure for Tansy that it helped to wipe out recent painful recollections. Friends of the Marsh family took her and Dickon in for the night at Lutterworth, and the following night they received similar kindness in Oxford. While looking for cheap lodging in the High Street, which seethed with lively groups of students, Dickon had the good fortune to meet one of his friend Piers Harrowe's brothers, who was studying at St. Edmond Hall.

"I will ask the porter at our gatehouse if he knows of anyone who can take you in," he offered, after Dickon had explained something of Tansy's story and exchanged news of London.

While the three of them stood there, looking in at the courtyard with its well and creeper-clad walls, it chanced that young Harrowe's tutor came out, a youngish bustling priest, followed by a servant bearing books and baggage. Intent on some journey of his own, he acknowledged his pupil's good wishes abstractedly. But, while wedged among them in the narrow entrance arch, he could not but overhear their unhopeful conversation with the porter and paused to see if he could help. "In an urgent hurry to get to London, are they?" he said to Harrowe. His glance shifted to Dickon, and he appeared to like what he saw. "If these are friends of yours whose honesty you can vouch for, and they can fend for themselves, there is no reason why they shouldn't sleep the night in my empty house, put their horses in my stable, and return the key to the porter here in the morning," he offered.

All three of them began to thank him effusively, but he was still looking hard at Dickon. "Since you have the key of my door, I had better know your name, young man," he stipulated. When Dickon told him, he laughed pleasantly and added, "My name is Richard, too. Richard Simon." And then, remembering the urgency of his own affairs, he left them abruptly and strode swiftly up St. Edmond Lane.

"What an extraordinary kindness!" exclaimed Tansy, suddenly aware of how desperately tired she was.

"He evidently took it for granted that we were married, and I would to God we were!" said Dickon, putting an arm around her. "But how does a young tutor priest come to have a house and stabling?"

"He takes younger pupils there, coaching them for their studies in college. But he is off to Ireland again, taking one of these boys home to his parents, perhaps," explained Harrowe. "I will show you the house, and I pray you give all my messages to my family when you reach London."

Tansy slept like a log in the housekeeper's bed while, in spite of her protests, her betrothed slept in the hayloft. "And it won't be the first time, as you very well know," he said, making light of his care for her good name. What she also knew, more surely than ever, was that his word was always to be trusted.

Her first sight of London temporarily banished the kindly priest and his house and all the tragedy in Leicester from Tansy's mind. Coming through Aldgate towards Lombard Street, they caught glimpses of the massive white keep of the Tower, then the gleaming river alive with masts, and the gabled houses on London Bridge stretching to the Surrey shore. And riding along Cheapside they could see the fine houses of the goldsmiths and the spire of St. Paul's. To Tansy, who had never been out of Leicestershire, it was breathtaking as a dream. And if she had to stay alone in this bustling strange city, with her betrothed bound to report immediately to his master, it was some comfort to sleep that night at the familiar sign of the Boar.

"You will have to share an attic with two of my maids," the busy Cheapside landlady told her. "We never seem to have a room vacant since this new King began encouraging foreign merchants and livening up trade. With all the shipping lying in the Pool, and the captains and traders coming ashore, my husband and I scarcely know which way to turn."

Tansy was quick to seize her chance. She said that her father had kept the Blue Boar in Leicester, where, as everybody knew, the late King Richard had slept. And that she would like to help. She was soon the center of good-natured questioning, during which it transpired that both inns had, with prudent haste, changed their Boar signs from white to blue. And so, with her fund of good sense and will to work, Tansy stayed on and soon became invaluable to the overworked hostess of one of London's most thriving taverns. If it wasn't home, at least the seafaring and foreign guests were interesting, and jovial Mistress Goodyear was considerably easier to work for than Rose Marsh had been.

The days were happy for Dickon and Tansy. They were both interested in their work and well trusted, and because they had little free time their hours together were all the more precious. Dickon took her to see the splendid house on the Strand that was rising for Sir Walter Moyle, and although his talk of corbels and quadrants and trace wheels left her puzzled, she was able to glow with some of his enthusiasm for the almost finished beauty of the structure. He presented her to his master whom she thanked so charmingly for allowing Dickon to come to Leicester that, apart from professional interest in his most promising pupil's work, Hurland Dale found himself taking a personal interest in their fortunes.

On Sundays they walked over London Bridge to Southwark or to Smithfield, so that Dickon could take part in some of the sports, or along the river past Charing village to see the royal palace and the Abbey at Westminster. Dickon could gaze indefinitely at dim vistas of arches and shafts of light filtering down from a finely carved clerestory, and told her with pride that it was Hugh Hurland, an ancestor of his own master, who had built the wonderful hammer-beam roof in Westminster Hall for Richard the Second.

"The King used to call him 'our beloved carpenter,'" sighed Richard Broome, the humble apprentice. "What would I give to create such beauty for a king!"—a remark which Tansy rightly supposed referred only to a Plantagenet king.

But often they would just sit beside the Thames in the sunshine, eating the midday food which she had brought and talking; making up time for all those months which they had spent apart; joyfully exploring each other's hearts and minds. The time together was never long enough. But even in talking of ordinary things, Tansy was sadly aware that she did not yet know Dickon as intimately as she knew Tom. There

were places in his mind which were still remote from her,
reactions which sometimes startled her by their vehemence.

"Have you ever seen King Henry coming in or going out of
the Palace?" she asked, watching a gilded barge moor alongside the royal wharf.

Dickon spat an apple core with unnecessary violence into
the rushes. "Once. Without intent."

"I saw him in Leicester, of course, when he was staying at
the Golden Crown. A mean-looking man. But they say he
works harder than most of his subjects."

"It may well be so. He was on his way to the docks to inspect some new merchant ships when I saw him."

Meeting this barrier of angry reservè, Tansy handed him a
pasty and hastened to change the subject. "I worried so much
about you last autumn, my love. When we kept hearing how
bad that epidemic of sweating sickness was."

"It was horrible," agreed Dickon, in more normal tones.
"One of our best carpenters died. Making us all laugh with
his bawdy tales at noon, and dead by midnight."

"We heard that even the Lord Mayor of London himself
died of it."

"Two Lord Mayors, within five days. And a whole clack of
aldermen. But the plague ended as suddenly as it had begun.
In time for the Tudor to have his coronation on the date he
had announced, of course. The Fates are always with him!"

And there they were, back on a topic which, however carefully avoided, was seldom far from their consciousness. "How
could the people accept him and shout for him so readily?"
murmured Tansy, tucking her feet under her lest they be
wetted by the gentle lapping of the encroaching tide.

"Most of them did. The merchants and shipowners with
good reason, perhaps. But underneath the prosperous face of
London there is still plenty of bitter muttering. You hear it at
every archery butt and tavern. Particularly because he declared all who had fought for my—fought on the Yorkist side,
guilty of treason. And then forgave most of them, so that they
should seem to owe their lives to his magnanimity."

"I know. People were raging about that in Leicester. How
could it be treason to fight for the man who was still their living King?"

"Even some of his supporters must have pointed out to him

the absurdity of it. Men like Stanley, perhaps—who should know all there is to know about treachery! So the Tudor began to count the date of his accession from the day before Bosworth. That Sunday, you remember, when I rode out after the army to the King's tent."

"With that unspeakable Gervase man who stole your money," said Tansy, thinking how Dickon could do with it now. "Lord Stanley has been created Earl of Derby for his pains, hasn't he?"

"Yes. He is very much the royal father-in-law now, although it is common knowledge that he and Lady Margaret Beaufort haven't lived together for years. And 'our dear Uncle Jasper' of Pembroke is now Earl of Derby. While loyal men like Lovell hide in exile somewhere, if they still live!"

"And what happened to dead Clarence's son, young Warwick? I heard milord Lovell telling someone that King Richard had him sent up north with the Lady Elizabeth of York for safety."

"To Sheriff Hutton, in Yorkshire. But the Tudor had him brought to London and put in the Tower. And that is another thing the people are muttering about. Some say that he has been done away with."

"Customers at the Boar in Cheapside are always talking about the new King's tardiness in keeping his promise to marry Princess Elizabeth. Complaining that even now, when she is Queen and has borne him a son, she has not been crowned."

"All the women seem to be enraged about that." Dickon brushed the crumbs from his Sunday doublet and turned to Tansy with his rare, attractive smile. "But why should we let the usurper and his sorry affairs spoil our few precious hours together?" he demanded, pulling her against his hungry heart.

"We seem to be living in such difficult times," she murmured, sadly aware that it must be much more difficult for him to shake off such thoughts than for any of his carefree fellow apprentices, even when the girl he loved was in his arms.

"It is bound to be difficult, living into a new dynasty," he said, looking down at her with tenderness. "But I promise you that whatever happens I shall always care most for my sweet wife and for my craft."

This was a promise which would become increasingly hard to keep. For Francis, Lord Lovell, was not dead. And John de la Pole, son of one of King Richard's sisters, had crossed to Dublin to join him, spreading a rumor that Warwick had escaped from the Tower of London and come with him. And the pupil whom Richard Simon had taken to Ireland at their instigation was no longer being coached in the classics, but in the far more dangerous game of being a Plantagenet pretender.

In England he was beginning to be talked about. He and his promoters were working for a Yorkist revival. Some people said he was only a baker's son. Others believed him to be the younger of the two Princes who had so mysteriously disappeared from the public scene after Bishop Stillington had sworn to the illegality of their mother's marriage and their Uncle Richard had accepted the crown. The Queen Mother was naturally intrigued, and another of Richard's sisters, the widowed Duchess of Burgundy, was only too eager to aid anyone who conspired against the man who had usurped her brother's crown and stopped her annuity. So publicity concerning this lad began to stir the placid pool of Henry the Seventh's apparent popularity—an impersonal popularity, fostered by a war-torn nation's longing for security and lulled by expectation of some era of extraordinary felicity when he chose for his son, born in Winchester, the legendary name of Arthur. For, astute and hard-working as Welsh Henry was, he lacked charm or a spellbinding personality. Unlike Richard Plantagenet, whom men either hated or fought for, some of them risking their lives for his cause even after he was dead.

It was difficult for Dickon, at work or in love, to keep his thoughts from his revival of old loyalties which so closely concerned him. He did his utmost to appear unconcerned and to hide his eagerness for news, but an uncontrollable excitement burned within him whenever he heard the doings of Lovell or Lincoln or of this young pretender being discussed. And although he had been entrusted to carve the pillars of a particularly beautiful hearth canopy, when he heard his mas-

ter and Sir Walter Moyle's steward talking, mind and hand
slipped from his work.

"It appears that when Lincoln joined the others in Ireland
he told Lovell that young Warwick had escaped from the
Tower," Hurland Dale was saying, as he led his companion
from room to room of the almost completed house. "So now
these crazy Yorkists are claiming that the lad is Edward, Earl
of Warwick."

"He must be a bright pupil to impersonate a royal earl,"
laughed the steward, his interest really more on whether the
house could be finished by the date of his master's return
from Calais.

"He would need to be bright as a Toledo blade to hood-
wink Henry Tudor," said Dale, whose ambition, as everyone
knew, was to be commissioned for work on one of the royal
palaces. "Weeks ago the King himself told Vertue, his master
mason, that he had sent secret agents to find out all about
this boy. He knows, for instance, that his real name is Lambert Simnel, and that he is the son of an Oxford joiner who
helped build this new college, called Magdalen, and who
saved enough money for him to be educated by a tutor
there."

The two men passed out of earshot and Dickon stood still
as a statue in his white apron, with chisel and mallet poised.
His mind was back in the narrow archway entrance of St. Edmond Hall where a kindly priest who was in a hurry to get to
Ireland had offered him and Tansy the use of his house. A
priest who was to pit his wits against Henry Tudor.

And then news spread like wildfire over England that the
Irish had received Lambert Simnel enthusiastically, and that
Lincoln and Lovell had had him crowned as Edward the
Sixth in Dublin Cathedral.

As soon as his week's work was finished, Dickon called in
at the Boar. He always had a kindly welcome from Mistress
Goodyear, although she warned him that she would never
forgive him when he took Tansy from her. However busy the
inn, she generally contrived to let them have a few minutes
together, and this night he wanted to tell Tansy of the coincidence about the Oxford tutor. "His name was Richard
Simon," he recalled. "He remarked on its being the same as
mine."

"And then he looked at you with that special kind of interest which always frightens me, and instead of mistrusting us he liked you and lent us the key," said Tansy. "I wonder what will happen to the poor man if the King ever gets hold of him?"

"But, Tansy, does it not occur to you that what these Tudor hangers-on say may be all a pack of lies? This lad may really be the Earl of Warwick!"

Tansy stared at him in pitying surprise. "Oh, Dickon, have you not heard? Of course, you have been stuck all day at your building. The town criers have been shouting the news all afternoon. The inn is seething with it."

"What news?" asked Dickon, almost sullenly.

"That the Earl of Warwick is alive! To prove it, the King has ordered that he be brought out from the Tower. He is to ride through the city. Up Thames Street, East Cheap, and past here to St. Paul's, and then back by way of Tower Street."

"When?"

"On Sunday. So that everyone may be free to go and see him for themselves—young folk like ourselves, and the older citizens who will recognize him."

Dickon did not answer. Only in that moment of surprise was he truly aware of how much his personal interest had been involved; of how much he had hoped that, one way or another, there might be Plantagenet kings again; that his father would be avenged. "So the trump card is with the Tudor again!" he said bitterly.

Among the babel of customers all discussing the same thing, Tansy could only press his arm. "Must you mind so much?" she whispered, compassionately.

He scarcely seemed to hear her, being lost in some intuitive study of the Tudor's inmost thoughts. "But he must have hesitated to use it, hated to use it," he muttered.

"Why, if it confounds his enemies?"

"Because if Richard's nephew rides through the streets of London again, even for one short hour, waves of sympathy will bring Richard back—into the hearts of the people, where he belongs. The Tudor is no fool. He must have faced this—weighed it against the value of proving himself no murderer and upsetting Lovell's plans."

"They say the Earl is to be brought out at noon. We shall both be free then. Let us go and see him."

"I must see him," said Dickon. "I have never seen or spoken to a relative in my life, except my father. By blood, this Edward of Warwick is my cousin."

Chapter Seventeen

Well before noon on Sunday, Dickon and Tansy took up their positions by the outer gates of the Tower. They could have watched the procession from Cheapside, but whereas most people just wanted to see the young Earl out of curiosity, Dickon wanted to share more intimately in the start and finish of his short, dramatic journey into freedom. Even so there were many spectators with them—warehousemen from Thames Street and dockers who worked on Tower Wharf. And all the way along the route to St. Paul's, the crowds were gathering.

"Coronations, executions, weddings, how you Londoners love them all!" A wool merchant from Flanders was rallying them good-humoredly. "But surely this is the oddest procession of all? Parading a man just to prove that he is alive."

"He is scarcely a man yet, this son of the murdered, attainted Duke of Clarence," a scholarly looking man told him.

"Do you remember seeing him, sir? Do you know what he looks like?" asked Tansy, partly because the man reminded her of Master Jordan.

"Why, surely. Most of us do," he assured her. "It is true that he lived chiefly up at Middleham, in Yorkshire, which the late King and Queen made their home. Not only was he King Richard's nephew, but also Queen Anne Neville's, her sister having married Clarence. But many a time have we seen the young Earl riding his pony among the royal party when they were in London."

"So you will recognize him when you see him?" persisted Dickon.

"Recognize him for his gentle, unassuming self, beyond all this nonsense of faked pretenders," chuckled their informant.

There was a stir among the guards; a trumpet shrilled somewhere within the thickness of the Tower walls; the crowd pushed forward but was held back in friendly fashion by the crossed pikes of men-at-arms. As the bells of All Hallows rang the hour, the great gates swung open and some of King Henry's newly formed Yeomen of the Guard marched out in charge of the Lieutenant of the Tower on his tall black charger. Then, discreetly guarded on either side by foot soldiers but with ample space before and behind so that all might see him, rode Edward, Earl of Warwick, a dark, slender youth attired in rich dark velvet, as became his noble estate.

Dickon and Tansy were so close that, but for the spaced-out pikemen between, they could almost have touched him. They saw him rein in his mount involuntarily, coming for the first time for months into the outside world. At sight of the straining, staring crowd he raised a gloved hand as if to shield his eyes from some unaccustomed glare. But it was Maytime and the sun shone and he was young, and after the first moment of shock they saw a smile of pure joy transform his gentle features as he rode forward eagerly, grasping at this unexpected illusion of freedom. A murmur of sympathetic welcome went up from most of the spectators. "Is it really the Earl?" the younger people asked, clustering around the scholarly looking man as soon as the gatehouse guards moved back to wait for the cavalcade's return.

"Yes, really the Earl," he assured them, speaking a little wearily perhaps because during the long Wars of the Roses he had seen so many titled people rise and fall.

As they stood about in groups they could hear their own murmurs of sympathy being echoed, and swelling in volume, all along Thames Street.

"Is it true, what some of the Palace servants say? That he is a little simple?" asked a 'prentice goldsmith, who had more than once taken his master's precious wares to Westminster.

"Henry the Sixth was simple. And look at the fighting we had then all up and down the land," someone reminded them.

"We want no more simple kings," agreed another.

"Better to cherish the one we now have, who keeps the peace," added a third. There seemed to be a little group of them, Lancastrians all, trying to damp down the old reviving loyalty.

"Peace at any price," murmured the scholarly man, to no one in particular.

"A capable ruler who had the sense to keep this rival decently shut up," went on the bulletheaded man, who appeared to be the leader of the Tudor faction.

"At least we know now that the malicious rumors were false. King Henry didn't have him put to death," crowed one of his friends.

"As Richard Plantagenet murdered his brother's sons," added the bulletheaded one with venom.

"Perhaps those rumors, too, may one day be proved false," suggested Dickon quietly.

The crowd began to drift away, but Dickon and Tansy moved out into the middle of the road, looking in at the open Byward Gate. In the inner ward, sunshine bathed the pathway leading to the royal lodgings, and some kind of fruit tree made a splash of hopeful green against the walls. "There are gardens and pleasant rooms in there, as well as racks and dungeons," said Tansy, holding half fearfully to Dickon's arm. "From the windows of the royal residence one could watch the shipping on the river."

"It must be reasonably pleasant, because it is a tradition that all our Kings sleep there before they are crowned," agreed Dickon, wondering if his father had done so.

Tansy edged a little nearer to the gate, and a kindly guard allowed her to peer farther in. Somewhere she could hear a bird singing, and it lightened her heart for the royal lad who would soon be going back there. "Dickon," she whispered, "do you suppose the two young Princes, Edward the Fifth and Richard, Duke of York, could still be in there?"

Dickon, whose brief love for his father had flamed fiercely, would have given much to know. "It is possible. But no one seems to think so," he said sadly, drawing her away.

The noisy group of Lancastrian enthusiasts were still there. "At least it is proved beyond all doubt that King Henry spared his rival nephew," one of them was insisting all over again.

Dickon stepped aside, avoiding him as if he were a particularly offensive clot of dung. "Were I any King's nephew I should find swift death kinder than lifelong captivity," he said quietly.

"Shall we not be going?" asked Tansy, both for her lover's sake and because she was growing tired.

But for once Dickon did not do as she wished. "It will take them at most an hour to go slowly to St. Paul's and back. Let us wait and see him return," he said, lifting her onto the wall of the moat that she might rest.

Most of the people had drifted away to stroll on Tower Hill, but for some reason or other the jovial wool merchant remained. He, too, sat on the wall of the moat to rest, and with mutual liking—or because they appeared to have equally disliked the departed Lancastrians—Dickon and Tansy fell into desultory conversation with him. He was English born, he said, but now traded wool to Flanders. His ship was moored just across the river. Before that he had been a soldier. As he had served Richard, when Duke of Gloucester, in some of the same places as Robert Marsh, it formed a bond between them. He asked them their names, and himself gave them the apt name of Weaver. The afternoon passed quickly until sounds of approaching voices warned them that the procession was returning.

"At least this Lambert Simnel has given the young Earl a morning's excursion," Jan Weaver said.

"Did you ever see him?" Dickon asked their new acquaintance, since he was obviously a much-traveled man.

"Yes, once, in Dublin," he said, after the faintest hesitation.

"What is he like?" asked Tansy.

"Oh, likeable enough. A strong, pleasant-faced lad. The trouble was he never held himself like royalty, but like the joiner's son he is."

"I am but a mason's apprentice," volunteered Dickon, with a grin.

Weaver glanced at the upstanding, well-knit figure beside him. "But now on Sunday, without your 'prentice garb, you might well pass for anybody," he said.

The crowd was almost at the end of Tower Street, so the three of them slipped off the wall and hurried to the gates. "Surely it was stupid to pick a pretender who did not look like the person he was supposed to be?" Tansy was saying.

"I thought so," agreed Jan Weaver. "This Lambert Simnel is no more like the Earl of Warwick than I am. Or you, or——"

He turned as he spoke, looked straight at Dickon, who was close behind him, and left his sentence hanging in mid-air, as if suddenly silenced by what he saw. Just then the sad little

cavalcade turned out from Tower Street, and the real Earl
approached the gates, still open like a hungry, unrelenting
maw to receive him.

They all turned to watch. Tansy wondered if it were her
imagination that he rode more reluctantly, moving more and
more slowly with every hoofbeat. Or it might have been that
the following crowds closed more protectively about him,
trying to block his path, as if reluctant to let him go. Most of
the women were weeping by now and stretching out their
arms as though they would hold on to some child of their
own; one hysterical young girl threw an armful of white may
she had been gathering so that the sweet blossoms scattered
over him. The low roar of protest from men's throats was
mounting and becoming dangerous. Yeomen thrust them all
back, far less gently this time.

Just outside the gates Edward of Warwick stopped, half
turning his horse, to look back at the city streets. With a gesture half childish, half despairing, he lifted a small branch of
may, caught in his horse's mane, to his lips. It was as if he
were thanking the Londoners for the love which he so much
needed in his lonely life.

Driven by urgent need to know more of his father, Dickon
seized his opportunity. He pushed his way between two pikemen. "Are they in there with you? Are they still alive too, Edward and Richard, your cousins?" he called.

"Yes, tell us!" joined in many of the crowd who were
within earshot.

The young Earl looked down at Dickon and smiled. He
opened his mouth as if to answer. But the Lieutenant rode
forward calling a sharp order, and Warwick's escort hustled
him forward so suddenly that the white blossom fell from his
hand into the dust. He passed through the archway, out of
sight.

"Oh, no! Merciful God, no!" cried Tansy, as the great gates
slammed shut behind him. She was only vicariously interested in rival royal claims, she had seen him only for a few
minutes, but the mothering heart of her was torn. Like most of
the other women milling about her, she felt her face wet with
tears.

"Poor parentless lad!" protested a fat market woman with a
baby in her arms.

There was nothing more to see. The crowd began to thin. Their excited, arguing voices grew fainter. "At least he is well cared for," said Dickon, trying to comfort his betrothed. "And, as you say, there are gardens in there. Listen, my love, yesterday I sold some carved figures to a shopkeeper for a good price, so today we will take a boat upriver and under London Bridge to Westminster. As we put off from Tower Wharf you will see the trees rising behind these grim walls." With an arm about her shoulders, he drew her towards the river.

"Oh, Dickon, he didn't answer you! We shall never know now."

"They saw to it that he had no chance," said Dickon, kicking an inoffensive stone out of his way.

He tried not to dwell on it but to give his whole mind to the happy present and the hopeful future. Tansy should enjoy her rare excursion on the river. "Soon I shall take my examination before some master mason," he reminded her, skillfully rowing their hired boat through the shipping on a slapping tide. "And if I do well, as I hope, I shall become a paid journeyman and a member of my Guild, and then we can marry. Tansy, my rare, patient jewel, where shall we get married and where shall we live?"

More quickly than ever the precious hours passed in seeing London from the water and discussing that inexhaustible, golden theme.

Chapter Eighteen

Unaware that Henry had already called their bluff, Lincoln and Lovell landed in Lancashire, bringing Lambert Simnel with them. They had raised some brave Irish troops who believed in him, and Margaret of Burgundy had sent well-organized foreign mercenaries. It was a desperate effort to revive the Yorkist dynasty but eventually only played into the Tudor's hands because of the way in which he dealt with it. His forethought showed him in a more favorable light. He had ports guarded and beacons trimmed all along the east coast in case the French should seize the opportune moment to invade, then went himself to Nottingham, that stronghold in the very middle of his kingdom, to await the advancing Yorkists. And after his army had completely routed them at the battle of Stoke, he once again won general approval by forbidding reprisals, pillage, or rape.

When the pretender and his tutor were taken prisoners, Henry was far too clever to inflame their cause by butchery. He brought them both back to London, damping down Yorkist sympathy by unexpected clemency. Knowing the value of ridicule, he quite humanely employed Lambert Simnel in the palace kitchens, which would soon put a stop to all grandiose notions, while leaving the lad chance of reasonable advancement.

"The chaff of his fellow turnspits will soon put all notions about being a belted earl out of his head!" laughed Mistress Goodyear, when she heard.

"But I doubt if it will put the recurrent fear of pretenders out of your new King's head," remarked Jan Weaver, who had become quite a habitué of her comfortable inn.

He had invited her and Dickon and Tansy to join him in drink, and if the two younger people would have preferred to be alone, at least the prosperous-looking merchant was entertaining and the way he sought their company quite flattering.

"You are probably right, sir. It is unfortunate for him that the fourth Edward left so many relations." Dickon grinned. The thought crossed his mind that King Richard had foreseen this very possibility.

"Well, at least one nephew, Lincoln, is now eliminated," said Mistress Goodyear, who wanted only the kind of settled peace which is good for trade.

"And Lord Lovell. Was he killed in the battle?" asked Tansy.

"No one seems to know," Dickon told her. "But it seems most likely, as he has not been heard of since."

"And the poor kind priest, Richard Simon?"

"Kind, indeed!" bridled Mistress Goodyear. "Why, King Henry would have been perfectly justified in having him hanged, drawn, and quartered. Enticing an innocent boy out of the country and teaching him to pretend to a lot of lies!" As the merchant rose with a shiver to pour himself another tankard of Burgundy, she added with concern, "Are you cold, Master Weaver?"

While she beckoned to a passing potboy to throw a log on the early autumn fire, Weaver murmured something polite about her rooms always being pleasantly warm, and a nasty mist which had chilled him down by the river. But once fortified by her good wine, he added anxiously, "Will your King really do this to him, do you suppose?"

"No. One of the city aldermen was in just now and told my husband that, with his usual clemency, the King will only imprison him for life."

"Why does throwing a man into prison for life always pass for leniency?" demanded Dickon.

"Just now you called this unfortunate tutor *kind*, Mistress Tansy. Do you know him?" asked Weaver, returning to his seat.

Tansy told him how Richard Simon had allowed them to use his house when they were on their way from Leicester to London. She was clearly much distressed for him.

"Yes, he is certainly kind, God help him!" agreed Weaver, staring down reminiscently into his empty tankard.

"Then you, too, know him?" she asked.

"I have met him," admitted Weaver noncommittally and, taking his leave less loquaciously than usual, went back to his ship.

He seemed to have been everywhere and met everybody.

What puzzled Tansy was why he should drop in at the Boar so often and seek her company. There were plenty of men who did, but they were mostly younger and of less consequence. Beyond the enjoyment of their laughter and the gratification of their compliments they meant little to her, and the kind of life she had led had taught her to keep them where she wanted them. Since she had grown to love Dickon, her natural interest in other 'prentices and dashing young city gallants seemed to have died. Besides loving him, she respected him in a way which made even the lightest giving of the least part of herself to any other man unthinkable. And in her inmost heart she acknowledged, half resentfully, that the knowledge that he was a King's son made this still more impossible.

"Does this man Weaver annoy you?" asked Dickon, one evening when Mistress Goodyear had been teasing her openly about the way in which their guest monopolized her.

"No, not really. One cannot help liking him," said Tansy. "But he keeps on deferring his sailing, and we are so busy. Often I feel I am neglecting something which the Goodyears want me to do, or thinking about something else. And they have been so good to me. It is as if someone kept putting other thoughts into your mind when you were trying to concentrate on some important piece of tracery for Master Dale."

"Do I not know, only too well! All this business about the rebellion, for instance. But, mercifully, that is over." He went and took her hands in his, looking searchingly into her eyes. "Tansy, he is not trying to make love to you, is he? Because if so——"

She laughed and kissed away the threatening frown from his forehead. "No, no, Dickon," she assured him. "It is nothing like that. He tells me about life in Flanders, making it sound so pleasant that I almost long to go there. But actually, we talk mostly about you. That is partly why I enjoy his company, I suppose. He seems very interested in you, and whenever we are alone he begins plaguing me with questions."

"What sort of questions?"

"Oh, where you lodge. Whether you have any privacy there, which I know you haven't, or he would probably come to see you instead of me. And things about your education. Whether you speak French, or can construe Latin. And, of all odd questions, where you were living during King Edward's reign."

Dickon glanced quickly around at the crowded inn parlor. "You don't suppose that he has met Gervase somewhere abroad, do you? That he suspects——"

"No. No. How could he? Don't worry, Dickon. I only tell you these things so that you won't get jealous."

"Jealous?"

"You were about Tom."

"And shall be again, when he returns."

"But why? Did I not leave Leicester and everyone there to be with you?"

"Not entirely. After all you had been through you *had* to get away from Leicester. But if Tom had come for you——"

"Oh, Dickon, why must you always think that?"

"Because you two are alike. Because you understand him better than a moody, plodding type like me. Because Tom has a kind of gaiety and brilliance—something which I envy him. Something which one is born with, but cannot acquire."

Tansy knew that he spoke the truth, that she still missed Tom's lighthearted laughter. "I could have married Tom if I had wanted to. But I didn't," she said slowly, consideringly.

"And life would have been much easier for you. Though I love you more utterly than he or any other man could, I expect I shall often be difficult to live with, my love. That is something which I was born with. And then, again," he added, looking at her remorsefully, "I probably care too passionately about my craft to make an ideal husband."

Tansy went to him and put her arms about him. "I understand all these things, and I love you as you are," she said simply. "Every day I thank God that I waited for you. Laughter is a lovely thing, but utter loyalty is rarer."

Dickon held her against his heart, knowing himself to be immeasurably blessed, and swore to conquer the thrusts of jealousy which, had he realized it, sprang from his innate humility.

Nevertheless, the next time he met Jan Weaver in the Boar he could not resist asking him pointedly when his ship would be sailing. "I noticed that the dockers finished her lading days ago."

"And a fine cargo of wool I am taking back for our weavers! But I have some private business to transact first. I will tell you about it. But not here."

"Why not?"

"Let us stroll down to the river."

"Why, what do you want with me?" asked Dickon surlily.

Weaver put a reassuring hand upon his shoulder. "Say rather, what have I to offer you? I am going on to Burgundy, and you might make your fortune there."

"Are the burghers of Dijon wanting some new bridges built there?"

"Not that I know of. But the Duchess needs the services of a dependable young Englishman like yourself."

"For some stonework on her palace?" inquired Dickon, rising to the bait.

The merchant picked up his cloak and moved towards the door. "Let us get away from all this chatter and I will tell you. Will you swear to keep your mouth shut?"

"I am no babbler. As soon as Sir Walter Moyle's house is finished I may be looking further afield. If this commission is something secret, I swear I will not speak of it to a soul. Except, of course, to Tansy."

Weaver stopped short in the doorway. "Women cannot keep a secret," he objected.

"Tansy has kept one for years."

Having so far persuaded his quarry, Weaver gave in with good grace sooner than let him go. "You trust her very much, don't you?" he said.

Every day and every hour I trust her with my life, thought Dickon, who still half suspected the wool merchant of knowing his own secret. He turned away to fetch her, and together the three of them went out into the darkness.

"I will take you aboard my ship," Jan Weaver offered, to Tansy's delight.

After they had seen the lights of London from the decks of the trim little Dutch merchantman and looked down into her tightly laden holds, they sat in Weaver's little cabin, in exactly the privacy he needed.

"After our meeting by the Tower gates, Broome, I gather you have little love for the Tudor," he began, wasting no time.

"None at all," said Dickon, looking with interest at the

smoothly fitted bulkheads of his unaccustomed surroundings. "What does the Duchess want?"

"To knock him from his stolen throne and avenge her brother's death."

The stark words struck like a sword thrust in the confined space. Dickon swung round and stared down at the speaker as he sat on his narrow, wooden bunk. Tansy watched shock, satisfaction, and excitement chase each other across her lover's sensitive face. Expectation of royally commissioned work abroad faded from his mind. Suspicious caution took its place. "And how could I, a mere mason's apprentice, help her towards that end?"

"By impersonating a Plantagenet."

"And ending up as a turnspit?"

"We mean to succeed this time. But even if you paraded your claims only before foreign courts, talk of you would still plague Henry Tudor. It is a nightmare to which usurpers lay themselves open, and Margaret of Burgundy lives to plague him."

Amazement held Dickon silent: amazement that he should be involved in one of these intrigues sponsored in high places; that he, of all men, should be approached; that such a cruelly difficult choice should be offered to him—dedicated mason and royal bastard—whose mind was so reluctant, whose heart so more than willing.

"Tansy was right, saying how foolish it was to choose a pretender who looked so little like the man he claimed to be," the Duchess's agent was saying almost lightly. "We do not intend to make the same mistake again. You saw Lambert Simnel following with the servants in the King's procession, no doubt?"

"Yes," agreed Dickon, who had not been able to resist watching.

"And a sorry figure he looked," admitted Weaver. "You must have felt that, even among the baggage wagons, you yourself would still have borne yourself so as to look the part."

It was so acute a thrust that Dickon reddened. He remembered very well how he had turned away from Tudor and all his followers that day, holding himself proudly, thinking, If I couldn't do better than that! He had been ashamed of thought. "Simnel looked a pleasant-enough lad, but he is past history," he said.

"I noticed that day at the Tower that you could have passed for Warwick far more easily than he. Hasn't anyone ever told you that you have something of the Plantagenet cast of features?"

"Warwick is here in London, alive, so the whole idea is played out."

"But there are others. Lincoln, for instance."

"Everyone is sure that Lincoln was killed at Stoke," said Tansy.

"Then Richard, Duke of York. Rumor has always had it that he was smuggled out of the Tower by boat."

So this was it: the thing which his father had warned him of was actually happening! "He is several years younger than I," objected Dickon.

Weaver rose with an expansive gesture and set wine before them. "Oh, it would not be yet, and time would make that less obvious. You would need to be trained. The Duchess would tell you all that King Edward's sons might be expected to remember. Put you *au fait* with family jokes and describe what his relatives and people about the court looked like. We should need to lay plans, to get supporters."

Dickon heard Tansy's sharp intake of breath and knew that she was frightened. "Master Weaver, you waste your time," he said, setting down his untouched tankard. "I am a mason. I have put all I am into my craft. In a few weeks' time I shall take my examination and hope to be received into my Guild. This is the life I have chosen, the only life for which I am fitted."

Jan Weaver looked up at him with his most persuasive smile. "A far more exciting one awaits you—both. Surely you are adventurous enough——"

"And I am going to be married," added Dickon, unmoved by the jibe.

"But do you not see, both of you, how your marriage would be made more easy? I imagine neither of you has much money. You are probably wondering how to buy yourselves a house. If you came with me you would both live in luxury, such luxury as you have never known, at the Court of Burgundy. There would be fine food—and lovely clothes,

Tansy. Often you would travel about, the two of you. See Paris, perhaps. And other cities of Europe. Talk to kings. There would be no more slaving like a dog from dawn to dusk to finish some rich man's house. No more waiting on tough drunkards and pert young blades for Tansy. And what do you stand to lose? You don't seem to have many ties here. Has either of you any parents?"

Tansy shook her head, half persuaded. "My father is dead," said Dickon shortly.

"All to the good," commented Weaver. "It might not be so easy if he were alive."

"No," agreed Dickon, smothering a sudden inexplicable snort of amusement.

"What was he?" asked Weaver, quickly reducing him again to wariness.

Tansy's hand shook, so that she spilled some wine down the front of her gown. But Dickon looked him straight in the eyes. "A soldier," he answered, with only an imperceptible moment of hesitation.

"Like Tansy's," remarked Weaver conversationally.

"They frequently fought on the same battlefields," Dickon assured him gravely.

"Which accounts for the way you two were drawn together in the first place, no doubt. And which should make you less afraid to grasp your interesting destiny, young man."

"I will think of it, sir."

"But never speak of it except among ourselves?"

"On that you have my word." And somehow, while saying that, Broome the 'prentice looked a more likely candidate than ever. Almost as if he were not pretending to be a Plantagenet, but being one.

How warmly the Duchess will commend me! thought Weaver, congratulating himself on his clever choice. And so anxious was he to please his patroness that he toyed momentarily with the idea of ordering the gangplank to be raised to prevent his guests' departure. But unwilling cooperation would be too dangerous. "Our overdue quitting of this berth begins to raise questions among the officials at the Customs House," he said, accompanying the young couple on deck. "So we must sail by midday tomorrow at latest. With all my heart I hope you will both be on board, prepared to meet my friends in Flanders and Burgundy."

"I will think of it," repeated the most convincing-looking pretender they were ever likely to get.

Chapter Nineteen

Dickon thought of it all night. In the apprentices' long dormitory in Hurland Dale's house, he lay sleepless among his slumbering, carefree fellows. Methodically, he tried to weigh the advantages of the Flemish merchant's glamorous proposal against the disadvantages. On the tempting side were ranged the chance to help the Yorkist cause, adventure, the luxurious married life which he would be able to provide for Tansy, and the lure of an unique task which he believed that he could accomplish. On the other hand he set uncertainty, his dislike of giving up his own identity and being used as a tool in other men's hands, the probability of leaving Tansy widowed young, and—above all—his urge to excel in the craft for which he was already trained.

The risk of doing as the Duchess and the Yorkist exiles wished would be great. Tansy, he knew, would suffer agonies of fear for him. For if he should be finally brought back to England impersonating young Richard of York, and the plot did not succeed, Henry Tudor would not make a turnspit of a second pretender. He would either kill him or imprison him for life.

Dickon preferred to be himself and to wield his own tools. But it was his dead father's words which decided him. He remembered them perfectly: "It is of such stuff as you—and even by means of chance likenesses—that pretenders are made. . . . Arrange your apprenticeship. . . . Live the enviable life of an industrious craftsman, marry some kind girl of ordinary station, mix with the uncaring crowd, and forget all that I have told you."

Before it was light Dickon walked quietly round to the back of the Boar and whistled, as arranged, beneath Tansy's window. "I remain a mason," he sang to the tune of "Come, gather ye May buds," and there was gladness in his voice because he guessed that she, too, must have slept little and would be much relieved. But at the risk of being late for work he could not prevent himself from running down to the river to take a last look at the Flemish merchant ship. All was bustle on her decks as her crew made ready to leave with the tide.

I could have sailed in her out past Greenwich and Tilbury to the Hague, seen the cities of Europe, savored such adventures as fall to the lot of few men, he thought, and come back with an army, perhaps, as a bogus King of England.

He went back, instead, munching a chunk of bread hot from the baker's ovens in Bread Street, to join his busy fellow 'prentices, to be reprimanded by the foreman, and to put the final touches to a fountain they were making in the forecourt.

"I am sure that you decided rightly," Tansy comforted him that evening, seeing how downcast he looked.

"I suppose we never seriously entertained the hare-brained scheme," he said, trying to hide his depression because life felt so flat and ordinary. "It was just that we were both carried away by Jan Weaver's enthusiasm. It was the very thing which my father warned me of, and at least I have obeyed him. But, oh, my pretty one, how I wanted you to have all those fine dresses!"

"So small an issue in so big a game!" laughed Tansy. "And what would they have meant to me if I had lost you?"

"You won't mind being poor? For even as a journey-man——"

She grew radiant at being able to reassure him. "Oh, Dickon, I was so relieved at heart about your decision that I forgot, in this first moment, to tell you! We shan't have to be very poor. While we were aboard the ship, the good chapman Gufford came. I was sorry not to see him, because he would have given me news from Leicester. But he left this letter with Master Goodyear for me." She pulled it from the pocket hanging at her belt and handed it to him. "It is from Master Langstaff, the lawyer. You will be able to understand it better than I. The inn is sold——"

"But not too well!" ejaculated Dickon, seeing the poor price.

"We could not expect it. He says no one made a bid for months. It had acquired a bad name." For a moment, as Dickon stood silently reading, she was plunged back again in all the unhappiness and horror of her last months there. But her busy and completely changed life had helped, and she shook herself free of frightful memories back into the happy present. "The loveliest news is that Master Jordan is coming to London," she said, catching at Dickon's arm and pointing to the end of the letter.

"He will be bringing your money, Langstaff says. Just as well, with so many thieves on the roads."

"*Our* money," corrected Tansy. "He is waiting a week or two so as to be here for our wedding."

"In time to give away the bride," said Dickon, kissing her and handing back the letter.

"It will be almost like having my father."

"Remembering the size of the Boar—the White Boar, as it was then—it seems a terribly poor price," reiterated Dickon.

"You knew it only during its brief days of prosperity, when the King was there," she reminded him. "My father had let things go, and my stepmother—God rest her poor soul!—was so pleasure-loving. What little trade there was—afterwards—has drifted away to the Three Cups, it seems. But at least, if Master Jordan arrives before we are married, the money will be enough to buy us a house. Perhaps one of those little cottages facing the Thames in Charing Village?"

"We both seem to have a yearning for green fields," said Dickon, smiling at her enthusiasm. "Though perhaps before actually buying a house we should know where I shall be working."

"But won't you go on working just the same for Master Dale? Except that you will be paid as one of his more experienced men, of course."

"I hope so. But you must remember that once this house on the Strand is finished, we may be working anywhere, and Charing might be less convenient."

By dint of hard work, Sir Walter Moyle's house was ready for him when he came home from Calais in the autumn, and he was more than pleased with it. Like the fine gentleman he was, he invited Hurland Dale and all the men who had worked on it to a feast.

After they had eaten, some of the principal guests stood about the splendid fireplace at the end of the great hall with their host and his family, discussing the various problems which had been overcome and receiving congratulations.

"Although Calais is like a part of England, it is wonderful

to be home again!" exclaimed his only unmarried daughter, Amy.

"And in time for the Queen's belated coronation!" Master Dale reminded her.

"We shall have to do a good deal of entertaining, and this will be a splendid setting," said its owner, looking round with vast satisfaction. "You and your men have indeed done well."

"As you probably know, Master Dale, my father was received in audience at Westminster yesterday," explained young John Moyle, who had come up from the family estate in Kent. "The success he has made of the Calais defences is so much appreciated that it is thought the King and Queen may come and visit him here. Your work may be seen and admired by royalty."

Carpenters, masons, glaziers were all standing about the hall, pricking their ears to catch such words of generous praise for their labors and being temporarily inattentive to the wives and sweethearts they had been invited to bring with them.

"Shall you be living here, sir, more than at Eastwell?" Master Hurland asked hopefully, seeing how valuable an advertisement this might prove for his architecture.

"I may have to be at court more often," agreed Sir Walter, jovial with well-earned success. "So it looks as if my son will have to run the Kentish estate."

"I ask for nothing pleasanter than to marry and settle down," said the younger Moyle. "Though my future wife will find nothing so fine as this in the old manor at Eastwell, I fear." He leaned across his sister's chair to look more closely at the excellently wrought pillars and canopy. "This really is a beautiful fireplace, Master Dale."

Dale glowed with pleasure. "One of my 'prentices carved it," he had the generosity to tell them.

"A 'prentice!" exclaimed John Moyle, running an appreciative finger over the delicacy of the scrollwork.

"Yes. That young man standing with the fair-haired girl by the serving screens. He will be taking his journeyman's examination next week."

"The girls over here seem prettier than our settlers in Calais. Is she his wife?" asked Amy Moyle.

"She soon will be. I gave him leave to fetch her down from Leicester. But he has amply made up for it by all the conscientious work he has put in."

"From Leicester!" repeated Amy, who evidently had some interest in the place.

At a word from her father, the master mason called to Dickon to come forward.

"I hear you have nearly finished the period of your indentures. What is your name, young man?" asked Sir Walter kindly.

"Richard Broome, sir," said Dickon, blushing and bowing.

"Well, we were admiring your carving here, young Broome. A very painstaking and efficient effort. How long did it take you?"

"I have no idea, sir. I just went on working each day until the light failed, it was such a joy to do."

They all laughed, including him briefly in their pleasant family circle. Amy leaned forward to whisper something to her father. "My daughter here has heard your name before and thinks you must be the fellow who sent that thrusting young fletcher, Tom Hood, so hotfoot after my good old fletcher's place."

"There was little work for him in Leicester after Bosworth. I trust he has served you well across the Channel, sir."

"As well as you men of Hurland Dale's have served me here. Though in a more, shall we say, spectacular manner," he added, with a reminiscent grin. "Quite a stir he made in Calais!"

"He is a more spectacular sort of person." Dickon laughed and would have withdrawn had not Moyle's daughter caught at his arm. "Did you live in Leicester?" she asked, lowering her voice.

"No, Mistress Moyle. I have been there only once," answered Dickon, in the same confidential tone. "But it was there that I met my future bride."

"That attractive fair girl with the generous mouth and adorable tiptilted nose?"

"Yes. Her father kept the Blue Boar where the late King stayed," said Dickon, liking his vivacious questioner all the more.

"Then she would know Tom Hood very well, wouldn't she?

I have heard him speak of her. And of you, with gratitude. Your ears should have burned."

"They are burning now, from the kind things your father and brother said."

"Oh, my brother is most interested in beautiful houses. I think he would have liked to be an architect, if my father hadn't made him study for the law. Do you know Tom very well?"

"Oh, yes, though only recently. We spent a good deal of our leisure time together when he first came to London."

"Then you can tell me. Is it true what my friend Mirabelle in Calais says?"

Dickon treated the scatterbrained little brunette to his most devastating smile. "Mistress Amy, I do not know your friend. How then can I even guess what she says?"

"No, of course not. My father is always saying that I am inconsequent, though I don't know quite what he means. But you heard him say that Tom Hood made a stir in Calais. Mirabelle says it was as much among the ladies as among the archers."

Clearly the inconsequent little beauty hung upon his words. "Really, you amaze me. Your friend must be very imaginative," he managed to blurt out, with admirable loyalty. "May I fetch you some of those delicious sweetmeats which the servants are handing round?"

She thanked him absently, and he beat a cowardly retreat before he could be pressed further on the subject. But when he returned with them she had flitted from the fireside, and he became involved in conversation with some of the senior craftsmen. It was not until some time later that he caught sight of her sitting in one of the familiar window seats with, of all people, Tansy. Dark head and fair were close together, and the daughter of the house appeared to be plying his beloved with yet more confidential questions.

As Dickon took his future wife back to the Goodyears' tavern, Tansy talked with a shade too much enthusiasm of the wonderful evening they had spent. "I wish you could work for the Moyles forever. They are a lovely family," she said.

Manlike, he failed to recognize the note of unhappy annoyance in her voice, for Dickon's own head was in the clouds after all their approbation. "Master Dale thinks I am sure to pass well. I made his head mason tell me exactly what these examinations are like. You go to the hall of your Guild, he says, and some eminent master mason is there to judge your work. He sits on a raised dais so that he can note every movement of mallet and chisel, and you all stand at benches before him. They give you each a block of stone, but you may bring your own tools if you like. Then some official calls out what you are to carve and you are given a certain time to work on it. You may all go about it in different ways. Master Dale once told me that they are very fond of setting ecclesiastic sort of tasks, such as making a holy-water stoop, or some head to decorate the corbel at the bottom of an arch. Someone times you by an hour glass and when the time is up they ring a bell and the judge comes down and looks at each 'prentice's work. He gives marks for originality of design as well as actual craftsmanship, of course. If you gain over ninety per cent, I wager any master mason would be glad to employ you. If only one knew the kind of subject which would be set, one could practice and practice. . . ."

He, who was given to long silences, had talked his way through several streets, intent upon his own concerns. They had come to the Boar before he was aware that they had crossed the Fleet ditch or walked through Ludgate or passed St. Paul's.

Tansy turned at the open doorway and shook him impatiently by the arms. "Dickon, you have been working too hard trying to finish that wretched house. You are all strung up and nervous."

"They say my father was always nervous before a battle," he recalled irrelevantly. "And he was the finest soldier that ever was. Perhaps, to do anything well, to put everything one has into it, one must be strung up first?"

Tansy gave up in exasperation. "Good night!" she said tersely, beginning to stride away from him with head held high.

Instantly, he was after her, holding her, turning her sweet, hurt face towards him. "Oh, my love, to make you angry I must have been intolerable! I told you, didn't I, that I cared too passionately for my craft to make a good husband?"

"You might at least pretend to take an interest in the social side of things, or other people's—hurts."

"But who has hurt you, my dear?" asked Dickon, completely mystified. "I thought that you were enjoying everything. Why, Mistress Amy said how attractive you were, and she seemed to be talking to you more than to anyone else."

"She was, indeed. And I couldn't help liking her," admitted Tansy, half mollified. "But it was only because she wanted to ask questions about Tom."

"She tried that on me." Dickon chuckled.

"And, of course, you stood by him like a rock. You men!"

"But what has Tom done that he needs any man's defense? A finer fellow never lived!"

"Of course! Of course!" agreed Tansy, trying to quell her exasperation and allowing him to kiss her at last. "And I *do* know how important your examination is."

"It is important largely because it will mean the end of all this parting," said Dickon, feeling how much easier it would be smooth out all their differences in a bed than in a public street. "This time next week I shall be seeing the priest at Bow Church about our marriage. You will belong to me then, Tansy."

When she had finally broken free from his remorseful embrace, she turned back again to reassure him. "And you need never be jealous of Tom, for all his gaiety and brilliance, any more!"

Dickon stared at her in questioning silence. He was beginning to come out of his man's world sufficiently to imagine what might have hurt her.

"He told that artless little Amy Moyle that I had always seemed like a sister to him, or you may be sure she would never have asked me all those lovesick questions."

Dickon's widening grin was a mixture of dawning comprehension, relief, and tenderness. "If Tom is half the gallant I think he is, that must have been hard to take."

"And Dickon——"

"Yes?"

"I want you to know that men have no monopoly in loyalty. I didn't give him away either."

Chapter Twenty

Dickon was filling in time, working with the rest of Hurland Dale's men on some repairs to a garden wall for the new Chancellor of the Exchequer. They talked and laughed as they scappled the rough blocks of stone, discussing the feast which had made such a happy termination to the months of hard work on their last assignment. For once the foreman did not reprimand them, and during the noon break they let off their high spirits still further by a particularly wild game of football through the streets. Like the rest of them, Dickon was dusty and disheveled by the time he returned to the garden and picked up his tools.

"Carve us that amusing face of the old tax gatherer again!" suggested one of his mates.

"Go on! No one will notice if you do it on one of the bottom quoins," urged another.

While they all stood around laughing, Dickon made a swift, ribald caricature of the much-hated chancellor on his own wall. He was just adding a devil's pitchfork by way of full measure when he became aware of a sudden hush and of the resumption of work among his mates, and then of a tall shadow falling across his irreverent labors.

"Very lifelike, but scarcely likely to amuse our client," remarked a familiar voice acidly, and there stood Master Dale, looking over his shoulder.

Caught in *flagrant delicto*, Dickon swung round abashed. "Sir, I *am* sorry."

"You will probably be sorrier if Master Morton himself sees it." Dale spoke grimly, but surprisingly he dealt out no well-deserved punishment, his mind seeming to be pleasantly occupied with something considerably more important. "Your examination, Broome, and yours, Lakin, will be at an hour past noon tomorrow, and I trust you will both do me credit." Since their master usually rested in his own house at this hour, he had evidently come specially to tell them.

"Tomorrow!" echoed Red Lakin, in consternation. "But, sir, we both thought——"

"I know. But it has been fixed for two days earlier. For you two, and another couple of promising apprentices, from Paternoster Row. The examiner would not be free to come at any other time. It is exceedingly good of him to spare time to come at all. And a great honor."

"Who will he be, sir?" ventured the eager redhead, since Dickon, who usually gave him the lead, seemed still too embarrassed to speak.

Hurland Dale, whose ancestor had built for Richard the Second, seemed to swell visibly with pride. "Master Robert Vertue himself!" he announced.

"The King's own master mason!" Young Lakin sank down with a muted whistle on the half-finished wall.

"Every member of the Guild will probably be there. A great honor," repeated Dale. "For me and for my two outstanding pupils of the year."

He looked round for some sign of elation from the far more outstanding of the two, but Dickon Broome, whose rare remarks usually came so concisely, was positively pale and staring in a kind of daze before him. "Yes, sir. The greatest mason in all England," he muttered with an effort. "And I shall most assuredly muff everything and die of fright."

A suppressed titter went round, and even their master had to smile. "Come, come, Broome. A capable craftsman like yourself has nothing to fear. It is a stroke of good fortune which most third-year apprentices would give their ears for and has come about largely because the Moyles were so pleased with your carving. It seems Sir Walter met Master Vertue at Westminster, and while telling him about his new house he mentioned you. I believe it was really young John Moyle who got him interested and persuaded him to come. Like all great craftsmen, Robert and William Vertue are always on the lookout for new talent."

"Sir Walter spoke to the King's mason about me?" Dickon was beginning to come out of his daze.

"Why, yes, you will remember how his daughter told him something about your having found him a clever young fletcher. And I imagine that energetic young man had more to do with the excellent state of Calais' defences than is generally known, because Sir Walter in his jovial way, 'One good turn deserves another.' If Robert Vertue passes you, you are made, Broome. Though I hope you won't be leaving me."

Dickon looked at him with great liking and gratitude, realizing that his good tutor, Paston, could not have chosen for him a better master. "It would have to be a very remarkable offer of work to tempt me," he said.

"I suppose, sir, you have no idea of what subject Master Vertue is likely to set us?" insinuated Red Lakin, beginning to share something of his fellow victim's sense of the magnitude of their coming ordeal.

Dale cuffed his flaming, disordered head good-naturedly. "None at all, Lakin. And if I had, I hope I should not be so unethical as to tell you." He called to the foreman to release the two apprentices for the rest of that day. "And have them take their 'prentice garb, which they appear to have been playing football in, to my laundry immediately, so that they do not shame us tomorrow. As both jerkins and hose look sadly outgrown, it is to be hoped that tomorrow will be the last time they will need to wear them."

"By all the Saints, how fortunate we are!" exclaimed Lakin, as they gathered up their caps and tools and prepared to depart, cheered by the good wishes of their fellows.

"Thank God, there is not long to wait!" murmured Dickon.

All afternoon he sharpened his tools; all evening he paced restlessly about the Dales' yard; all night he tossed and turned, thinking at intervals, This time tomorrow it will all be over! His enormous admiration for the architectural genius of the Vertues humbled him hopelessly.

He envisaged himself failing. Not being qualified to do increasingly interesting and intricate work. Not being able to afford to marry. Failing Tansy—Tansy, who had come with him to London and trusted him, who had worked in a stranger's inn so that she might wait for him. By the time he turned up at the hall of the Masons' Guild in Basinghall Street in a clean, neatly belted jerkin and apprentice's peaked cap, he was almost frantic.

It was all just as he had been told. The hall was packed with members, not because they particularly wanted to watch the efforts of four promising apprentices, but because they were supremely honored by the presence of the leading exponent of their craft. Dickon and the other three young men standing for trial were behind their benches with a slab of rough hewn stone and their tools laid out before them. Instinctively, Dickon's hand reached for his chisel. Somehow the familiar feel of it calmed him. He even dared to look up for the first time at the great master mason to see what manner of man he was, and to his amazement the gray-haired genius who had built Bath Abbey smiled down at him, almost as if he understood that absurd shaking of a novice's hands. The comforting thought occurred to Dickon that perhaps many years ago the great man had stood nervously at this very bench. And he was more sure than ever that nothing worthwhile was easy, that all fine creative work must take something physical out of one to the point of exhaustion.

After asking them a few questions about cusps and mullions and fan vaulting, Vertue, being big enough to break away from custom, announced, "I am not giving you four candidates any set task but am leaving you to choose, each according to his inclination. So shall we, and you, learn in which direction your best gifts lie."

A bell rang. Each pupil stood motionless or fumbling with his tools, momentarily embarrassed by the unexpected but welcome freedom of choice. And in that moment the last shred of Dickon's tension relaxed, leaving him cool as steel.

Just as my father, after a sleepless night, charged confidently into battle, he thought, with the hint of a smile curving his lips. Somehow that thought took him back to the King's bed at Leicester with its two panels of exquisite carving, and to King Richard explaining carefully to his landlord's daughter that they represented the Holy Sepulcher. Because they were something so intimately connected with his father, they were indelibly impressed on Dickon's memory. He remembered every relief and outline as clearly as though he had seen them only yesterday. Steady in mind and hand, he began without more ado to carve one on the virgin stone before him. His mates were fashioning corbels, bosses, or caskets which would be of some material use, but he was re-creating a vision from a far-off land fit to decorate some royal throne or cathedral sanctuary. And, as with Sir Walter Moyle's fireplace, he lost all sense of time or awareness of his surroundings until the bell rang again.

Ushered by an official, and followed by some of the finest

masons in London, Master Vertue stepped down from the examiner's chair. As the candidates moved respectfully aside, he stood consideringly behind each bench. He was patently pleased with all he saw. But he stood silent so long behind Dickon's bench, and examined the small carving so carefully, that men pressed and peered from behind to see what had caught his attention. "Is it entirely original?" he asked.

"No, sir," admitted Dickon, standing respectfully, cap in hand. "Rather a copy from memory of something I once saw and admired. It represents the Holy Sepulcher."

"It would make a very suitable design for a crusader's tomb," remarked Robert Vertue, obviously impressed. "There is great demand for elaborately carved tombs just now. And vast need, alas! for more originality."

He said no more, but when the results of the examination were announced the name of Richard Broome headed the list, with only two marks lost—for the lack of complete originality, presumably.

As soon as the great master was gone, lesser men crowded round to look. "Fine work for an inexperienced 'prentice!" they said. "But what an extraordinary subject to choose!"

Some of them, whose 'prentices had never achieved anything half as clever, spoke with envy. But Hurland Dale, having seen the King's mason to the door, came back and wrung Dickon by the hand. He was inordinately proud. "Master Vertue is a man of few words," he told him. "But such commendation could well make an ambitious young builder's fortune."

"Sir, you have taught me all I know, and all my life I shall be grateful," vowed Dickon.

"I am proud to hear you say so. Next week I shall want you to take charge of the new cloister for those monks at Richmond. But remember, Broome," added Dale generously, "if at any future time work should be offered to you which is more important than mine, I shall not stand in your way."

Dickon was almost speechless with happiness. When their betters had departed, he and Red Lakin thumped each other on the back in mutual, incoherent joy. Their ordeal was successfully over. As they gathered up their tools, congratulations flowed over them and fellow workmen crowded round trying to plan some sort of celebration. But there was only one person whom Dickon wanted to celebrate with at that moment. Hurrying along Cheapside in the direction of the Boar, he seemed to walk on air and knocked into at least half a dozen citizens without so much as apologizing.

The inn parlor seemed particularly full of people, but he scarcely saw them, save as a background to the girl he loved. Although usually undemonstrative before strangers, he rushed to her and caught her to his heart. "Tansy! Tansy! I have passed!" he cried breathlessly. "It was Master Vertue himself, and he seemed very well satisfied. He put me first."

"Oh, Dickon, how wonderful!" Turning as best she could from his embrace, she tried to include other people in the good news, but he was still unaware of them. "What did you have to make?"

"He let us choose. We were so surprised, all of us, that we hadn't an idea what to do. But it was better so. Guess what I sculptured, Tansy." Suddenly, seeing her eager face, he remembered that the subject might bring back all her past horrors, but his wise insistence that she should show him the bed had worked well. When he told her she did not flinch from the memory. "Master Vertue asked if it were original, but how could I explain?"

At that moment someone slapped him on the back and pushed a brimming tankard into his hand, and he began to realize that they had an audience. He was as much the center of an intimate, admiring kind of gathering as if he had a family circle of his own. It gave him a warm, good feeling. There were people whom he knew well, like the Goodyears, customers whom he had come to know by sight, and strangers whom he had never seen before.

"He had just passed his journeyman's examination," they were explaining, one to another. "Commended by the King's own mason, he was."

Tankards were raised. Mistress Goodyear kissed him with affectionate tears in her eyes. "Now you will take her away, I suppose, you brute!" she accused, torn between regret and romantic delight.

But best of all, a man's arm was fondly about his shoulders, its owner as generously radiant as if the triumph were his own. "Pardieu, I always knew that you would do it, Dickon!" said a familiar voice. It was Tom.

Dickon turned and seized his hand, and they stood laughing and shaking each other's hands in a renewal of past good comradeship, as united as if nothing had ever threatened to come between them. "We thought we should see you at the supper Sir Walter gave. You can only just have landed."

"Two days ago, at Dover. And this is the best news I have had since I came ashore."

"It's good to have you back, Tom. By all accounts you yourself did brilliantly—in Calais."

Tansy was pulling at her betrothed to meet someone else. "It has been a day of arrivals," she said happily. "See who has come from Leicester: our beloved schoolmaster, Master Jordan! You have never met him."

"No, but I have heard enough about you, sir, to fill a book."

Young man and old looked into each other's eyes with mutual liking. Will Jordan knew who he really was because Tansy, in the midst of her troubles, had confided in him. But not a sign of this knowledge passed between them, and Dickon instinctively trusted him.

"Langstaff had to send someone trustworthy with the money for the sale of the Boar," Jordan was explaining. "So it was arranged that I should take it and assuage a long desire to see Tansy at the same time."

"And of all inspired thoughts, he brought Jod along to mind the horses!"

"Or help mind the money bags," laughed Will Jordan.

Dickon left them all and went to the old ostler, who was standing, grinning toothlessly, in the background. "Welcome to London, Jod," he said. "I do not forget your help, but most of all you mean a great deal to me because you have served and protected Mistress Tansy since she was small. She and I mean to show you the sights of our city." And Jordan, watching him, recognized in his voice and movements something of the grace and dignity of his royal father.

Returning to his group of friends, Dickon found Tom and Tansy with their heads together over Jordan's map of Leicester, laughing over old times. Not that he minded any longer, but he considered it time to stake his own firm claim. "Shall we invite them now to our wedding, Tansy?" he said clearly. "At Bow Church, next Sunday. I lost no time in speaking to the priest."

"And here, for a wedding breakfast, afterwards," invited the Goodyears in unison.

"It would not be my real wedding without them all," said Tansy, kissing the landlord with almost tearful gratitude.

"I hope you have come *in loco parentis*, Master Jordan, to give away the bride," said Dickon.

"And *locum tenens* for Master Langstaff. Our good host has put your money away in a safe place, Tansy. But there will be some signing to be done."

"And you, Tom, must be my man and hold the ring," invited Dickon. "For who knows when you yourself will need similar support?"

"Who knows, indeed?" echoed Tom, with unaccustomed gloom.

Indeed, so lugubrious did he look that Dickon found occasion to draw him aside. "At Sir Walter Moyle's house we had the pleasure of meeting at least one charming girl who might help you to answer that question, Tom."

Tom brightened immediately. "You mean, she spoke of me?"

"Of nothing much else, either to Tansy or myself. I do not imagine that we should have attracted the attention of a daughter of Sir Walter had she not wanted to question us about you. Particularly Tansy, who has known you all her life."

"It is not conceivable that her father would ever agree. And Amy herself is such a provocative tease. . . . But if you think she really likes me—" stammered the charming, successful fletcher, with quite unaccustomed modesty.

"You seem to have dented her heart."

"She has completely shattered mine," murmured Tom. "What sort of questions did she ask?"

"The main qualm in her mind seemed to arise when her father said you had made quite a stir in Calais. She wasn't sure whether it was a stir among the ladies or the archers."

"Whatever it was then, it is only Amy and the archers now. As, with you, it is Tansy and your everlasting transoms." Then, as if bothered by an uncomfortable thought, he inquired anxiously, "Exactly what did you both tell her?"

Dickon grinned and punched him rallyingly in the chest. "Exactly nothing," he assured him.

Chapter Twenty-one

The following evening, as soon as his work was done, Dickon was due to be on City watch with the other liverymen of his Guild while Tansy, forgetting her work altogether, sat talking with Tom Hood and Master Jordan in the room which the latter had hired at the Cheapside Boar. "They are little white cottages facing the river with a view of green fields across the water. Charing is a pleasant village, and every day Dickon would see the lovely cross for Edward the Third's *chère reine*, which he so much admires," she was telling them ecstatically.

"You could easily afford to buy one with the Leicester money, of course, if there is one to be had," said Tom, who preferred towns.

"There is one for sale. Dickon and I have been to look at it many an evening."

"But it is not real country, dear child, and may soon cease to be a village at all, what with the city encroaching on one side and Westminster on the other," warned Jordan, smiling at her enthusiasm. "And, seriously, would it be wise to buy a home now that Dickon is a journeyman and may be sent to various places?"

Both men knew that there was sound truth in what he said but hated to damp her radiant happiness. "We could take rooms for a time, perhaps" she sighed, seeing her dream of a peaceful country cottage fading in the light of common sense. "But I am so tired of living in other people's houses!"

"My poor, sweet Tansy!" Tom put a comforting arm about her while he racked his inventive brains on her behalf. "I wonder," he said, after they had sat for a few moments in despondent silence, "if young Master Moyle could do anything for you."

"How could he?" and "Why should he?" the other two asked, in unison.

Tom, who was nothing if not an optimist, sat tapping his knee as he weighed the chances. "He shares some mews out Richmond way with a friend who is equally keen on hawking. They took me with them only yesterday. There seemed to be an empty, rather neglected-looking dwelling house of some kind beside his falconer's cottage. If I could persuade him to let you rent it, Dickon could soon put it to rights. It stood on the edge of a park not far from the Thames and there was, as I remember, some stabling."

"Stabling!" cried Tansy, as if he had offered her the keys of Heaven. "So far we have managed to keep Mopsy and Pippin at the Boar by letting them on hire to foreign visitors. But now we fear we may have to part with them. Just when I might have time to ride Pippin again!"

"Nevertheless, Jod reports that both animals are in fine condition. When we rode into Goodyear's yard and he saw them, it was like the reunion of a parent with long-lost children," Jordan told Tom.

"Oh, Tom, do you really think you could persuade Master John Moyle to let us rent that place?" entreated Tansy.

"I doubt if he will need much persuading, seeing that it is just within the wildest realms of possibility that he may one day be my brother-in-law." Tom grinned, with some of his old swagger. "And, as you probably gathered for yourself when he talked Master Vertue into that examination business, he is rather taken with that future husband of yours."

The future husband joined them at that moment, jubilant because he had caught a pilferer on his first watch and his wedding had been fixed. He was immediately interested in Tom's idea. "If I have somewhere to keep the mare I shall be able to get to any building site where Master Dale is likely to send me."

"I will ask Amy to put in a word for you," promised Tom.

"Tansy and I are certainly blessed with good friends," said Dickon gratefully.

"And so are we. John Moyle is putting in a word for us with his father."

"So Amy has really said she will marry you!" exclaimed Tansy, any twinges of previous jealousy wiped out by her instinctive liking for the girl.

"She has really said so at last," confirmed Tom, so much enamored that his smile was almost fatuous. "But even with her brother on our side, how can one expect Sir Walter to allow his daughter—who is being wildly sought after by at least three heirs of manors—to marry a mere fletcher?" he added, coming down to earth. "You two ought to be thankful that you are both sprung from ordinary parentage." He turned to his friend of only a few years' standing, suddenly realizing how little he knew about his background. "By the way, Dickon, what *is* your father?"

Though the other two occupants of the room might hold their breath in sharp uncertainty, the late King's son had his reply rehearsed and ready. "He was a soldier," he said calmly, for the second time within a matter of days. "And in any case, since none of our parents is living, there is no one to say us nay. Or, for that matter," he added regretfully, "to bless us."

They sat talking for a while, and listening to news from Leicester.

"What happened to the King's bed?" asked Dickon, bending to buckle his shoe with elaborate casualness.

"The man who bought the Blue Boar does not intend to keep it. He would have made a show piece of it again, but his wife is fearful of ghosts. And so might his customers be," Jordan told them. "He may be putting it up for sale. Personally, I doubt if he will get much for it now the country is settling down again."

Dickon looked up eagerly and opened his mouth to speak but, seeing Tansy shake her head, suggested nothing. "It was a fine piece of craftsmanship," was all he said.

In a few days, thanks to the quick wits of Tom Hood and to the easygoing kindness of the younger Moyle, Dickon and Tansy had a remarkably cheap rented home waiting for them.

A thin November sun shone and the streets of London were already decorated for the Queen's belated coronation, when Bow bells rang out for their wedding. Since they themselves were such a likeable couple, it was not nearly such a quiet occasion as they had planned. Of all their guests only the elderly schoolmaster, who gave away the bride, and a humble ostler knew that she was marrying a Plantagenet. And of all the guests who returned to celebrate at the inn afterwards, only two were utterly unexpected—Master John Moyle and his sister Amy. Her beguiling glances strayed more frequently than they should have done to the debonair

best man, but since her brother escorted her, Sir Walter had
made no objection to her coming. The wedding party was
greatly honored, and the happy bride could not thank Amy
enough for her efforts to assure a pleasant home for the
friends of her father's fletcher.

Scatterbrained, warmhearted Amy Moyle had sent some
spare furniture from the stately house on the Strand. Mistress
Goodyear had supplied all the pots and pans. The obliging
chapman Gufford had brought from Leicester on his cart the
oak chest which Robert Marsh had given to Tansy, together
with a few of her mother's favorite household possessions.
And Jod had spent two whole days cleaning up the disused
stables.

"Do you realize, my beloved, that this is the first home I
have ever had?" asked Dickon, when at last they had left their
friends and the lights of London behind and stood alone in
rural, evening silence at their gate.

"We shall be able to ride out through the country lanes on
Sundays," murmured Tansy, resting her head on his shoulder.

Dickon glanced up at the gables, washed white by moon-
light beneath their thatch. "I shall be able to make this into a
really attractive house. Quite half my mates have offered to
help me," he said, his voice richly deep with content.

"As soon as spring comes I am going to sow golden marigolds in the little garden," said Tansy.

"As Master Jordan said, we should have been most ill-ad-
vised to buy. From here I can ride out early each morning to
work, wherever it may be. Now that I am a competent craftsman and a member of my Guild, there is no foreseeing what
work may come my way. My only regret is that it is not my
earnings which are paying for this particular bit of Paradise."

"That will come later, love, when we are older. When you
are a well-to-do master builder like Hurland Dale you will be
able to buy me all those fine dresses which that scheming
merchant promised me at the Court of Burgundy. You will
never regret not going there, will you, Dickon? The risks
would have been so great that I scarcely know how we ever
came to contemplate it. Whereas in England you will almost
surely rise to be well known in the world of architecture. And
for the present, what more could we ask?" Tansy spread her
arms wide, as if gathering to her heart all the happiness she

had ever longed for. "Here we can hear the birds sing, with no smell of stale ale nor noise of traffic and street brawls. And yet we shall still be by the sweetly flowing Thames."

"And we shall be, for the rest of our lives, together," said Dickon, drawing her into the firelit living room and bolting their door on the rest of the world.

"You don't mind—about the King's bed?" asked Tansy shyly, when they had climbed the little winding stair to their room beneath the eaves. "I knew that when you heard it was going cheaply, you had half a mind to buy it. And we could have afforded it, perhaps. But for me it has later memories. I could not bring myself to——"

Dickon pulled her down onto the very ordinary bed they possessed. "No, no, my love. You were right. It is something out of our past, fraught with sorrow for us both, and no resting place for the happy future of young lovers."

It was a happy present indeed, the more precious for every day they had waited for it. And the future which stretched before them promised all the greater blessing because it had not been easily won.

It was not only the first time Dickon had had a home, but the first time he had had somewhere to keep his precious book, *Sayings of the Philosophers*, and to be able to dip into it whenever he wished.

"Always I have kept it locked in this box, which I made for it as soon as I first got to London. And only occasionally in all this time have I been able to take your gift out from among my gear and read parts of it."

"Only when you were alone," commiserated Tansy, picturing him very young and gawky, as she had first known him, perplexed by the babel of a strange dormitory and aching sometimes for privacy.

"Not that my work mates would willingly have harmed it," he hastened to explain. "Some of them came from families who had books and lamented that they had not been apprenticed to printing, since it is the most modern craft. But there were others who had no idea of a book's value and might have set guttering candles down on it or hurled it at one another in their horseplay."

"Well, now it will be taken every care of, and I promise you I shall not feel shut out if you are reading. I shall think of how often you must have wanted to, with no place of your own. Let us keep it on the table Red Lakin made for you, with a piece of my mother's tapestry for a cover."

"But not, I think, down there, where people might pry and ask awkward questions. Unlocked, I think, beside our bed."

And so, like all newly married couples, they took pride and pleasure in arranging their first home. Every now and then John Moyle and his friends came hawking, and Tansy would set out refreshment for them. Sometimes he brought his sister, and inevitably Tom Hood happened to turn up on such occasions. He seemed to have become very much a part of the Moyle family.

By the time spring came and the marigolds had begun to show green in the garden, Dickon, with much willing help, had refaced the front of the house, made a window to lighten Tansy's kitchen, and repaired the roof.

One day, after his friends had gone, John Moyle stayed behind specially to see what had been done. "Hood says you have made great improvements to my old property," he said, "and I am glad to know this before I return to Kent, where our old manor becomes a source of worry and expense because of endless necessary repairs."

"With your permission, sir, I have used my own initiative in this," said Dickon. "Chiefly in the matter of building a better fireplace in the living room and letting in more light wherever possible."

Moyle, with his keen interest in creative work of any kind, appeared to be well pleased.

"And he has mended the bedroom roof where it leaked between the beams," said Tansy proudly. "May we show you?"

Together the three of them mounted the winding stars and stood looking round the sunny little room. "What a pleasant place you have made of it!" commended Moyle. "And that ingeniously contrived shelf or desk against the wall." Instantly his beauty-loving eyes were attracted to the handsome leather-bound volume which lay upon it. "I see you have one of William Caxton's printed books!" he exclaimed, less surprised that Dickon should read it than that he should possess one.

"It is Earl Rivers' *Sayings of the Philosophers*," said Dickon proudly, unfastening the great metal clasp and opening it at the place where he had been reading.

For some absorbed minutes they stood there, talking about layout and translations and bindings, as booklovers will, until the falconer from next door called from the open doorway and Dickon excused himself and ran hurriedly downstairs.

Tansy, who was still standing on the small landing, saw how lovingly, almost enviously, their landlord turned the pages. Rich man's son as he is, he may not possess one, she thought. And then she saw him turn back to the title page where *Ricardus Rex* was written in the late king's clear, flowing hand. Unaware that he was being observed, he stood there staring down at it for a long time. Then closed it thoughtfully, refastening the clasp very carefully. When he turned and saw her he said nothing. But when he came down and joined the others in the living room, Tansy noticed that he was unusually silent and that he glanced several times at her husband in a puzzled sort of way. She wondered why he did not ask outright how Dickon had come by so rare a treasure. The wild thought even crossed her mind that he might not like to ask in case Dickon had stolen it. But, knowing how well the Moyle family served the new Lancastrian king, she did not mention the incident to Dickon in case the matter should worry him.

"Well, at least he made no objection to any of the alterations I have made," said Dickon with relief, when Moyle had gone to see the sick hawk his falconer had called about, before returning to London.

"He was clearly impressed and should be very thankful that you have so improved his property," said Tansy. "But you have been working too hard, Dickon, constructing that new vault at the Exchequer during the day and beginning work again here in the evenings the moment you have supped."

"And I have been neglecting the sweetest wife a man ever had," he said contritely, pulling her down onto his knees. "On Sunday we will forget all about building and take some of those delicious pasties of yours and some home-brewed elderberry and ride out to see the riverside monastery at Hampton."

But they never did. As Dickon was setting out for work next morning, they were surprised to see Red Lakin push open the garden gate and come running breathlessly up the path. "The master wants you!" he panted.

"Well, I am just coming, Red. What is the hurry?" said Dickon, glancing round at the scarcely risen sun as he fastened his saddle girth. "I am not late starting, surely?"

"Not to the Exchequer. He doesn't want you there. At Westminster."

"At Westminster?"

"He called to me, just as he was starting out, to tell you to meet him there. Master Vertue wants to see you."

"Master Vertue!" Dickon paused with one foot in a stirrup and Tansy stood stock still on her way down the path to bid him farewell.

"Yes, Dickon. I don't know what it can mean," said Red, recovering his breath. "All I can tell you is that Master Dale was wearing his best doublet, the one he wore when we had our examination, and that he wants you to meet him at the Vertues' lodgings by the Abbey."

"Oh, Dickon, you don't suppose it is some much more important work?" Tansy, the practical, ran to take Mopsy's reins and tether her to the mounting-block hook. "Better come in quickly and change into your best doublet, too. I pressed it only yesterday. And, Red," she called back over her shoulder, "you will find some cool beer in the brewhouse."

"If you get up behind me, Mopsy will carry you as far as Westminster, Red," offered Dickon, reluctantly wasting precious minutes while Tansy gave due wifely care to his appearance.

"If Master Vertue himself wants to see you—oh, I shall pray all the time you are gone that it may be something good!" whispered Tansy, proudly fastening his belt.

He caught her up in his arms and kissed her. "Yes, pray," he urged, "and when I come back I may have some good news for you!"

She tried to hold him back a moment. "And I may have some good news for you," she whispered. But he was gone, without hearing her, eagerly mounting her father's mare, with all his mind already straining forward to fresh work.

Chapter Twenty-two

Dickon rode as fast as he could along the river to Westminster, trying to quell his mounting excitement and curiosity. After dismounting Red Lakin and making impatient inquiries of a palace guard, he found the royal mason's lodgings and saw his master's horse already tethered outside. Some of the windows overlooked the Abbey, and he was all agog to see the interior. A servant admitted him, as if he was expected, and opened the door of a living room where three men were talking. So deep were they in discussion that Dickon stood, cap in hand, for some minutes before they noticed him.

He had time to notice the lovely beamed room and its occupants. Robert Vertue himself sat at a long table strewn with architect's designs and lists of figures which looked like quantitive surveys. He seemed to have aged considerably since Dickon had last seen him. It might have been because his brother William, standing beside him, was a younger edition of himself, or possibly, Dickon suspected, because he was a sick man.

Hurland Dale was standing on the other side of the table, picking up one design after another with suppressed excitement. Clearly he had been invited to look at them and was amazed by their merit. As soon as he looked up and became aware of Dickon's presence, he smiled encouragingly. "My man, Richard Broome, whom you asked me to send for," he explained to his companions. "You told me you remembered him, Master Robert."

"Certainly, I remember him, and his odd carving of the Holy Sepulcher," agreed the senior builder, waving Dickon towards the parchment-strewn table with a friendly gesture which seemed to include him in the conclave. "I sent for you, young man, because I am convinced not only of your ability but of your devotion to your craft. An apprentice who stops work only when the light fails must be thinking more of perfection than of profit. It takes a burning creative urge to drive one on regardless of time and hunger."

"Robert is gathering a small nucleus of assistants for a very large undertaking," explained his more matter-of-fact brother.

"Particularly craftsmen who use their tools but not their tongues," warned Dale, knowing by long experience how well his maddening reticent erstwhile pupil qualified for the part. "And, as I have already told you, I shall not stand in your way of advancement."

By the rules of their Guild he could not, now that Dickon was fully qualified, and they both knew that he hoped to gain professionally through obliging the Vertue brothers, but Dickon's sense of obligation still remained. "Is it something secret which these gentlemen are about to build?" he asked, puzzled by the aura of importance and guessing that, as the King's mason was in charge of it, the project must have something to do with fortifications.

"It is not so much what we build, as what we shall first have to pull down," explained Master William. He moved to the window, as he spoke, and beckoned to the young journeyman to follow him. "You see the Lady Chapel over there?"

"Why, yes. Built in the thirteenth century, it was, and part of the pride of the Abbey."

"Exactly," agreed Master William. "And that is why there will be such an outcry when we pull it down."

"Pull it down!" echoed Dickon, in horror."

"Like yourself, Broome, the Londoners will probably make loud protest about it. But the King is set on doing this, and, after seeing some of these wonderful designs for a new chapel, even the Abbot of Westminster is half persuaded."

Seeing the genuine concern on Dickon's face, the elder Vertue took the trouble to explain the matter as carefully as he would have to any senior architect. Through long experience he knew that the only way to draw out the best in his assistants was to share with them his own thoughts, and he had high hopes of this unknown young mason who could, at a moment's notice, produce a piece of carving worthy of the finest setting.

"I well understand your feelings, Broome, and those of many Londoners who have known and loved the Lady Chapel all their lives. And no one knows better than I the grief it will be to the nuns who serve it. But they will build elsewhere with the fabulous price which his Grace has arranged to pay. And the fact is, the present fabric is so sadly in need of repair that it might well cost Abbot Islip almost as much as to rebuild. And, then again, one must consider the cause for which the King so urgently desires it.'"

"But why, sir, must his Grace have that particular site?" asked Dickon, weaned from all initial shyness.

"Because it is for the reinterment—the homecoming, as one might say—of a king."

"A king?" Dickon scarcely breathed the words, being almost tempted to believe that after all this time the Tudor's conscience might be troubling hil.

"A murdered king whose present resting place is unworthy of him."

The words fostered still further the wildly improbable idea. Dickon's thoughts went back to the Gray Friars' garden beside the Soar. A pleasant resting place, kindly tended, but utterly unworthy of the sovereign who had ridden out with such splendor over Bow Bridge and fought with such high courage. Could it be that his poor mangled body would be honored and brought to Westminster?

"The last Lancastrian king, Henry the Sixth. That gentle saint who was murdered by Yorkist venom in the Tower," Dale hastened to explain, having known Dickon long enough to guess where his dangerous sympathies, like those of many others, really lay.

Dickon immediately knew himself for an optimistic fool. No usurper could afford to stir up past loyalties. "Forget all that I have told you," his father had said. Forget! Forget! he was always saying to himself. But it was never easy. By an effort of will, back from Leicester to the sober room at Westminster came his foolish thoughts. The designs and models became just an extraordinarily good job of work to him, the august personages about the table a sign of unexpected, marvelously good fortune. With all his carefully garnered technical knowledge he listened intelligently and appreciatively to their discussions, even putting in a question at times which they answered with kindly patience. It would be wonderful to work with such men, where nothing was petty and no detail unimportant, where one would be learning all the time.

For a few brief moments his mind went back to Tansy,

praying at home for his success, and to his gaily flung half promise that he might bring her back good news. Now he was warmed by the certainty that he would have the joy of bringing news beyond their highest hopes that very evening. How happy they would be! The cottage would still serve them. He would have work in Westminster for years. Progressive work, which would be talked of throughout the land. His fortune and—wildly alluring thought—even his fame might be made. Everything that he had, every skill that he might acquire, would be put enthusiastically into this project of the Vertues'. Given in good measure to the last glimmer of daylight, he vowed smilingly, out of gratitude.

He was carried away by their talk of roof vaulting and dazzled by the prospect of carved statues. But it all seemed of a richness, and designed on such a scale as to be too large and sumptuous even for the tomb of a king. Moreover it seemed that a dispute was going on between Westminster and Windsor about the removal of poor Henry's corpse from the royal chapel there, a dispute of which the issue was still so uncertain that it must be referred to the Pope himself. To pull down and to build on such a scale on the chance of gaining his Holiness' permission to re-inter seemed to Dickon the height of imbecility, and in all that Henry Tudor had so far done he had shown himself to be no fool.

While he wondered about this, the Vertue brothers went on talking about vaults: vaults beneath a marble tiled floor. As far as Dickon knew, all important personages were buried above ground, their coffins placed within their carved tombs. Wooden effigies, clothed in the best garments of the deceased and complete with painted waxen faces, which had been made like masks upon the dead by chandlers, were placed on biers beside them until moths or time destroyed them.

"It is a new idea to put the coffins on shelves beneath the tombs," explained Dale, seeing how puzzled he was.

"But so—so impersonal," complained Dickon. "When one looks at a beautifully wrought tomb one likes to think that the body of the person it commemorates is in it."

Robert Vertue leaned forward, holding out to him the rough sketch of a grand tomb with stairs leading down to an immense vault in some crypt below. "But, you see, Broome, the tomb as we know it has limitations. There would be room for man and wife, and perhaps their children. But with this idea of family vaults, there would be ample room for more than one generation. For—shall we say?—a whole dynasty."

Dickon saw that perfectly but was still mystified. "But poor, simple, saintly Henry the Sixth. His wife and son are both dead. And he seems to have been, by all accounts, a slender weakling." Dickon waved a hand towards the drawing and treated the master mason to his most attractive smile. "His slender bones could scarcely fill all this."

There was a suggestion of embarrassment in the ensuing silence, so that for the first time Dickon felt that they had been holding back something of importance from him. But either because Robert Vertue was bemused by the smile, or because he needed everyone's full cooperation in order to get the work set in train before his own strength failed, he decided to take the young mason into his complete confidence. "You may as well know now as later, since Master Dale vouches for your discretion," he said, leaning back rather wearily in his chair. "The honor to be paid to that other Lancastrian monarch is only a beginning. A popular move, perhaps, to gain the Abbot's consent and to raise the necessary money. For what we are going to do will cost vast sums of money, hundreds of those shining new sovereigns which the King is having minted. It will be an age-long memorial to the Tudor family, to a whole flourishing dynasty. And now that his first son is born his Grace is all the more anxious that we should overcome the initial obstacles and begin."

Slowly Dickon laid the wonderful drawing down on the table. Slowly full comprehension seeped into his brain. Incredulously, he strove to accept it. "You mean, this will be Henry the Seventh's chapel, to house his family tomb?" he stammered, too aghast to put his question more formally.

Robert Vertue, seeing him so overcome, warmed to what he supposed to be the astounded excitement of his questioner. "Yes. And every spare moment he devotes to it. Although it may be months before we can clear the site and begin, he is already making plans and inventories with his own hand. He is a better businessman than many of his Treasurer's clerks, and a genius at raising money. He is as proud of his kingly Welsh ancestry through Cadwallader as of his blood through John of Gaunt, Duke of Lancaster, third son of King Edward the Third. This tomb and chapel will hold him forever in men's memories as the founder of a great Tudor dynasty."

While the mutilated body of the last Plantagenet lies mouldering and unmourned beside the Soar! Dickon found himself carrying on a silent conversation, as Tansy used to when she dared not comment aloud to her stepmother.

"Abbot Islip himself is beginning to be caught up in our vision, and he is no mean builder," went on Robert Vertue. "There will be a fine east window; the roof vaulting will be talked of from here to Rome. You will meet some of the finest architects, designers in glass, joiners, and bronze workers in the world. The King is thinking of persuading the celebrated Torrigiano to come from Italy to make the actual effigies on the tomb itself. He has even thought up an apt and effective device to be carved recurringly upon the corbels or possibly upon the surrounding grill."

"What sort of a device?" stammered Dickon, accustomed only to the old escutcheon of leopards couchants and fleurs-de-lys used by the Plantagenets.

"A golden crown resting on a thornbush, in memory of Bosworth," put in William Vertue, unwittingly adding the final factor to a half-formed decision.

My father's treacherously stolen crown, echoed Dickon's mind. And I am expected to decorate a Tudor's memorial by carving them—recurringly!

"It will not be only men of note who will be working on it. There will be other young men, too," said Robert Vertue kindly, noting the young mason's silence. "Men of promise like you, because we must keep alive the art of building in this land. I myself may not have long to live, but before I go I long to see something of this beauty rising. And after my brother and I are dead, who knows but what you yourself might rise to be King Henry's master mason?"

Dickon saw the other two men looking at him with fresh interest, almost with awe. But I would sooner die than be Henry Tudor's mason! said his inmost mind.

They went on talking technicalities and discussing how much labor they would need, while he stood there cold and still as one of the statues they had described.

Presently Hurland Dale thanked them for inviting him to

see their plans and, as the meeting seemed about to break up,
turned with an air of relaxation to depart. "Well, Broome,
you are made," he said cheerily, clapping him on the shoulder, "and no one is more pleased than I."

"One moment, Dale, I shall need you," broke in the busi-
nesslike voice of William Vertue, who was gathering up his
estimates. "I need scarcely tell you, Broome, that it may be
weeks before we start work. We will let you know, of course.
I understand you live at Richmond, not far from my brother's
country home. But there is a contract to sign, including a
promise to keep silence about all we have told you until such
time as it becomes common knowledge. You had better sign
now, while Master Dale is here to witness it." He held out a
pen with one hand, while holding down an unrolled sheet of
parchment with the other. "Come, sign, man, so that we can
all get to our dinners," he added impatiently, tired of holding
out the pen.

"Come, come," urged Dale, shamed by his protégé's slow-
ness. "There is no difficulty. Builders' contracts are not in
Latin now."

No, my father changed all that, thought Dickon. Not that
it would make any difference to me if it were. But he knew
his tenants and soldiers personally and was human enough to
appreciate their difficulties.

"All you have to do is to sign here," went on Dale, with a
guiding finger on the document. " 'I, Richard Broome, agree
to give my services as a mason in the building of King Henry
the Seventh's chapel at such and such a salary,' or whatever
the exact words are."

"And since the King himself will be paying your salary, it
will be considerable!" commented Master William drily.

To take money to glorify the Lancastrian dynasty, I should
need to be a second Judas! thought Dickon.

"Well, young man, are you struck dumb?" demanded the
King's mason testily.

Dickon moved, then, and came closer. He looked across
the table at the aging master mason with heartfelt admiration. "Sir, if I lived a hundred years I could not express my
gratitude, or the deep—the humble—gratification I feel because you have judged my work worthy to be of use to you.
But I can neither accept nor sign."

Unconsciously he opened his fine skilled hands in a dramatic gesture of renunciation, as if he were relinquishing something as precious as the Holy Grail.

Dale stared at him aghast. "Sirs," he intervened. "He is always like this. It is lack of self-confidence, nervousness, I know not what. You remember, Master Vertue, how he was before his examination?"

"Yes, I remember. And I understood. The humility of an artist who would give all he has, but fears it is not good enough." He looked at the young man, marveling how one so unhappy could look so coldly proud. "But this time I do not understand. It is not that he *fears* to sign but that for some mawkish reason he will not." With quiet dignity he rose from his chair and turned away, finished with the matter.

"You mean, you refuse?" exclaimed the two other men.

Dickon turned to Hurland Dale almost pleadingly. "It is something which I cannot do," he began, but Dale cut him short in envious fury.

"It is something which any other jumped-up nobody would give his eyes to do!"

"I would sooner go on as I am," Dickon forced himself to say.

But Hurland Dale flushed with anger. "That you will not do, by Heaven!" he vowed. "Ingrate that you are, you have made a fool of me and insulted the greatest men in our craft. I wash my hands of you."

"Let the dog lie, who is too dull to hunt his chances," soothed Master William. "There are plenty of others. Though none, I fear, from your kennel, friend Hurland."

They bent over a list of names, discussing them, striking out a name here and there. Dickon left them at it and walked blindly towards the door. As he opened it he looked back at the comfortable room, comparing his feelings of elation, when he had first seen it so short a time ago, with his present misery. He knew himself to be infinitely worse off than if he had never entered it. Already, to the three men at the summit of his craft, he no longer existed. There would never be any niche for his name upon any future scroll of fame.

Chapter Twenty-three

"No one in London will give me work now that Hurland Dale has dismissed me. It is not fair to you. But say that you understand," entreated Dickon. "Say that you know I could not bring myself to help beautify a memorial to the Tudor."

"I think that I should have despised you if you had," answered Tansy slowly. "Though I am sure that many, placed as you are, would have done it for the dazzling prospects and the money."

"There cannot be many who are placed as I am," said Dickon bitterly.

It was long after midnight, and he and Tansy were still crouched over the dying fire in the cottage where they had known such happiness.

When he had first come home and told her, all their high hopes had turned to gall. He had stumbled in from the stable, and she had not stirred. Although she had been waiting for him all day, she had not even recognized his step, which was usually so firm and buoyant. But when she looked up and saw his face she had run to him, comprehending his misery, before ever he spoke a word. He had looked much as he had after the mob had chased him in Leicester—wan with strain and suffering—and she had pulled him inside and shut the door as she had then. "I have lost even what work I had," he had said, with complete and instant honesty. She had drawn him to a chair, brought him reviving wine, and listened with her whole compassionate heart, just as she had listened to his story after Bosworth.

"I am a poor sort of husband. You would be well rid of me," he said. "It is not right that you, too, should pay the price of bastard Plantagenet birth."

"You are the husband I want," soothed Tansy, kneeling on the floor beside him. "And if the celebrated Vertues sent for you, what went wrong? Why am I to be pitied?"

He had told her then, word for word, everything that had happened. The shock of it had nearly caused her to swoon, but she rested her forehead on his knee and said nothing until the faintness passed.

"I could have grown rich—famous, perhaps—by making a fine monument to my father's murderer," he said more than once.

"King Richard was killed in battle," corrected Tansy.

"As he would have wished to be. But it was murder by treachery. By sheer quality as a soldier, he should have won that battle. From the little hill where I stood I saw him hack his way through the Tudor's bodyguard, one man against scores, until the Stanleys betrayed him and struck him down. Only a few more paces, and he would have killed this usurping Tudor in fair fight, and the Tudor knew it. Singlehanded, he was no match in skill and courage. And had he been slain the treacherous Stanleys would have pretended they were still on Richard's side. Such grasping curs must always be on the winning side. And I, had I accepted this alluring offer, should have been a bigger traitor than any of them. A Judas, betraying my master for money."

"It would not have been for the money alone," said Tansy, with maturing insight. "Through love I can share your feelings, but I doubt if any uncreative person can know how much it cost a craftsman like you to refuse."

"It was a terrible temptation," admitted Dickon more simply, beginning to relax. "But had I succumbed I know that I should not have been able to put in my best work. Something would have held me back. And that would have been perhaps the worst punishment of all. Anyway, my sweet love," he added, achieving a tender smile, "I am glad that the awful moment of decision is over."

"And I shall always be proud beyond words that you did not succumb."

Tansy had coaxed him to sup then, and made some pretence of doing so herself. He had eaten ravenously, with no idea what he swallowed. Between them, they even achieved a kind of rueful merriment. "You must think that my sole accomplishment is to refuse delectable offers," he said. "That fantastic pretender business, and now this." Unfortunately, "this" was his whole life, and he almost broke down, covering his face with both hands. "I, who worked so hard as a 'prentice and was so sure I would achieve something worth while!"

"But how you were handicapped, my love!" consoled Tansy, drawing his bowed head against her breast. "One offer was made, and the other refused, because of your strange birth."

They had sat by the fire, far into the night, trying to face frightening reality with common sense. In those quiet hours Dickon came to learn that even the fierce, tender ecstasy of physical love was by no means the crown of marriage, and even to guess, perhaps, that any woman who is capable of motherhood must always have known this. He realized that although he had more wisdom of the mind, Tansy had a deeper intuition of the heart. And in the close communion of shared difficulty and disappointment, the spiritual side of their marriage was consummated that night.

"Are you certain that Master Dale will not take you back?" she asked, after they had sat silent for a while.

"A man does not easily forgive being made to look foolish before his superiors. Nor condone such apparent ingratitude. No one could expect him to."

As they talked quietly in the firelight, Tansy saw her husband's profile grow set and strong again against the glow. "We must accept it. The whole trade will hear that he has dismissed me. No builder in London will employ me."

"You are at home now, where no one condemns you."

"Tansy, Tansy, what a sweet fool you were to marry me!"

"The problems that kings create when they beget illegitimate sons!" she sighed pitifully, smoothing back his disordered hair as he bent over her. "I have often wondered, Dickon, do you not sometimes wish that King Richard had never told you?"

He turned her hand over and kissed the palm slowly, giving the matter thought. "No. Particularly as he cared for my upbringing. Knowing has made me somebody. Having no people, no background, I was nothing before. I grew accustomed to it, of course. But sometimes when I heard other fellows talk of going home for May Day or Twelfth Night, or saw their mothers smile at them——"

"Oh, Dickon, that must be why I sometimes feel like both wife and mother to you!"

"You are the whole world to me."

"Except your craft. Alas! I cannot make up for what you have lost in that."

"No. Nothing and no one can. But I must learn to face it. It is no longer a matter of ambition and high success. The simple facts are that we must eat, and that I have no employment at all."

"We can live for quite a long time on the money from the Boar."

"Do you think I have no pride, Tansy?"

"You are eaten up with it." She laid a hand quickly on his arm, to wipe out the asperity of her words. "But it is the right kind of pride. And, oddly enough, it is counterbalanced by your true humility."

Seeing how tired she looked, he rose and lit a candle to light them up the stairs. "Even though our whole world be changed, we must get some rest. Tomorrow I will go out and look for work," he said.

Most of the night they lay awake, each, for the other's sake, pretending to sleep. He could not have heard me, when I called after him yesterday that I might have good news for him, thought Tansy, as the light of dawn began to glimmer through the willows along the riverbank. If he had heard he would surely have asked me about it. He loves me too much just to forget. But I cannot tell him now. Since he has no wages coming in, perhaps my hope that we are going to have a child is not such good news after all!

She rose with the sun to sweep the hearth and set out the platters for their breakfast, but Dickon did not come down. She found him lying, hands clasped behind his head, staring at the ceiling. "I thought you were going to look for work," she said, almost reproachfully.

He swung his legs over the side of the bed and transferred his gaze to her troubled face. "I have been thinking, sweet. As we decided last night, it would be quite useless for me to see any London builders. They would want a reference, and the only name I could give would be Hurland Dale's. And one may not work outside one's Guild. I must go to Oxford, where new colleges are being built. There is great demand for good masons there."

"Oxford! Leave here, and go to Oxford!" repeated Tansy,

looking round the room they had striven to make so pleasant and feeling as if the bottom were dropping out of her world.

"I will go alone first and get employment, and then find some place for us both. Don't look so desolate, my dear. You remember how fortunate we were in Oxford before."

Tansy did not answer. She had not been married then. Once one was married and carrying a man's child, one did not expect to be separated like this.

"I should not be long. A few weeks, perhaps," Dickon was saying.

"And suppose Master John Moyle comes to hear of this, through Tom or someone?"

"You mean—oh, no, Tansy! He would not turn you out. Not until my return, at any rate. He is too fine a man. And hasn't his sister always shown herself to be your friend?"

He pulled on some clothes, and they discussed his idea in more detail while breaking their fast. "If you think this best, go soon," said Tansy, thinking only that the sooner he went the sooner he would be back.

"I will go this very day, so put me up some food for the journey," he said, with all his father's decisiveness. And with all his own pride, he refused to take any of her money for his needs. "I shall soon be earning there, even if I have to take unskilled labor until I find something better," he assured her.

His determined cheerfulness brought tears to Tansy's eyes, and seeing them his decision momentarily waned. "I hate to leave you here alone. Specially at nights."

"I shall not be afraid," lied Tansy, trying to emulate his courage. "After all, the falconer and his wife are not far away."

"How I wish Will Jordan could be with you!" exclaimed Dickon, when his tools had been carefully greased and wrapped and put into their special box, and both his saddlebags packed.

"He will be leaving London tomorrow, or his pupils will have forgotten everything they ever learned." The thought of school-books carried her on to something more erudite. "What about *Sayings of the Philosophers?*"

"I must leave that in your care."

"It is so valuable. . . . Dickon, do you know what I

should like above everything? If Jod could come, instead of returning to Leicester with Master Jordan."

"To guard my book instead of money bags? A splendid idea! But for me the main advantage of his coming would be to guard you. Before turning left onto the Oxford road I will go on to Cheapside and ask him."

"He told me he had been hiring himself only for odd work in Leicester. He wasn't happy at the Blue Boar after I left. Do you think——"

"Yes?"

"That we could keep him with us? Even after you have work, and we are together again, I mean. He could look after the horses, and do the fires in winter——"

Dickon noticed how pale she was, but put it down to the shock and anxiety they had been through. "I should have thought of it before," he said gently. "As Tom always says, the old fellow would commit murder for you. I will ask him to ride out before nightfall."

The thought cheered her immediately. "Give my dear love to Will Jordan, and to the Goodyears." But on second thoughts, she wished he need not see them. "At an inn, with so many people going and coming, and Red Lakin dropping in, they are sure to hear some garbled version of what has happened."

"I suppose they will all think me mad," agreed Dickon, miserably. "But I don't have to explain my actions to anyone but you. Surely, a man is free to choose his own work. I have done nothing to be ashamed of. The shame would have been if I, a Plantagenet, had accepted."

But neither of them would ever be able to explain this. And, womanlike, Tansy wanted others to think well of her man.

Parting so soon after their marriage was a cruel wrench, but Dickon promised her it would not be for long.

Before nightfall Jod came, and she was partly comforted. The next day was full of small homely happinesses, arranging for the old ostler's simple needs in one of the lofts above the partially disused stables. "I never had nothin' but bare boards and straw afore," he said, looking almost reverently at the woven mat and truckle bed she had provided. "But best of all will be able to stay along o' you, Mistress Tansy—or Mistress Broome, as I should recollect to say. And to have Pippin and the mare again to care for."

"You can take things more easily now, without a yard full of horses and impatient customers shouting for them all at once," she told him, noticing how frail he looked.

"But I can still chop wood, and fetch and carry for you and Master Broome. An' mostly I can fend for myself."

"But I shall see to it that you have at least one good hot meal a day," insisted Tansy, feeling that part of her old home life had come back.

But Jod was not her only visitor. A day or two later, when she was sitting mending her husband's workaday hose, she heard a familiar voice, clear and friendly, calling to Jod, then a quick step on the path, and tall Tom Hood was ducking his head to come through the open door. A finely dressed Tom these days, and at the moment full of urgent indignation. "What is this I hear about Dickon losing his job?" he demanded, throwing his fashionably plumed velvet cap across the table.

"Master Dale no longer wants him," answered Tansy, trying to keep her voice and fingers steady.

"Then it is true?" Tom threw himself down on the fireside settle. "Oh, my poor Tansy! I put off a deputation of defense people from the Cinque Ports and came out immediately to see if I could do anything to help you both. Where is he?"

"Gone to Oxford."

"To Oxford!"

"Where there is much building going on. To try to find work." As she crossed the room to put away hose and wool, Tom's quick eye noticed that she walked almost like an old woman, with all the delicious spring and youth gone out of her. "He would not get any in London—now."

"But he is one of the finest craftsmen! He passed his examination so splendidly! And that redheaded friend of his rushed into the Boar last evening with some wild story about the Vertues themselves sending for him. And I thought, 'Good God! The Vertues. He must be made!' And afterwards I heard this rumor that Dale had dismissed him. The man who told me was in his cups, so I simply laughed at it. I knew Dickon was as well on his way to success in his craft as—

well, as I am in mine." Tom leaned forward on the settle.
"Tell me, did Hurland Dale make difficulties about losing
him? He was the best craftsman he was ever likely to have. I
can tell you now that most of the features in that house on
the Strand which pleased the Moyles were things which
Dickon had either designed or made."

"Far from making difficulties, Master Dale had done everything to help him. That was why he was so furious. . . ."

"Why, what happened, Tansy? Did the Vertue brothers
really send for him?"

There was nothing for it but to tell him. "They offered him
some wonderful work, of which I may not speak. Something
for the nation, like your new appointment as arms adviser to
the King's bowmen. And—he refused."

"Oh, come, Tansy! You mean he wasn't quite good enough.
Oh, I know your loyalty! For who," he asked, with a shame-
faced grin, "should know it more gratefully than I? When you
first met Amy, I mean. And now you just can't bring yourself
to admit that Dickon failed. But, my dear, I do assure you
there is nothing to be ashamed of. The Standard of the master masons of England is renowned all over Europe."

"It is very high indeed, and he more than satisfied them.
They offered him this important work," repeated Tansy, with
golden head held high. "And he refused."

Tom sprang to his feet. "Refused! You really mean it! He
had a chance to work for the King's mason, and he refused?"

"He had a reason," said Tansy, standing wretchedly by the
window.

A fury of exasperation rose in him against his friend,
largely on her account. "It would need to be a very strong
reason," he began, almost contemptuously.

"It was," said Tansy quietly.

He knew her well enough to be sure that he would hear no
more. "For a nameless young man of any guts or ambition at
all to refuse a chance to rise to the very top of his profession
is something which I simply cannot understand."

"I am quite sure, Tom, that you could not understand!" she
said angrily, pushing his fine plumed cap aside so that it fell
to the floor.

He accepted her estimation of his character with a shrug.
"And now he leaves you here alone. Well, it is none of my

business, except in so far as it affects you, for whom I have always cared. And I do care, Tansy. Oh, not in the way I thought at first," he added, careful not to touch her. "But even if I ever win Amy as my wife—and I adore her—I shall always know that you are the finest woman I have ever known."

His surprising words, and their obvious sincerity, were such a heartwarming comfort to her that she turned away to hide a rush of tears. "Thank you, dear Tom. It is not true, of course, what you say of me. But that you should feel that way means so much to me. Particularly just now, when things are going wrong. I only hope," she added, with a sudden radiant smile shining through the tears, "that you may one day find out just how fine my husband is!"

He stood for a moment or two picking thoughtfully at the broken feather in his cap. "I think I do know, really," he said slowly. "There is something unusual about him, almost as if he were set in a finer mold than most of us. Some of our mutual friends feel it, too. Somehow, he is both sensitive and strong. Quiet and ordinary in his behavior, yet when he chooses he can make men heed his briefest word. He always entered into every kind of sport with the rest of us, and yet there is—an apartness about him. As if he knew, sometimes, an intense loneliness."

Tansy looked at Tom with new appreciation. She had always admired his lively quickness of mind, loved his infectious gaiety, but never before had she credited him with such serious insight, or with thinking any more deeply than he spoke. "It is for me to prevent that apartness—that loneliness—from pressing too heavily upon him," she said. And then, because it was not usual for them to be so solemn, she added lightly, "Will you not stay and eat, master fletcher?"

"*Non, non, ma chere,*" he refused, treating her to his new French mannerisms. "A glass of your homemade wine, *et voila tout.* I am a busy man these days."

"And deserve to be," said Tansy, rising generously above her own bitter disappointment. "That is why it was so very kind of you to come."

"When you want me I will always come."

Tansy drove from her mind the thought that when she had wanted him most he had, quite reasonably, put ambition first.

She would always be unutterably glad that it was Dickon who had come. But across the brimming tankard she handed him they smiled, liking each other better than they had ever done before. "I am sorry I broke the fine feather in your cap, Tom," she apologized, wishing that she had not hit out at it because it seemed symbolic.

Chapter Twenty-four

Tansy was so overjoyed when Dickon came home from Oxford a month later that she scarcely worried because he said nothing about any fresh employment. He was very quiet, with that ruminative sort of quietness which suggested that his thoughts were elsewhere. His preoccupation made her feel left out, so that more than ever she missed Tom's easy talk and laughter. Yet Dickon himself did not seem to be particularly worried or unhappy.

"It was good of him to come, especially when he is doing such important work," he said, when she told him of Tom's visit. "And I am relieved that Moyle's bailiff asked no awkward questions when he came, soon after I left, to collect the rent."

"Then you don't think we shall be moving to Oxford?" asked Tansy, realizing that things were beginning to look grave for them, and that her own money would not last for ever. She wondered how, if her husband had returned with no prospects, he could seem so disinterested—so concerned with something else. "Just what did you do all those weeks you were away?" she asked, after he had been home for nearly two days. "You have told me so little about it. Nor," she added, out of her private hurt, "have you asked much about me."

He was all contrition at once. "Something happened which has put money, employment, and everything else out of my head."

"Even me, your wife?"

"I am afraid so, at the time. Tansy, it was one of those extraordinary coincidences. I still can't believe it really happened. And before I talked about it, even to you—and I could not speak of it to anyone else—I had to sort out my mind." He sat down on the settle beside her, absently drawing onto his knee the small white kitten which Amy Moyle had sent her by the bailiff for company.

"All you told me yesterday was that you had been in

charge of repairs at some big mansion," she said, settling herself within the loving warmth of his arm.

"Yes. I never worked on any of the colleges at all. Directly I arrived and began making inquiries I was told that a responsible mason was needed out at Minster Lovell."

"Minster Lovell!" exclaimed Tansy. "Why, that must be the home of poor Lord Lovell, God rest his soul!"

"Yes. The name attracted me at once, of course. A fine mansion it is! And, like the homes of many other Yorkists who fought at Bosworth, it was confiscated by the Tudor."

"Given to one of his supporters, I suppose?"

"This particularly fine mansion he is giving to his uncle, Jasper Tudor, I think. Or to his precious mother, the Lady Margaret Beaufort."

"They say he thinks far more of her than of his wife."

"It may well be, since Queen Elizabeth is my father's niece, whereas the Lady Margaret is married to Lord Stanley. Anyway, he has given her so many mansions that she cannot use them all."

"While some folks need a roof over their heads!"

"So Minster Lovell stands empty, except for an old caretaker. And naturally it is getting into a sad state of disrepair. I was given a couple of indifferent journeymen and told by some royal official what work was necessary. Food was supplied to us from a cottage on the estate, and we were left very much to ourselves. One of those skinflint jobs it was, and we had finished in just over a fortnight. I wasn't worrying because the contractor who asked me to do it had promised me plenty of better work if I went straight back to him in Oxford. I was going to look for lodgings for the two of us as soon as I arrived." Rubbing the kitten's soft fur, Dickon sat staring in front of him. "But I never did go back."

"Why ever not?"

"Because I stayed—for something which I was privileged to do. I didn't seek it, this time. It just happened. And I wasn't even paid for it—not in money, that is."

Tansy sprang up and seized the astonished kitten from the lulling movement of his fingers. None too gently she set it down on the floor beside a bowl of milk. Anything to rouse him from his mood of crazy reminiscence.

"Dickon, I implore you, don't be so mysterious! Do you

know, you have been quite different since you came home?
Your mind is only half here. And yet"—she stood with hands
on hips and head on one side, studying his sensitive face—"in
some strange way you look more settled, more contented than
I have ever before seen you."

He rose and pulled her down beside him. "How well you
understand me!"

"I doubt if anyone really does," retorted Tansy.

"I warned you, did I not, my love, that you would find me
difficult? But here is the coincidence that so shook me. The
house was not really unoccupied. Lord Lovell himself was
there, in hiding."

Exasperation gave way to amazement. "Then he wasn't
killed at Stoke?"

"I think I realized almost from the first that there was
someone. . . . There was a room at the end of one of the
wings with shelves full of books. I confess that when the
other men had packed up their tools and gone I used to stay
and browse. I had never before had such a chance. Sometimes it seemed to me that one or another of them had been
moved. Or a marker put at some different page. And then
early one morning I was up on the roof seeing to some broken
slates and found myself looking down into a narrow walled
garden, which I hadn't realized existed. Some sort of private
garden for the monks, I suppose, when the place had been a
monastery. I saw a man walking there. I could only conclude
that he was some local friend who had the use of it and who
perhaps came into the library sometimes, by arrangement
with the old caretaker. There was a locked door in the library
which might well have opened into another room or into that
garden.

"And then, the last evening I was there, I went back into
this room where the books were to finish a chapter of *La Forteresse de Foy*. I was completely absorbed in it when I heard
the sound of a key being turned cautiously in a lock. I swung
round to find the door open and a man framed in the entrance to a smaller room.

"I stood there, like a frightened fool, twisting the wedding
ring on my finger as a kind of talisman against the supernatural. But he was no ghost. He was the same man I had seen in
the garden. And he looked far more frightened than I. But at

the same time unutterably glad. To my amazement he called me by my name. 'Richard!' he exclaimed, with a kind of awed joy.

"I stammered some sort of apology, something about loving books. And then, completely astounded that he should seem to know me, I asked, 'But how did you know my name, sir?'

"The gladness was dying out of his face by then. And the strange wonderment. He came farther into the room and looked at me more closely. 'Then it is your name? What is your full name?'

" 'Richard Broome,' I told him.

" 'Broome. Yes, it could well be. But don't do that!'

"He spoke as sharply as if he were in sudden pain. 'Don't do what, sir?' I asked, horribly conscious that I had been taking liberties with his precious books.

" 'Don't stand there turning that damned ring on your finger. *He* always did that in moments of stress or thoughtfulness. And what with that and your facsimile of a face, I really believed for a moment——'

"He came and perched on the table, shading his face with his hand, so that I shouldn't see how badly he had been shaken. But he soon pulled himself together, with a shrug and a smile. 'Broome. Of course, I remember. Broome for Plantagenet. He sometimes used the name himself, when we slipped away from court or camp and he didn't want to be known. And God knows, he had time for too few of such carefree hours! You are so like him at that age that you can only be his son. That by-blow he was so concerned about during his first campaign, no doubt.'

"It was then that I knew he must be Francis, Lord Lovell. Only you had said he was stocky, and this man was almost gaunt. But I remembered that he must have fled from place to place, through Flanders or France, then back to England, in danger of his life, and was probably half starving. At the same moment that this occurred to my bemused mind, he said quite abruptly and without ceremony, 'Can you lay your hands on any food, young Dickon?' He trusted me like that from the first moment of our meeting.

"To my joy I remembered that in my eagerness to finish the work and return next day to Oxford, I had been too busy to finish the food in my bag. I hurried to fetch it and when I returned, Lord Lovell had seated himself in what was, I suppose, his own chair by the window and the evening light was on his face, so that I saw how worn he was. 'The old caretaker has worked for my family all his life. He brings me what he can get from loyal cottagers on the estate, but now, with workmen hammering all over the house, he is afraid of giving away my hiding place,' he explained. And then, as I was rummaging in my bag for bread and meat, he saw my tools. 'So you are one of them? I could not imagine how you came to be here, reading one of my favorite books.'

" 'Yes, I am a mason,' I told him.

" 'Thank God for that!' he said, and sat munching ravenously until the last crumb was gone, while I wondered what caused such fervent gratitude for my particular calling.

" 'I wish I had more, sir,' I said, grinning at the obvious inadequacy of my offering.

"He grinned back and motioned me to sit opposite to him. 'Now that your noisy mates have gone, old Jacques will be able to bring me something in the morning,' he said. In all the two weeks I was with him it never once seemed to occur to him to treat me as anything but an equal—as his friend Richard's son.

"He knew that Minster Lovell had been given to the Tudor's mother and feared that, now repairs had been ordered, the place would no longer be left empty. 'And that will make it more dangerous for me,' he said.

" 'Everyone thinks that you were killed in battle,' I told him.

" 'I know,' he said. 'It is probably only because of that I was eventually able to make my way back here. Actually I escaped and swam across the Trent on my horse.'

" 'You mean you had the glorious effrontery to come and hide in your own house?'

" 'Surely the last place where any pestering Lancastrian is likely to look for me?'

" 'Too true,' I had to agree. Color had come back into his face, and some of the devil-may-care expression into his laughing blue eyes, and I thought what a wonderful companion he must have been! 'But surely, milord, you do not intend to go on staying here *now*, with people living in the house?' I asked.

" 'It is still the safest place from Henry's spies. And I have made this a center of our plans. But I must have that door blocked up. That is why during the last few days I have been wondering how, cooped up here, I could find a mason whom I could trust. Trust beyond bribes or blabbing in his cups, I mean. For it is not only my own worthless life now, but notes and documents'—he nodded to the small inner secret room, in which I could see a table strewn with papers—'which would endanger the lives of many ardent Yorkists whose names would surprise you.'

" 'You know that I will do this,' I said instantly. 'But how would you get in or out? You would be immured.'

" 'You must find me some way to get out into the little gar-den. It is surrounded by a wood thick with shrubs and great spreading trees. Through that one can get out onto the Ox-ford road. But I do not know how to make an exit in the stone wall which will not show. One would need to be a clever mason, Dickon, to work that out, and also to brick up the inside wall so that it looks like the original.'

" 'Leave that to me, sir,' I said.

" 'You sound very confident.'

"So then I told him about my examination and Master Vertue's offer and my mad refusal. And that, I think, brought us closer together than anything else could have done.

" 'We should have to begin immediately, and work at night.' 'This very night,' I said, saying farewell to all my high hopes in Oxford.

"I was amply rewarded when he said, 'How like your fa-ther you sound!'

"And, Tansy, when he said 'we' it was no polite expression. Belted earl as he was, and King's bosom friend, we worked in shirt and hose together like slaves. Apart from my hours with you, it was the happiest time of my life.

" 'Let us go out into the garden now before the light fails,' he suggested.

"After examining the walls from inside the little room and from outside in the wood, I decided to hollow out a small passage space and low inward swinging stone doorway in one of the buttresses.

" 'This buttress, beneath the biggest tree,' he suggested. 'It will be better hidden.'

"I demurred, I remember. 'If that tree should fall you would be trapped,' I pointed out.

"'How could such a mighty beech tree fall?' he argued.

"'It could be struck by lightning in a storm,' I said. He laughed at me for the world's worst pessimist, of course."

"You have probably saved him from discovery and death," said Tansy, marveling as much as he and Lord Lovell about such a God-sent coincidence. "And you must have learned more about your father than you can ever have hoped." She could judge what this meant to him by the love she bore her own.

"And learned about him not just as Duke or Regent or King, but as a man among his friends. Francis Lovell let me give him all the tedious tasks—I had to, because he knew nothing of the craft, of course—and while we filled in the existing doorway with some old stones from a disused cloister, or sat on a tree trunk sharing my lunch, he described how they used to live in Warwick's household at Middleham, and how my father fought against his natural delicacy, becoming a fine horseman and practicing hours a day with sword and mace and bow. I had never realized how despondent he felt sometimes because his two elder brothers were of such fine physique, while he was always small-boned, lean as a whippet, and of only medium height, like me. Or how he worshiped the kindly, handsome Edward, and after he became King devoted his whole life to serving him. He used to say that if he were no courtier, at least he could fight for him, and he'd go on swinging that mace of his long after Lovell and the rest of them ached for their beds. And fight for him he did, commanding an army when he was little more than a boy. King Edward was so pleased he sent him butts of Gascony wine which, considering the successful young general's usual sobriety, may possibly have accounted for his begetting me! He had the knack of winning his men's hearts as well as their willing hands, Lord Lovell said.

"'That I know,' I said, smoothing the face of the stone he was working on so as to hide all recent joins, 'for my wife's father was one of them: Robert Marsh, who kept the Boar in Leicester. A fine type of man he was.'

"'So you are married, and I have been monopolizing you

day and night! And have scarcely the wherewithal to pay you.'

"And then I told him about you. And, Tansy, my dear, he remembered you! 'A sweet, fair girl,' he said. 'Quick for the comfort of her father's guests, yet interested in other things.' And after we had gone on working in silence for a while, he said, 'Dickon, how strange that out of all the girls in England you should marry one whom your father saw and actually spoke to—and who, I am sure, pleased him.' That has often been a great source of happiness to me, Tansy."

"And to me. Was that all that milord Lovell told you?" asked Tansy, held spellbound.

"No. He spoke often of his plans—his and the Duchess of Burgundy's—to bring back a Yorkist dynasty."

"I do not think they will ever succeed now. As Master Jordan says, the country is too settled, too prosperous."

"But they will never give up. He knew the priest, Simon of Oxford, of course, and—as you know—he and Lincoln organized the disastrous Lambert Simnel affair, although he thought the young fellow badly chosen. They had several secret agents over here on the lookout for likely young men to impersonate one or other of the Plantagenet princes. I told him how the Flemish merchant had tried to persuade me to be a second pretender, and how I had been sorely tempted at the time but had refused.

"'You have never regretted it?' he asked. 'We have found a young Flemish fellow called Perkin Warbeck. With training, he may do. But you, with your Plantagenet features—'

"I could see that he wanted me. And how we could have worked together, I thought!"

Tansy caught at his arm. "Not again, Dickon?" she cried.

He bent to kiss her, and all the preoccupation was gone from his face. He was eagerly alive, and all hers. "No, my beloved, not ever again. I told him that I had the most precious wife in all the world, that I had let her down when I refused to work on the Tudor's chapel, and that every hour of the rest of my life was hers."

In spite of material difficulties, both of them felt that they were entering into a more secure, complete period of their marriage. The room was already full of shadows, but they had scarcely noticed it. He put the kitten in its basket and lit their candle. "So your visit to Oxford wasn't very lucrative?" laughed Tansy, the practical, too happy to care much any more.

"No. Not in terms of money. I doubt if he had any. Anyway, he didn't offer me coins, and I was glad. I told him, when we parted, that to have been able to help one who had risked and lost so much for my father was the greatest happiness I could have. He gave me his copy of *La Forteresse de Foy*, which had belonged to him, and the complete trust which is between friends, and some precious glimpses into the private life of the last Plantagenet king." Suddenly Dickon burst out laughing. "And even if we never meet again, I shall always remember the most inept and lovable mason's mate I ever had to bear with. And those most precious hours when we hewed and heaved, and toiled and talked together. Please God his plots prosper and he is now safe!"

Rising from the settle, Tansy stretched her arms and felt as if she were coming back from some gripping legend into their everyday world. "It was all wonderful, Dickon, and I cannot tell you how glad I am for you," she said. "But I ought to remind you that my inn money will soon be gone, and with dear old Jod we have three to keep"—she paused for a moment, but still could not bring herself to add to his pecuniary worries by telling him that before half a year was out they might be four—"and what do we live on now? Tomorrow, and all the other tomorrows?"

But Dickon, her conscientious husband, seemed to have learned something of Lord Lovell's optimistic gaiety. He grasped candle in one hand and willing wife by the other, "*Dominus providebit*," he pronounced piously. "But tonight we live on love."

Chapter Twenty-five

Next morning, when they had finished a late breakfast of bread and meat and ale, Dickon unwrapped the book he had brought from Lovell Minster and showed it proudly to Tansy. He had scarcely translated more than a few words of the front page for her when they heard hoofbeats and Jod's voice bidding someone good morning.

"The bailiff!" exclaimed Tansy, hurriedly clearing away their pewter platters. "It is just a month since he came with the kitten. Will you get the money, Dickon? It is in the safe place you made beneath the bedroom floorboards."

Dickon rose to get it and saw that the tall, fashionably clad figure passing their window was no bailiff. It was Master John Moyle himself.

"Hurland Dale must have told him what I did, and that I am out of work. I warrant he is here to tell us to go," he muttered, hurriedly closing the book.

"Tom and Amy would never let him do that!" breathed Tansy.

And it certainly seemed to be the last thing which was in young Master Moyle's mind. He was in the soaring high spirits of a man recently betrothed. He remarked cheerfully on the beauty of the early spring morning, stopped to admire a small statue of Saint Francis which his tenant had carved on the lintel, looked round their room approvingly and, before finally settling himself in the chair they pulled forward for him, exclaimed, "You have improved this shabby old place out of all knowledge, Broome!"

"I am glad you think so, because some things I have done without your permission. But I think we showed you most of them, sir, when you came before. Will you try some of Tansy's homemade wine?"

"And thank your sister again for sending me this adorable pet," added Tansy.

"She thought you would be fretting while your husband was away," he said, stretching out a hand to stroke it.

211

"So you know all about—what happened?" stammered Dickon.

"My dear Broome, no one who is interested in building could help but hear. It seems you infuriated Hurland Dale and set your Guild by the ears by refusing work from the Vertues. No one seems to know what, but as I am concerned with raising funds for the King, I have a pretty shrewd idea. Did you manage to get work in some other city?"

"Nothing permanent, sir," confessed Dickon.

It was at that moment that Moyle's beauty-loving eyes caught sight of the well-worn copy of *La Forteresse de Foy.* He rose and began leafing through the pages, taking so much pleasure in it that he seemed almost to have forgotten them.

"We thought—perhaps you have come for the rent? It is here," offered Tansy, nervously.

"By all means, if you wish." Without removing his gaze from what he was reading, he picked up the coins and pocketed them. "And I hope it will be for the last time."

They both stared at him aghast.

"You mean, because Master Dale has dismissed me?"

"In a sense, yes. This is indeed a lovely book. Almost as lovely as one I once saw upstairs." He looked across the table at Dickon, then down again at the exquisitely bound volume. Very deliberately he turned to the title page. With his fine long fingers holding it open, he looked up searchingly again at its owner. "It is true, then, what I thought," he said.

The blood mounted slowly in Dickon's face. He stood there saying nothing, unaware that he was inevitably adding to Moyle's conviction by twirling the ring on his finger.

"I saw King Richard's own signature in that other book you have upstairs. At the time, I wondered, but kept my mouth shut. But now, because I did see it, and now see it again, I can guess why you did that mad thing at Westminster: smashing your own career sooner than add beauty to the Tudor tomb."

Still Dickon did not speak.

"You are King Richard's son, aren't you?" he asked outright.

"His bastard," admitted Dickon at last, his head held high.

He knew that it was a disastrous admission, that his likeness to his father would always be a hazard to him. "I know that all through the Wars of the Roses your family has been firmly on the Lancastrian side. You can throw us out now. Even if my Guild in London will have none of me, by the nature of our calling we journeymen must have lesser Guilds in other towns. Or at least I can always get work as an unskilled laborer." He gave vent to an odd little reminiscent laugh, explicable only to Tansy. "I have seen better men than myself doing it."

Thomas Moyle closed the book smartly and hurried to him, shaking him by the shoulders. "Richard Broome, what do you take me for?" he demanded. "I am a loyal Lancastrian, yes. With my specialized knowledge of financial law I hope to rise high in King Henry's service. For my father's sake he has already shown me favor. I admire him for an acute businessman and a hard worker. Even those of you who look upon him as a usurper must admit that when he took the crown he took all the responsibilities with it. And Welshman as he is proud to be, he strives equally for England. On the continent we are no longer looked upon as an unimportant little island but, thanks to him, begin to take our place in trade and culture with the countries of Europe. But I know courage and loyalty when I see them, no matter on what side. And I seem to have hit by chance on the reason why you refused such profitable employment on his chapel." He turned back for a last look at *La Forteresse de Foy*, but this time touched it only absently. "I only hope that in your place I should have had sufficient courage to do the same."

"My father chose *Loyaulte me lie* as his personal motto, and the least I can do is to live up to it," said Dickon, overcome by such generous understanding. "But as to courage—I have never fought in battle and have been avoiding recognition ever since I learned the truth."

"There are different kinds of courage, Broome. Yours was of your father's 'Loyalty binds me' kind. I can imagine the dilemma you must have been in, between conscience and the well-being of your wife and any family you may have. And as an artist, albeit an amateur one, I can appreciate what you gave up."

"I have a wife who should be happiness enough for any man," said Dickon, drawing her to him and hating her to feel that she was in any way responsible for his professional loss.

"And by keeping in obscurity I shall be doing as my father bade me."

"Well, I am glad he told you that. He, of all men, must have known the sharp penalties that go with fame—or infamy. But let us hope it will not be complete obscurity." Relaxing, Moyle sat down again and sampled Tansy's wine. "Since, for my good fortune, you have no other work, I have a proposition to make. And, believe me, I have formed so high a regard for your skill that it is no mere compensating kindness. Sit down, both of you, and listen. Your wine is good, Mistress Broome, and if this obstinate husband of yours will come and work for me in Kent you will probably find yourself making it for my entire household!"

"Work for you in Kent!" they both exclaimed, with excited anticipation beginning to break through the anxiety on their young faces.

"At Eastwell Court. I am going to be married to a relative of my late mother, who was of the wealthy Drury family. So, with my father's permission, I intend to pull down most of the old house and rebuild. My father may not live much longer, and then the title and both houses, there and in London, will be mine. I shall need a house convenient for court, of course, but my betrothed and I are both country lovers and hope to make our real home at Eastwell. You know my ideas about building, Broome, and I should like you to be in charge of both places."

Dickon was almost speechless with relief and gratitude. "Here indeed is something which I accept with joy," he managed to say.

"Do we have to thank our good friend Tom Hood for this?" asked Tansy.

"In a very small measure, perhaps. But I liked the work you did on that fireplace of our London hall, and the fountain. And, as I told you—and in spite of what is being said of you—I liked your refusal to Robert Vertue. Also, I intend to make Eastwell one of the most beautiful houses in England, and I believe that you are the right man to help me do it."

He went to the open door, called to Jod to bring a satchel from his saddle, and began laying drawings on their table. Soon he and Dickon were bent over them enthusiastically, with no other thoughts in their minds. String courses, spandrels, mullions for the windows, and hammer beams for the roof of the hall, they discussed them all while Tansy, silently executing an ecstatic *pas seul* with the Moyle kitten clutched in her arms, watched this strange, splendid man, half lawyer and half artist, who held the rest of her life in his capable hands.

"After my marriage we shall be away in France for some months on the King's affairs, so I should want you to be on the spot to work it all out in your own mind and begin the demolition work."

"Since you will be in France, sir, could you possibly order a shipload of stone from Caen?"

"It will come expensive with the freightage, but I know the late King used it for King's College chapel and most of the many castles he repaired."

"May we bring our horses, and old Jod?"

"By all means. You will certainly need a horse. I should want you to keep an eye on the Strand house, and to scour the neighborhood for the best team of local workmen you can find. They can begin by pulling down the west wing. If you and your wife will ride with me to Kent next week, my people will see to bringing all your household gear."

And then, for Tansy, came the most splendid miracle of all.

"Here, by the orchard wall," Master Moyle was saying, stabbing some spot on the rustling parchment with a decisive forefinger, "you can build yourself a cottage while I am away. Some of the men will help you. Make it your first job, and while you are about it, build big enough for your family, Richard Broome, because it looks as if you may be with us for the rest of your natural life!"

As Master Moyle began to roll up the precious parchments, Dickon raised his head at last and met his wife's ecstatic gaze. He knew then that, as far as she was concerned at least, nothing which he had hitherto refused to do had been in vain. "I think you would find it difficult to get rid of us with such a generous master," he said laughingly. "But for one who scarcely knows me, you seem to put remarkable trust in me."

"I hope to enjoy some of that hard-proved loyalty of yours. And don't forget that I have heard much of you both from Tom, whom you sent to my father in the first place, and who seems to be completely incapable of relinquishing the hope of becoming my brother-in-law."

"Do you think he ever will?" Tansy could not resist asking. "Mistress Amy will be so desperately unhappy if she is forced to marry someone else."

Moyle smiled kindly at her anxiety. "Well, she is proving remarkably stubborn for so small a person, and my father has not beaten her yet."

"I have known Tom all my life, and no one could help loving him," said Tansy.

"But we have never told him about—my birth," put in Dickon, anxiously.

"Our loyalty will count both ways," promised Moyle. "I shall never tell either him or my chatterbox of a sister. Nor, if this is what you are both fearing, will I ever tell the King."

"Any fervent Lancastrian who knew the truth might think it wise to get rid of Dickon."

"You are probably right, Mistress Broome," agreed Moyle, gathering up his papers and preparing to depart. "So do you not see, his best chance of security, and of your happiness, lies in honorable anonymity? That I can give him, with comfort and a fair wage, though I cannot give him the fame and fortune which his skill deserves."

Hand in hand, they stood to watch him go. All bustle of removal would come after.

"*Dominus providebit*, I prophesied casually last evening," recalled Dickon. "And indeed the Lord *has* provided, although in a way that I could not possibly have foreseen."

"But then the unexpected always *does* happen to you," Tansy reminded him.

Though it is unlikely to from now on, thought Dickon, looking ahead rather ruefully into what seemed to be the even tenure of a happy but uneventful life. To have had first adventure and then fame within his grasp, and let them go, had not been easy. To exchange cheerfully the excitement of notoriety even for security and happiness would take discipline. But when he thought of everything which Lord Lovell had given up, he felt himself to be in good company and was strengthened.

Now that they knew of their change of fortune, Tansy drew him back into the shelter of their first home and told him that they were to share the joy of parenthood. And Dickon, in common with most expectant fathers, hoped that pride in his own achievements might one day be transmuted into a vicarious fulfilment of himself in the successes of his son.

Chapter Twenty-six

It was appleblossom time in Kent. White and pink, they waved above the orchard wall at Eastwell, every now and then scattering petals as if for a bride on the Broomes' garden path. Tansy sat at her spinning wheel just outside their cottage door, with honeysuckle scenting the air, while her small son pranced on his hobby horse towards the open gate.

"You have the best carved horse in the world, Robin," she told him.

The fair-haired three-year-old nodded vigorously. "Dear my horsey! Dick-Dick made it," he confirmed proudly, not as yet being able to pronounce the word father.

"Well, ride horsey down the path and up to the house to where Dick-Dick is working and tell him to come home to dinner," said Tansy. As Robin set off at full canter with only a few spills, she glanced back over her shoulder and called through the open doorway to the young wench from the village who was setting the table, "The master will be in soon."

These days 'the master' meant Dickon, for he had a dozen men, including carpenters, tilers, and glaziers, working under his control.

From where she sat Tansy could see across courtyard, lawn and terrace to the manor house, where the fine new wing was rising beside the best part of the old. She could see her husband among a group of workmen pacing out some important measurements, and presently saw Sir John, who had recently inherited both house and title, come across the terrace to join him. They stood there talking, measuring and gesticulating. She had no idea what they were discussing, but as usual they seemed to be enthusiastic and in the utmost accord. Presently some of the workmen caught sight of young Robin Broome, trying to reach them on his fiery-looking, unmanageable steed, and stood around to give him a laughing welcome. When he fell off for the third time, seeming to think it all a splendid joke, his father turned and caught him up in his arms. What Dickon made of her message transmitted through

218

such a limited vocabulary, Tansy could only imagine. But she laughed aloud, thinking how good life was.

The sun shone. There was scarcely a cloud in the early summer sky. And so it was with her. Her home had been built to her own desires. Her husband had found contentment in his work, their child grew strong and tall in such healthy surroundings, and they all three seemed to have become part of the Eastwell household. Only a few days ago Tom and Amy, now married with her brother's consent, had been staying at the manor, and the rich Drury heiress who was now Lady Moyle, instead of resenting the successful fletcher's humble origin, had been completely captivated by his charm. So, as with us, their troubles are over, thought Tansy.

Her husband was striding up the garden path, his precious plans in his hand and stone dust in his hair, and, as usual, joy in his eyes at seeing her.

"Where is Robin?" she asked anxiously.

"Having a plaster put on his nose," said Dickon, sitting on the low garden wall and wiping the sweat from his face. "Horsey had the ill manners to throw him again, and Lady Moyle is comforting him. Sometimes I think they could not pet him more if he were their own child."

"It is because she aches for one of their own, which may the good Lord soon send her," said Tansy. "How is the chapel work progressing?"

"Excellently. This morning we have hoisted my carved reredos into position. I have always wanted to build a chapel. And although this is but a small private one, when it is finished it will compare with any in the land."

She guessed at once at the comparison which was in his mind. "And into this one you are able to put your best creative work?"

"It has been a joy. And using Caen stone, too. In the chapel at Westminster I should have been only an underling, seldom free to use my own ideas. Whereas here—" Dickon stopped short as if some thought had cut short his pleasure.

"The Moyles are inordinately pleased with it, aren't they?" asked Tansy, puzzled by the half-humorous, half-angry grimace on her husband's face.

"So pleased that they have persuaded the Tudor to dine with them next week on his way to inspect the new defenses at Dover. Lady Moyle is sure to ask him to inspect the new chapel as well."

Tansy sprang up, her unwound wool winding about her. "King Henry—coming here! Oh, Dickon, you will hate that! As likely as not he will ask to see the head mason."

"His visit betokens sure advancement for Sir John. And, anyway, there is nothing I can do."

She went and laid a hand on his shoulder, as if to still the tumult of his feelings. "Here, surrounded by so much peace and kindness, it has been so easy to forget."

"Easier, yes," qualified Dickon.

"Holy Church tells us to forgive our enemies."

"It takes the end of living memory to wipe out a war."

"You mean, that there need be no bitterness in Robin's generation?"

"It is always easier to forget what one has heard of than what one has actually seen. He will not have been forced to see King Richard's body, naked, stabbed, and bloody, thrown across a packhorse and brought back with a felon's halter about his neck—and hear Lancastrians jeering. His hackles will not rise as instinctively as a dog's at sight of any Tudor."

"The Tudor may not have known. After all, he gave permission for your father's burial as soon as the Abbot asked." But Dickon was not to be propitiated. "Then, when he is older, you will tell Robin?"

"I think not. Do you suppose I could tell him dispassionately about Bosworth and not make it 'come real' as he calls it when we tell him stories now?"

Tansy tried to hide her disappointment. "We called our first son Robert after my father, but I should be extraordinarily proud to tell him about yours," she said. "And a long time ago, when I asked you, you said that—even with all the dangers and disadvantages—you yourself would rather have been told."

"But not wholly because my father was King. It was because I had at last found someone of my own, some sort of background. It was before I had met you, beloved." Going towards the gate, Dickon laid an arm about her shoulders in passing. "But our lad has no need of love and security, and I would not have him know that awful sense of apartness from his fellow men."

"Apartness. That is the word dear Tom once used, when speaking of you."

Dickon swung round. "But he does not know."

"He said it without knowing. He must have felt it. Tom is more sensitive than you suppose."

An affectionate smile warmed away the strain which was now so rarely on Dickon's face. "One day I should like to tell Tom," he said.

He went to meet his master and his son. Robin's happy face had been carefully patched, and Sir John was carrying the wooden horse. "We had trouble with our mount this morning," he said, handing it across the fence to Dickon.

Robin ran to his mother, announcing that he was hungry. "It must be a perpetual state, for my injudicious wife has just been stuffing him with sweetmeats," remarked Sir John, amused. "I came across to tell you that I think you had better find time to build a new parapet to the well, Dickon. The kitchen maids are grumbling that it is not safe. And soon we shall have an adventurous little horseman to think about."

"We have been praying for that good news," said Tansy.

"I will see to it, sir," promised Dickon.

But clearly that was not all Sir John had come about. Although it was past the dinner hour at manor and cottage he did not go immediately, but stood picking a sprig of honeysuckle and thrusting it through a buttonhole of his doublet with rather unnecessary care. Then, quite abruptly, he said, "I am not too happy about that subsidence of the river wall along the Strand. We might get the water into our town house with any high spring tide. I think you will have to leave things here for a few days and ride up to London to see about it for me."

There was a moment's silence, while only the birds chirped in the apple trees. Both of them were very well aware that the worst of the spring tides were over. Then the eyes of knight and master mason met in a long look of mutual understanding and regard.

"Thank you, more than I can express, for everything," said Dickon. "I will start tomorrow."

"The day before the King comes," murmured Tansy, gazing at their benefactor with deep gratitude.

Sir John must have heard her. He turned and leaned for a

moment or two on their garden wall. "His Grace is not likely
to have forgotten what Richard Plantagenet looked like on
the only brief, terrifying occasion when he ever saw him."
And then, as if lightening the dangerous subject, he nodded
towards their son. "Do you intend ever to tell him?"

Although it was the first time he had alluded to the circumstances of Dickon's birth since that day in their old cottage at Richmond, save implicitly by occasionally borrowing
their books, they both knew what he meant.

"How strange!" exclaimed Tansy. "We were speaking
about that just before you came, sir."

"Not so strange, Tansy. The King's coming must have put
it into your heads," said Sir John. "And what did you
decide?"

"For myself, I should have liked Robin to know," she said,
gathering the boy against her skirts. "But it is more Dickon's
concern than mine. And he says no."

Dickon faced him with easy confidence and his most
charming smile. "Considering the wisdom and kindness with
which you have reshaped our lives, I think that it should be
for you, sir, to cast the deciding vote."

Sir John looked at the robust fair-skinned boy consideringly. "How like his mother he is!" he said, realizing cause
for relief. "No need for him to be handicapped by any fatal
family resemblance or bitter memories! Let him grow up zest-
fully, without prejudice, into this bravely expanding new
Tudor world."

Author's Note

This is a story set in a framework of authentic history, but some of it is based on very plausible legend and much is fiction. Most of the events really happened, but in some cases I have condensed them into the space of a few years rather than a lifetime.

Dickon is mentioned by his real name in John Heneage Jesse's *Memoirs of Richard III* and also by John Harvey in *The Plantagenets*, and his burial in 1550 is recorded—with the mark V which signified that the deceased was of noble family—in the register at Eastwell in Kent. Actually, it was Sir Thomas Moyle, John Moyle's son, who had the home built for him there, when Dickon was an elderly mason, and even today the site of it is known as Plantagenet Cottage.

The Blue Boar at Leicester was pulled down in 1836, but before the demolition a Mr. Henry Goddard made careful drawings and descriptions of it, which are preserved in the City Library. The original High Street, in which the inn stood, is now known as High Cross Street. Blue Boar Lane and the King's bed still exist. The fate of the landlady is recorded in the city archives of Leicester, but she was in fact a Mistress Clark, who lived and owned the bed at a later date.

Many years after the battle of Stoke workmen repairing a chimney at Minster Lovell came upon a walled-up, secret room. To their amazement they saw, seated at a writing table, the body of a man which disintegrated almost as soon as the air penetrated. This was always believed to be Francis, Viscount Lovell, about whose disappearance there had been so much conjecture.

My thanks are due to the Leicester City Library and the Ashford branch of the Kent County Library for putting so much helpful information at my disposal, and to the Isle of Wight County Seely Library for getting me so many reference books.

MARGARET CAMPBELL BARNES

FRESHWATER, ISLE OF WIGHT